I0690385

Flaming Crimes

by

Chrys Fey

Disaster Crimes Series

Flaming Crimes

Cover Art by *Kim Mendoza*

The Wild Rose Press, Inc.
PO Box 708
Adams Basin, NY 14410-0708
Visit us at www.thewildrosepress.com

Publishing History
First Crimson Rose Edition, 2018
Print ISBN 978-1-5092-1878-3
Digital ISBN 978-1-5092-1879-0

Disaster Crimes Series
Published in the United States of America

Beth's heart clenched

at the sight of the smoke stacks, as if a fist had driven through her chest and was squeezing the meaty human drum, paralyzing it. She gripped the door handle. The faster Donovan drove and the closer they got to home, to those tiers of billowing, dark smoke, the more anxious she became. Donovan's words replayed in her head.

It looks like it's right next to our house.

Her heart woke from its coma and punched her ribcage like a boxer attacking a speed bag. Perspiration dampened her underarms and slicked her palms. *Please, God, no. I can't lose my home again.*

The smoke stack was soon right in front of them, right where their home was located. Donovan turned down their street, and the tower of smoke loomed above them. Fire consumed the empty lot next to their house. Flames ate their way up the bark spines of pine trees. Orange flickers slithered along the length of the branches, reaching toward the roof. The fire was descending upon their forever home as a raiding army would race toward a city with swords drawn.

Donovan floored it down the street and brought the truck to a jerking stop in the driveway. He jumped out of the truck without taking the key out of the ignition. Beth shoved the door open and stumbled out onto the driveway.

"Call the fire department, pack some clothes. I'm getting the hose." Donovan raced toward the fire and slipped around the side of the house.

Praise for Chrys Fey and...

HURRICANE CRIMES:
"*HURRICANE CRIMES* by Chrys Fey is a pure delight. It is a romance first and a suspense novella second, but both are combined in a perfect formula for a wonderful afternoon's reading."

~Readers' Favorite

~*~

SEISMIC CRIMES:
"Action packed is the only way to describe this exciting, sizzling love and adventure story! Between the steamy private scenes and the made-for-TV shoot-outs and natural disasters, there is adventure that keeps your heart pumping on every page."

~Readers' Favorite

~*~

TSUNAMI CRIMES:
"Ms. Fey's strong and compelling visual storytelling coupled with the overwhelming uncertainty facing Beth and Donovan make this a powerhouse novel."

~InD'Tale

Dedication

To my family,
who were there with me during the 2001 fire.
RIP Angel

Chapter One

Beth paddled down the Little Manatee River. The four and a half miles of flowing water was one of her favorite stretches to canoe. Upstream, she had to wind her way through the twisting path around cypress, willow, and cedar trees. Each turn was a challenge but rewarding once she saw the scenery beyond. Every twist, dip, and rise offered her something new to see. Overhead, the canopy was thick. Trees leaned over the river like archways. She maneuvered her canoe around the obstacles in her path, occasionally bumping a tree with the back of her canoe.

Flowing water and the greenery filling the banks and stretching above the river brought her a sense of peace. As she made her way downstream, she let her mind go. Her muscles moved mechanically, knowing what to do. The current's speed slowed, and the water's level lowered. She knew this would happen. With no rain for weeks, the land was dry, and the rivers were dropping. With the shallower water, she could see the sand below. She pulled the paddle out of the water and lay it across the canoe. Sunlight touched her skin, and a breeze tickled her sweaty neck. She floated in the middle of the river and took a deep breath. The air had a faint smoky smell to it. There were so many fires popping up throughout the state you couldn't go anywhere without smelling the evidence. At least it wasn't so thick in this sanctuary, for that she was glad.

As she drifted with the slow current, she thought about the past year and a half. As Oahu rebuilt after the tsunami, Beth rebuilt herself. While seeing a psychiatrist, she slowly ventured back to the beach with Donovan—first for a simple stroll along the shore, letting the shore tickle her toes, and then to sit on her surfboard as she worked up the courage to face a wave. Panic attacks plagued her for months until she could stand up on her board and ride a wave. For her shoulder, she took physical therapy until the gunshot wound no longer caused her pain. She also spoke to a therapist about the tsunami, the girl she tried to save from the rapid torrents, her kidnappers, and every moment she spent locked in the closet with a GSW and broken fingers. After eight months, both doctors declared her well, but Beth continued to work on herself by getting reacquainted with the things she loved, especially those that involved water. The last time she had canoed had been through the floodwaters Hurricane Sabrina left behind. She had decided to do this adventure solo, despite Donovan's request to accompany her, because she *needed* to do it alone. Later, she promised to take him on a trip, to share the magic of canoeing with him, but she needed this time to reflect.

The fear she had brought back from their honeymoon had paralyzed her for a long time. She felt sorry for Donovan now, having to deal with that when they should've been experiencing the bliss of new marriage. But he loved her and had been there through it all. He stood by her side in her darkest moments when she needed anti-anxiety medication and woke up screaming from nightmares every night.

She was much better now, though. No medication, no nightmares. And she didn't try to hide her GSW scars anymore. For months, she had stamped large bandages over the round, rough scar on her shoulder and asked Donovan to do the same to the matching scar on the back of her shoulder. From the mirror, she could see his reflection as he smoothed it over her skin; the pain in his eyes visible. After going through several boxes, she eventually stopped hiding them. Rather, she'd make sure the straps to her workout tops covered them. Each morning, she'd ask Donovan if they were visible, and he'd reassure her they weren't. Although she wasn't doing either of those things anymore, to this day, she still hated the sight of them.

Beth lifted her paddle and cut it through the water to start moving again. While making her way downstream, she had to get out of her canoe a few times to glide it over the lowest levels of water when the bottom of her canoe touched sand. She didn't mind, though, as it let her stretch her legs and back. Near Tampa, the end of the stretch, she floated next to a manatee lazing in the water. He was so peaceful she couldn't stop from smiling. She hovered her hand over his body, wanting to touch his smooth body but restraining herself. Although manatees were no longer considered an endangered species, they were still protected, and she respected them. Ever since she was a little girl, manatees were her favorite aquatic mammals.

She moved her hand a foot over his head. "Hi, handsome. Thank you for letting me share the river with you."

The manatee lifted his head out of the water and

looked at her. When he bobbed his head and dipped back beneath the surface, she smiled.

He nodded at me. Feeling blessed by his acknowledgement, she removed her hand and carefully glided her canoe past him.

At the end of her trip, she utilized the offered transportation to get back to the car waiting for her upstream. With her canoe strapped to the top, she climbed into the driver's seat and blasted her AC. With the engine running and car in park, she picked up her cell phone to call Donovan.

"Hey, beautiful. How was it?"

She smiled at his greeting and leaned back in the seat. "It was nice. Serene. I think I have a new boyfriend."

There was a pause on the other end. "Really?" Donovan's voice was deep. "And what is this new boyfriend's name?"

"Manny," she said, biting her lip. "Manny the Manatee."

Donovan's rolling laughter touched her ear. "Well, damn, I can't compete with that."

"Nope, no, you can't." She giggled. "I was just calling to let you know I'm heading home."

"Okay. See you soon. Love you."

"Love you, too." She hung up and backed out of the parking space. Driving down the interstate, she passed two separate fires consuming the dry wildlife beside the road. Flames flickered beside the concrete barrier. Smoke seeped through the vents. She crinkled her nose and breathed through her mouth. Traffic slowed as police cars directed cars out of the outer lane, away from the fire. She slipped between two cars and endured a crawling pace until they passed the fires and broke out of the obscuring smoke.

In her hometown, she encountered another fire; this one dangerously close to homes. Firetrucks clogged the road. A cop stood behind a roadblock. Detour signs were set up, pointing her down a side street. She sent Donovan a quick text.

20 mins away. Detour.

Following the detour signs, she passed a section of woods that had been devoured by the fire. Smoke drifted from the ash-covered ground. Palmetto bushes had been fried down to blackened stumps. Trees stood like burnt giants. Their leaves and branches were gone; their bark was like charcoal. Seeing the black, sparse land was a stark contrast to the lush, green woods on the other side of the road. The blackness went on for two blocks, and then suddenly, everything went back to green.

She drove the rest of the way home while peering at the smoke stacks in the rearview mirror. They shrank the farther she drove, but they remained menacing. Living in the Sunshine State, you got used to hurricane season and fire season, but you weren't always impacted by them. Until you were. And this fire season was proving to be harsh. Already twenty individual fires had erupted just in Central Florida. Two hundred acres in total burned to a crisp. Authorities didn't see it ending any time soon, either. Not with the drought. Several fires were said to have been set by the hands of arsonists. She didn't understand why anyone would get a kick out of starting fires. Back when she was in school, learning about psychology, she did a paper on arsonists. They loved fire because it was alive—it breathes, eats, and moves. They liked starting fire for the thrill of it, the rush. Striking a match was like arousal. And they enjoyed that they could use it as a weapon for vengeance. Power. Fire was a power they could unleash on anyone, anywhere. Seeing things burn was a game of foreplay; hurting people was climax. They enjoyed every blazing second.

The only forms of fire Beth thought sexy were candlelight and fireplaces. Fire that burned away nature and wildlife habitats hurt her soul. And seeing those fires so close to homes made her heart heavy.

She pulled into the driveway of her stunning two-story house. She felt blessed to be living in such a beautiful home with Donovan, on the same lot where her childhood home had been, on the same street where she grew up. It was a home built on promises and full of possibilities.

She walked into the house and dropped her keys on a side table by the door. "I'm home!" She ran up the stairs to their bedroom. Donovan wasn't there, so she kicked off her shoes and stripped out of her sweaty clothes. In the shower, water streamed down her body, taking away the sweat clinging to her skin. The wet drops beating against her head relaxed her. She lingered beneath the spray after her hair had been washed and all the bubbles from her body had slithered down the drain. After stepping out of the shower, she wrapped a towel around her body and tucked the corner between her breasts. With an extra towel, she shook the access water from her hair. Standing in front of the mirror, she caught sight of the scar on her shoulder. A clenching sensation in the middle of her chest had her looking away. The jagged circle and uneven skin was hideous.

She brushed her hair over it before stepping out of the bathroom.

Donovan came into the bedroom at the same time. He stopped suddenly. She paused in the doorway. "Hey," she said. "I didn't see you when I came in."

"I was on the patio." His gaze lowered to her legs. Drops of water slipped down her shins to her ankles. He came toward her, and she knew. She knew what he wanted—her. The look in his eye and the way his chest rose and fell were clear signs. His fingers trailed lightly across the pink skin on her chest. Beads of water converged and leaked down the crevasse between her breasts. His hands molded around her shoulders and roamed down the length of her arms. Droplets fell from her fingers. He lifted her hand and sucked the water from her fingertips. The contact made her mouth go dry. Her breathing quickened, straining the towel around her chest, making it tighter and tighter.

"You're never more beautiful than when you're wet," he said.

She arched a brow at the double meaning.

It only took him a second to realize it, too. He grinned at her as he pulled her close. Lips touched her neck, kissing and sucking. Clutching his shoulders, she dipped her head back. His warm lips traveled down her neck to her chest. His hand brushed her upper thigh. The feel of his work-roughened palms against her skin made her quiver. Then two fingertips stroked her center. Heat exploded. Those fingertips circled the heat, drawing out more and more. They became slick with her pleasure as they tweaked, and she sighed. He caught her most sensitive flesh between his fingertips and rubbed until she let loose a moan.

Heart pounding, center humming and screaming for more, she moved her mouth to his ear as he sucked on damp skin. "I just canoed a river, Donovan. My arms are tired."

His head rose. "You won't need your arms."

With her back against the wall, he unzipped his pants, whisked opened her towel, exposing her naked body, and lifted her off her feet. Twining her arms around his neck and locking her legs around his hips, she gazed into his violet eyes. He slipped into her slowly, filling her completely. Her eyelids fluttered, but she kept them open so she could watch him as he watched her. Her mouth parted as her breath escaped. He moved at a leisurely pace, as if wanting to savor this moment, their contact, their binding. Each sedate stroke had her core quaking. Her leg muscles worked with his steady pace, pulling him deeper. Every other stroke, when he was fully enclosed within her, he stilled, holding himself in place. Like this, he'd stare into her eyes, and their breathing would synchronize. Then he'd retract. Her toes curled. Her leg muscles flexed around him. Finally, it became too much. She couldn't hold her eyes open any longer, so she let her lashes stay sealed. After a moment, his body pressed into hers as he buried his face in the crook of her neck. Her nails trailed up and down the back of his neck, a touch she knew could soothe and seduce. His pace eased into a faster tempo.

Their moans blended.

"Baby, let go."

Donovan's deep voice in her ear had her core contracting. She pulled him into her and held him there as she shattered. And he shattered with her.

Donovan set her on her feet, zipped his pants, and

staggered back. He lowered onto the floor. His body was shaking as he tried to catch his breath. She wrapped the towel around herself and slide to a sitting position. Curling her legs beneath her, she sat across from him with her head against the wall. She looked at him. He was leaning back on his hands, with his legs bent. He looked as though he had played a tough game of basketball and was now cooling down on the court, unable to move. His eyelids opened, and his gaze settled on her. She probably looked as stunned as he did; her center still hammered.

A slow grin took Donovan's mouth, enticing a matching smirk to appear on her lips. They laughed at the same time.

"I guess I should go canoeing alone more often," she panted.

He shook his head and laughed. When he caught his breath, he said, "You're magnificent."

"You're just saying that because we had sex. Great sex."

He shook his head again. "I'm saying that because it's true. I don't know another woman sexier or fiercer than you."

"If you met one, I'd have to kill her."

He chuckled. "That would never happen."

****

After dinner, Beth answered the ringing phone and heard the voices of Donovan's mom and grandma greeting her simultaneously.

"Hi, Meredith, Lily, how are you?"

"We're fine, sweetie," Meredith said. "We had an unexpected cold snap, so we're a bit envious of your Florida weather right now."

"Oh, don't be too envious. Florida skipped spring and went straight to summer. It's brutally hot here, and the fires are spreading like crazy." Beth sat down at the kitchen table and put the phone on speaker when Donovan joined her.

"Hi, Mom. Hi, Grandma."

"Donovan," the women gushed his name. Their love for the boy they raised oozed from the phone, making Beth laugh.

"Grandma and I have been talking," Meredith started.

"Uh oh. That's never good." Donovan chuckled.

Lily tsked into the phone. "If I could smack you in the back of the head for that, I would."

Beth reached over to lightly slap Donovan on the back of the head. "I did it for you."

"Thanks, Beth."

"No problem. Whenever you want me to smack him, just call and I'll do my duty." She winked at Donovan, teasing him along with the women who raised him.

"We'll keep that in mind," Meredith said. "Like I was saying, we've been talking…"

Donovan glanced at Beth when his mom gave a dramatic pause. "Yes?"

"And we want to know if the two of you are on the baby making train."

Beth covered her eyes with her hands, wanting to pretend she was no longer in the room. Her cheeks warmed. Talking to Meredith and Lily about the future always ended up embarrassing her, especially when babies were brought into the conversation.

"Yes, Mom, we're on the baby making train." They

had been on it just hours before.

"That's good, but, umm, how long have you been trying?"

"Since our one-year anniversary." It was a promise they had made each other. As it turned out, instead of using that first year to enjoy married life without a pregnancy taking over it, it had been plagued by her efforts to heal from multiple traumas.

"And you haven't been using condoms or birth control pills?"

Beth cringed. Hearing her mother-in-law say "condoms" was horrifying. "No and no," she said, hoping that was the end to the discussion.

"Well, we couldn't help but notice that six months is a long time to be baby making."

Beth peered at Donovan through sad eyes. She looked down at the table, unable to form an answer for the women who were optimistically, and understandably, hoping for a new addition to the family.

Donovan took her hand in his. The touch warmed her. "We're just grateful to have each other right now."

She squeezed his hand, thankful for his words.

"You're right. Absolutely." Meredith's voice was sympathetic. After they returned from Oahu, Beth had spoken on the phone to Meredith every day, needing the comfort of a mother and missing her own dearly. She took solace in Meredith's soothing voice and the advice she gave her about taking things slowly and leaning on Donovan for support. "Beth, dear, are you sure your body is completely healed?"

The implication she was at fault somehow was there, however unintentionally, and it hurt. She had thought the same thing many times—that her body was damaged and would never produce a baby—but she had been checked out by doctors and everything from her ovaries to her uterus were in tip-top shape.

She cleared her throat. "Yes, I'm sure. I had ultrasounds, pap smears, blood work, everything you can think of. It all came back normal. My body is healed, but it's just not the time right now." She glanced at Donovan. He nodded with a small smile, letting her know he believed the same thing.

"Maybe it's the sperm!" Grandma Lily's enthusiastic shout made Beth blink. When she registered Lily's words, she clamped a hand over her mouth. She peeked at Donovan's face. His mouth was open in speechless shock.

"Grandma! My sperm is fine."

"Are you sure?"

He sputtered as he tried to form a response.

Beth's chuckle escaped, despite her attempt to keep it buried.

"Well, maybe you're not doing it right," Lily accused.

Donovan's cheeks turned a bright pink. "I'm doing it right!"

"How do you know?"

Donovan held up his hands as if the women could see the gesture and caught Beth's eye. "Believe me...I know."

"Hmm. Well, if you need any pointers—"

"All right, that's all the conversation we can handle tonight. Bye, Mom. Bye, Grandma. We love you." Donovan snatched up the phone and ended the call to Beth's laughter.

****

While lying next to Donovan in bed that night, the insecurity she felt during the phone call, before Grandma Lily intercepted with jokes, came back to her. She realized then that Lily's jests at Donovan had been for her benefit, to make her laugh and forget about the possibility that it was her body to blame for the fact she wasn't pregnant.

She rolled over and gazed at Donovan's profile. They had turned off the lights five minutes ago, so she knew he wasn't asleep yet. She gathered her courage and asked the question that had been weighing on her for a long time.

"Are you disappointed?" Her voice came out in a whisper. She wasn't sure he heard it until he turned his head to her.

"Disappointed about what?"

"About me not being pregnant? Are you disappointed...in me?"

Donovan shifted so he was looking down at her. He embraced her face with his hands and pressed his lips to her forehead. "I could never be disappointed in you, Beth. Getting pregnant is not something you can just do when you want it. I want to have kids with you, but I'm not in a rush. I truly believe that when it's time, we'll have our first little urchin."

She had been so worried, and stayed silent for so long, that it was a relief to hear those words. She smiled at the last thing he said. "Urchin?"

"I think it's better calling a baby an urchin than a peanut or nugget. Besides..." He lay a hand on her stomach. "There will be water in there with him, so urchin fits better."

"Your philosophy makes sense, Dr. Goldwyn."

He chuckled, and then he kissed her smiling lips. When he leaned back, he peered into her eyes. "This was spurred on because of what my mom said, wasn't it?"

She nodded.

"I'm sorry." He combed his fingers through her hair. "Don't let either of them get to you. You're perfect, and our baby will be perfect. Our future urchins couldn't have a better mom."

She twined her fingers with his. "Or Dad."

Chapter Two

Donovan woke the next morning with Beth curled next to him. His thoughts drifted to their conversation before they fell asleep. He didn't want Beth to ever feel responsible for not being pregnant, though he knew women always blamed themselves. His grandmother's words came back to him, and he had a moment of panic thinking he was the reason they weren't expecting yet. He looked at her and stole a moment to stare at her sleeping form.

Brunette hair was spread out over her pillow. Sleeping lips were pink and pouting. A tug in the middle of his abdomen had him wanting to plunder those soft lips. His gaze continued to rove over her. He saw the circle of patched-up skin below her collarbone and the scar stretching across her chest from a tree branch with talons. Everything they ever did together resulted in a bad memory forever etched on her skin. Dread and guilt ripped his heart to shreds, until he was sure his heart resembled a pile of Sloppy Joe meat. What he wouldn't give to erase those scars with a brush of his fingertips, to banish the disastrous moments that took place during their relationship, but then he wondered how much would be left? Their life together couldn't be plagued by disasters forever, could it?

He lifted his hand to touch the thin scar near his eyebrow, which he acquired during a fight in San

Francisco. At the same time, he saw the small, shiny scar on the back of his hand from a burn, also picked up during their stay in the Golden City.

They both had scars.

With a sigh, he rolled out of bed and headed downstairs for the kitchen. The coffeemaker was already gurgling. He pulled out eggs and bacon from the fridge and set about frying his breakfast. He was frying extra crispy bacon for Beth when he sensed her presence. Turning with the spatula in his hand, he saw her smiling at the entrance. She wore a spaghetti strap shirt, that showed the points of her nipples, and a pair of basketball shorts. *His* basketball shorts.

"You're so cute when you cook," she said with a voice thickened by sleep. "I should buy you one of those 'Kiss the Chef' aprons." She winked at him as she went to the cupboard. She brought down two cups and poured their coffee. "Are you making my bacon extra crispy?"

"And the yolk of your eggs extra runny," he confirmed.

She wrapped her arms around his middle and pressed her body to his back. "You know me so well."

He rubbed his free hand along her arms. "Be careful. I don't want the grease to splatter on your arms."

She pulled away, shifted beside him, and pressed her lips to his cheek. She didn't have to say anything to show her love for him and his protective ways.

They ate their breakfast and started to get ready for their day. Donovan grabbed his keys from the side table and tossed Beth hers. She caught it one-handed. At the door, he teasingly tugged her high ponytail. "Have a good day at work."

"You, too. Don't get too crazy in that truck."

He grinned. "Crazy? What do you mean?"

She rubbed her fist into the center of his abdomen and leaned in to kiss him. "I mean it," she said. "No death-defying stunts."

He twined her ponytail around his hand and gently pulled on it so her head tipped back. He stared into her whiskey-brown eyes. "I'm a married man now. I'd be an idiot to do stunts like that," he said and took her lips on a slow ride, tasting the fruity lip balm she had applied moments ago. "Besides, I'm saving the death-defying stunts for Wednesday."

She whacked his arm.

He chuckled.

"Don't worry," he added. "I'll be good."

****

He went to his garage on a patch of private property he bought years ago to entertain his monster truck practices. In two days, he had a competition. His first challenge would be a race with five other fast, skilled drivers. The second challenge would be jumps. The one truck with the biggest air, farthest reach, and best landing would win. He planned to be the champ of both.

He opened the door to his garage. Inside, his neon-green monster truck waited for him. He felt like fist-bumping the grill. On the side of his truck a black Cobra posed to strike. Along its scaly body, green letters spelled *VENOM*. That was the name he had given his truck. His fans and competitors often speculated that he didn't run his truck on the usual methanol that was required of all monster trucks, but rather that he filled it with real snake venom, and that's why he was undefeated. A few believed he had venom in his veins, and that's why he was fearless behind the wheel. They were partially true. He had something burning through his veins, but that burn had dulled since Beth came into his life. He didn't have the desire to be as reckless as he once had been, because he had a life outside of his truck now—a wife, a future.

He checked the air pressure in the tires and the level of fuel. Both were satisfactory. He was cleaning the windshield when a truck came down the dirt road and pulled in beside his truck.

A man wearing a raggedy baseball cap, mud-splattered jeans, and a Speedway T-shirt came out.

He headed toward Donovan with a stop-watch and measuring tape in one hand and a blow horn in the other.

"Hey, Don."

"Hey, Mitch."

Mitch was Donovan's manager. Well, he had started out as Donovan's manager when Donovan first took on monster truck driving. Now, Mitch sat back and let Donovan do his thing, but he still came out to help Donovan prep for a competition and was present for each one.

"How's Beth?"

Donovan smiled. "She's great."

"Damn, to be young again with a woman like that."

Donovan threw the dirty rag he had been using to clean the dust off the windshield into Mitch's face. "Get my wife's body out of your head."

Mitch chuckled as he removed the rag. "It's hard, but I'll do my best." His laughter grew louder when

Donovan scowled at his word choice. "Are you ready to get this beast dirty?"

Donovan hopped off the tire. "Yeah."

"Let's go."

Donovan climbed into the driver's seat, and Mitch clambered into the passenger's seat. He drove around the garage to the track in the back.

"Now remember, the track Wednesday will be twice this size, so you'll have to go around yours four times before I hit stop." Mitch lifted the stopwatch.

Donovan dropped him off at the finish line. He positioned his truck and gripped the steering wheel. His foot itched to come off the brake and punch the gas pedal. He didn't look at Mitch but kept his eyes trained straight ahead. When the blow horn sounded, he slammed onto the gas. The truck took off, lifting onto its back tires. After a moment, the truck dropped back down, and he whipped the wheel to maneuver the truck around a sharp turn. The track was solid and dry from no rain. Dust floated in his wake. Having a dry track was better for the drivers. He had been in many muddy races where trucks fishtailed and took out competition. Wednesday, though, the playing field would be level. Mud wouldn't compromise anyone's times. That meant he'd have to be faster than usual.

He finished the four laps and braked. A cloud of dust blew past his truck and drifted away. Mitch walked up to the driver's side and held the stopwatch up to the plastic covering. The stopwatch said 00:02:42.

Donovan shook his head. "Not good enough. I need to get those seconds down to half that."

"My thoughts exactly."

Donovan blew around the track, doing four laps

each, several times. Each one he knocked a few seconds down on his time. He refueled and kept at it until he reached 00:02:21.

"Happy with that time?" Mitch asked him.

Donovan nodded as he guzzled water. "Much." He pulled out two sub sandwiches from the mini fridge in his garage and handed one to Mitch. They sat at a workbench and consumed the sandwiches with gusto. Once the subs were gone, they went back to practicing. This time to do jumps.

Donovan lined up his truck to the biggest ramp on his track and revved the engine while he waited for the bull horn to sound. The second it blared, he shot up the ramp. The engine roared as the tires ate up the dirt. At the top of the ramp, the truck sprang into the air. It rose and rose. For several seconds, a feeling of weightlessness overtook him. Then the truck started to descend. The tires hit the ground, jostling Donovan. He eased to a stop and waited for Mitch to measure the distance.

"One hundred and fifty feet," Mitch said.

Donovan punched the steering wheel. "Shit." That was far from his best jump, which measured in at two hundred and fifteen feet. He checked the tires and went again. Getting closer to two hundred with each jump. Every time he tried again, he adjusted what he did, learning from each attempt. He wouldn't have a redo tomorrow. He had to nail it the first time. But there was no key to making a perfect jump. There were several factors, such as the angle of the truck when you hit the ramp, the speed at which you lift off, and even the wind was at play. His final jump for the day ranged in at 205 feet. He banged his fists against the steering wheel in triumph.

"Yes, that's what I'm talking about!" He drove to the front of the garage and jumped out to give Mitch a high-five.

"Kid, you're something."

"Thanks, Mitch." He hosed down the truck, refilled the tires, and locked the garage. "I'm gonna go home and make love to my wife." Adrenaline still rushed through him. He needed a release and the best release was with Beth.

"Now you're just showing off. Try to take it easy tonight. You have a big day coming up."

Donovan grinned. "I will. Afterward, I probably won't be able to get out of bed."

Mitch flipped him the bird as he walked away. Donovan roared with laughter.

On his way home, he saw three looming smoke stacks in the distance. From their positions, he noted they were away from civilization, burning acres of unoccupied land. He hoped none of the fires got close to his track and garage, though.

He passed his neighborhood fire station. A sign posted near the road said the fire threat was "High." *No kidding.* If there was a level above high, like dangerously-high, meaning a fire could be in your backyard, that's where they'd be.

He got home an hour before Beth. By the time he had showered, grabbed a beer, and started the first load of laundry, she was pulling into the driveway.

"Hey, honey, I'm hoooome!"

Donovan laughed. "I should be the one saying that to you."

She smiled at him. "Then you need to come home

later." She gave him a kiss hello. "How do Sloppy Joes sound for dinner?"

Donovan recalled his thought this morning about his heart being like Sloppy Joe meat and was repulsed by the idea. "I'm not really in the mood for Sloppy Joes."

"Okay. What about Reubens and steak fries?"

"Sounds good." He got out the ingredients while Beth took a quick shower. On the way back from the fridge, he caught sight of the calendar on the wall. In a box, he saw his own handwriting alerting him to Beth's birthday in five days. While preparing for his competition, the days had gone by in a rush. He had a gift for her, but realized they hadn't talked about doing anything special. If she had it her way, her birthday would be like every other day, but Donovan wanted to celebrate his wife.

Together, they put together the Reubens and fried them on a skillet. At the table, Donovan studied Beth over his plate. Every night before bed, Beth crossed off the day on the calendar, but she never said anything about her approaching birthday. He took a bite out of his sandwich and washed it down with a swallow of beer.

"What do you want to do on Saturday?"

She shrugged. "I don't know. What do you want to do?"

"I want to celebrate the day my wife was born."

She bit into a fry. "You know I don't like a big fuss."

"It won't be a big fuss. It'll be the two of us."

She sighed. "Donovan—"

He cut her off. "For me."

She blinked.

"If not for you, then for me."

A smile broke apart the frown on her face. "Okay, so what do you want to do with me on Saturday?"

He picked up his bottle by the neck and gazed into Beth's eyes. "I'll think about it and surprise you."

"A Goldwyn surprise is my favorite kind."

After dinner, they caught the end of the evening news. Most of the coverage was about the fires burning through Central Florida. A reporter stood in front of black rubble. "Five houses burned to the ground in this neighborhood in Volusia. Five families left homeless with not a possession left other than the clothes on their backs. One family even lost their two dogs."

Beth moved her head back and forth on Donovan's shoulder. "That's so sad. Gosh, I couldn't imagine."

On the television, an image of Central Florida came on with little flames to indicate active brush fires. Seven.

"I wish this would end," Beth muttered sleepily. "Pretty soon, there's not going to be anything left."

Chapter Three

Beth tightened the pony tail at the back of her head as she went down the stairs. The wide-screen television in the living room was on. She paused beside the couch for the weather. The temperature in the corner said her city was at eighty degrees, a rather warm April day. She listened to the news about the fires. One had been put out, but two more had cropped up during the night.

Someone was out there setting those fires. She was sure of it. The first fire, maybe even the first two, might have been because of the dry earth and blazing sun, but the rest had to be malicious. She knew that ashes and embers from one fire could start another fire blocks away, but these fires were separated by many miles. They were in all different cities. Since this started, every city had at least one fire. Her city seemed to be the main target, though.

The fire fighters were working day and night and were stretched thin. Trucks from down south and farther north were coming to Central Florida's aid. Even trucks from Georgia were heading down to offer assistance. Beth hoped the fires came under control soon, or what she had said last night would become reality.

She met Donovan at the kitchen counter.

"Good morning, milady."

Beth snorted at the term. "You're way too happy in

the morning."

"Only when I see your beautiful face." He kissed her on the lips as she rolled her eyes.

She accepted the cup of coffee he gave her. "Do you want something for breakfast?"

"I was just thinking about cereal."

"That's another reason why I love you," Beth said as she took down the Cocoa Puffs. "We think the same."

They ate a bowl of cereal then left—Donovan to look over his truck for the big day tomorrow and Beth to teach self-defense classes.

During the drive to her studio, she went her usual route, bringing her to the neighborhood that had been bursting with flames the day before. The roadblocks and firetrucks were gone. She slowed her car as she looked. The houses had been miraculously spared. Blackened earth circled each lot, but green grass in their front and backyards remained intact.

On the highway, she glanced toward the southbound side to see the land over there charred by the flames that had been flickering dangerously close to her car. The fire was out now, but piles of ashes still smoked. Smoke-tinged air seeped through the vents and dominated the tropical scented car freshener. When she got off the highway, the smell dissipated. The good thing about being in a big city was that brush fires couldn't reach it, because concrete couldn't catch on fire. In the heart of the city, she felt safe.

She parked along the side of the strip mall and entered her studio. The orchids on the front desk sweetened the air by the front door. She inhaled the scent, filling her lungs with it. Closer to the mat, she smelled the antibacterial she used to wipe down the equipment between classes. Beneath that was the tang of sweat. Sweat earned.

She picked up the vanilla bean room spray from behind the front desk and decompressed the nozzle while she made a full circle around the room. Then she checked to make sure the small refrigerator near the front door was well-stocked with bottles of water.

From the storage closet, she hauled out a bag full of boxing gloves to the blue mat and went back for the helmets. Many of her students came with their own equipment, but her beginner students didn't, and that was the class that started out each day. She opened the first bag, took out a pair of gloves, dropped it at her feet, and set a helmet with them. She did this several more times until she had enough equipment out for her students.

Corissa, her front desk receptionist, arrived shortly after. She had recently graduated with a Master's Degree in psychology and was looking for jobs at psychiatrists' offices. Until then, she would continue as Beth's receptionist. Part of Beth, the selfish part, didn't want to see Corissa go. She had hired Corissa when she was fresh out of high school and kept her on during her college years. They had developed a friendship, and at times, Beth felt motherly toward her. She'd hate to lose Corissa to a psychiatrist, but she also wanted Corissa to follow her dreams.

The beginner's class was always Beth's favorite. She enjoyed teaching nervous, scared students how to find the confidence to defend themselves. The techniques were simple. Anyone could do them. She had students as young as sixteen and as old as sixty.

Each of them were treated the same. They came to her for all different reasons. Some wanted to be stronger. Some just wanted a good workout. Parents sought her class for safety lessons for their adolescent children. Others needed her classes to stay alive.

After the beginner's class, she had a moderate class. Then lunch and a second beginner's class. The final class of the day was always the advanced students. For this class, she relied on an assistant. She had hired Dave two years ago when she needed the help. Donovan disliked the man, saying Dave purposefully flirted with Beth in front of him. She reminded him of another man who purposefully flirted with her, their good friend Detective Thorn.

"The difference is I know Thorn would never do anything inappropriate," he had said.

"He kissed me full on my mouth once."

"Yeah, well, I had wanted to hit him then. The point is, I trust Thorn, and I like him. I don't trust or like your assistant."

The topic had been dropped, but his death glare whenever he saw Dave near her hadn't escaped her notice. She knew what Donovan was saying. She had noticed Dave's flirtations, too, but had ignored each and every one of them. Many times, she had even put him in his place, but that didn't make Donovan feel any better when Dave had to put his hands on her during lessons.

Beth always had thirty minutes before the next batch of students usually started to arrive. She went to her office, shut the door, and stepped into her private bathroom. She stripped out of her sweaty workout clothes and used wet disposable towels to freshen up.

From her bag, she pulled out the second change of workout clothes she always brought for a mid-day change. She slipped on black, paint-splattered yoga pants and a teal jog bra. She applied more deodorant, a spritz of body spray, and redid her ponytail before turning to leave and nearly running into Dave.

Seeing him there, watching her, sent chills down her spine. She had been naked moments ago. And she was doing things, like putting on deodorant, that no man had ever seen her do, with the exception of Donovan. "What the hell are you doing? How long have you been standing there?"

He frowned at her. "I just got here." He backed away from the door, letting her pass.

She looked toward her office door, the one she had shut, which was now cracked open. "I didn't hear a knock."

"I didn't knock," he said. "Corissa said you were back here. I thought you were working at your desk."

She didn't believe him. Any normal person would've called out her name after not seeing her sitting behind her desk. She would've told him she'd be out in a moment and would've hastily shut the bathroom door to ensure her privacy. And she wasn't completely sold on him not having seen her naked, either.

"What do you need me for?"

"I was wondering if we could discuss people assisting you during the moderate classes."

She frowned at him but didn't say a word.

"I think the moderate students could use some extra training before the advanced classes, to learn a few maneuvers that require partners."

"They do work in partners."

"Yes, I know, but some of the maneuvers we teach the advanced students in the beginning could be taught during the moderate lessons."

She arched a brow at him. "Are you saying I'm not teaching my students what they should be learning when they should learn it?"

"I think we're wasting our time—"

She cut him off. "I know my students. I know what they're capable of and I know when they're ready for certain techniques. I only move students up to the next class when I feel they have a good grasp on the previous lessons and can handle a tougher routine. I never push them ahead of schedule. All of my classes are tailored to my students' strengths and weaknesses. The advanced students aren't professionals when they start. They have to work up to it. I know what I'm doing."

Before Dave could reply, she stalked out of her office to the main studio. She usually wouldn't have gotten so heated so quickly, but after he snuck up on her, she couldn't contain her anger. Besides that, where did he get off telling her how to do her lessons?

"Set up the equipment, Dave," she called over her shoulder as she went to the front desk where Corissa was reading a book.

Corissa slipped a bookmark into place. "I, uh, sort of heard you talking a little loud back there. What's going on?"

Beth flipped through the sign-in sheet to make notes of who, out of her frequent students, had missed the day's lessons. She liked to catch up the previous week's absent students in the next lesson so they wouldn't be behind. "Dave walked into my office, no knock, no nothing, when I was changing."

Corissa gasped. "Seriously? I told him you were changing."

Beth looked up. "You said that?"

"Yeah. I mean, come on. It's not rocket science. You always change now, but when he said he wanted to talk to you, I warned him. Did he…see anything?"

"I honestly don't know. He said he didn't and made it sound like an accident."

"Donovan wouldn't believe that," Corissa said with her right brow quirked.

Beth knew exactly what she meant by those words and with that look. "No, Donovan wouldn't." She glanced at Dave, wondering what she would do with him when the door behind her opened and the bell jingled.

"Hi, Beth."

She smiled at Amanda, her best student. Amanda was eager, skilled, and smart. She reminded Beth of herself when she was an assistant for the self-defense instructor who taught her everything. Amanda had her strawberry-blonde hair in a bun atop her head, and she wore light pink workout pants with a gray fitness top. She always appeared bright-faced and happy, despite her past with an abusive boyfriend who had once stabbed her in the stomach, a secret only Beth and Donovan knew.

All the other students arrived shortly after, and Beth began class. Today's lesson was about getting out of choke holds. Beth went around to every pairing to correct positions and offer tips to help them use their differences of height, weight, and strength to their advantage. Every one of her students was different. Male and female. Victims, teens, grandparents, business people. They were her family. If they cried, she cried. If someone was hurt, everyone stepped in to offer support. Watching them grow filled her with pride. Many of them came looking like frightened puppies with tails between their legs, but they all found their courage with each lesson they completed. Nothing made her happier than seeing her students blossom.

Once they accomplished the escape, she showed them a new maneuver with Dave's assistance. After that, they had free-style time. This was her students' favorite practice. They each took turns being the bad guy by grabbing their partners from behind. They had to find some way to get free. With the advanced students, the game was always fun. Because they were good and knew what to expect, it took more work for them to get away.

Beth and Dave went around selecting individuals at random to test. Beth chose Amanda. She planted her feet and locked her arms around Amanda's waist. Amanda went for the typical points of attack. She lifted her foot to stomp on Beth, but Beth snapped her foot out of the way. She thrust her elbow back, and Beth twisted clear. She threw her head back. Beth dodged it. When she struggled from side to side, looking for the leverage she'd need to send Beth flying over her to the mat, a shout hit the air.

Amanda froze.

Beth released her as she looked for the source of the shout.

"You touched me, you sick bastard!" One of her students, a young woman named Maria, was pointing an accusing finger at Dave. Her entire body shook. Tears rolled down her cheeks.

Beth hurried over.

Maria went to her as if she was a child needing consoling. "He touched me, Beth."

"No, I didn't," Dave said.

Beth ignored him and blocked him from the girl's view. "Tell me what happened."

"H-he put his h-hand between my legs and touched me. He grabbed my…crotch," she whispered the last word. Her cheeks were a searing red.

Hearing Maria's statement and seeing her distress enraged Beth. She knew this girl to be soft-spoken and shy. Getting her to come out of her shell had taken a lot of gentle coaxing on Beth's part. Maria had been raped by her uncle. She was fragile, and from past experience, Beth knew she would never lie, not about something like this.

Beth rotated stiffly to Dave. Her chest was tight. She wasn't breathing. She glared at her assistant, daring him to speak, to lie, to make an excuse. Working closely with people while teaching self-defense meant there was some degree of touching that couldn't be avoided, but grabbing a private area couldn't be done by accident. Never in her entire career had she ever grasped anyone between his or her legs. It just didn't happen. And when you worked with individuals who had experienced trauma like rape and molestation, you were especially careful.

Dave's upper lip was beaded with sweat. His cheeks were flushed, and he was breathing heavily. Usually that would've been a sign of a heavy workout, except for one thing—the bulge in his pants. Dave tried to hide it with his hands and sweaty T-shirt, but there was no hiding it.

Given what happened before class, she did not believe this was an accident. The girl behind her had a figure that could get the attention of any man, especially in tight workout clothes. If Dave could flirt with Beth and stare at her body, then he could do that with any of her female students. She felt awful for not realizing it before, for not seeing the potential danger she was putting them in. She had always thought Dave was her problem, but she was wrong. She hated that she let it get this far.

She faced Maria. "Let's go to my office." While leading Maria to the back, she paused next to Emmett, a black man she lovingly called Bear, and told him to make sure Dave didn't leave.

"He's not going anywhere," Emmett said in a deep voice.

In her office, Beth ushered Maria to a loveseat she had positioned along one wall. She gave her a bottle of water and a tissue. "I'll be right back, sweetie." Before leaving, she turned on her radio to let a soothing piano melody fill the room. She used it whenever she had to calm distraught students. Many tears had been shed in her office.

Angry at Dave, with herself, she marched back into the main room. Everyone was clustered in a group on the mat, looking toward Dave who stood near the front desk. Bear was blocking the door with his arms crossed.

Beth went straight to Dave. "Outside." Bear shifted to the side, and Beth followed Dave out the door onto the sidewalk. She tried to speak softly, but it took all her restraint. "First, you're inappropriate with me. That

I could get over. One thing I will never forgive, or forget, is you being inappropriate with one of my students. How dare you take advantage of a girl who was raped."

"Aren't you going to ask my side of it?"

"I think your side is in your pants. That's all I need to know. You're fired."

Dave's face turned red. His eyebrows drew together. Rage radiated off him. "You bitch!"

He advanced on her.

She lifted her chin and stood her ground. "You really want to do this with a room full of people well versed in the art of self-defense inside? You'd lose, so get out of here before I call the police."

Dave stood there a moment. His body visibly vibrated. Beth expected him to swing a punch at her, and she was ready for it if he tried. He didn't retaliate, though. He whirled around and stalked to his car in the parking lot.

Curse words drifted to her; words that would offend many women. She let them roll off her back as she returned to her waiting students. Seeing them standing there around the front desk, in case she needed them, made her smile. She nodded at them. "It's handled. He won't be back."

Chapter Four

Donovan came home after his day practicing jumps and racing to see Beth sprawled on the couch in her work clothes, with a beer in hand. She never popped open a beer before eight o'clock, and she always took a shower to wash away the day's sweat as soon as she got home.

On the TV was one of those mind-numbing, egotistical, totally BS reality shows that she detested. Seeing her that way immediately told him something was wrong. He set his keys on the counter and went to her.

"Hey." He sat on the coffee table next to her feet. "I never thought I'd see you watching this show."

She pointed her bottle at the TV. "Her boyfriend is a complete ass, but she stays with him for some undefinable reason. And her sister is starting a new business, which makes her mad for another undefinable reason." She took a swig of beer while frowning at the bickering unfolding on the screen.

Worried, Donovan shifted in front of the TV, blocking her view. "Babe, you're scaring me. What's going on?"

She blew out a breath. "I just needed to veg out to something mindless."

"Bad day?"

She looked at him in a way that told him it was

worse than a typical bad day. "I fired Dave."

A slow smile stole across his face. Since the moment Donovan met Dave, he despised the man, and he hated knowing he got to put his hands on Beth, something he was sure Dave enjoyed for reasons unrelated to teaching.

"It's about time." His pleasure and smile faded as he realized Dave would've had to have done something horrible to get the ax from Beth. "Did he touch you, because if he did I'll—"

"Not me," Beth interrupted. "Maria."

Donovan dropped his head into his hands. "Shit. She's such a sweet, wounded girl." He lowered his hands. "What did he do to her?"

"Grabbed her crotch."

Donovan's back straightened as anger flowed through his veins, setting them afire. "What?"

Beth nodded. "And he got off on it, too."

He clenched his jaw. He had sensed something off about Dave. How he'd look at Beth had always made Donovan uncomfortable. He had to restrain himself from ripping Dave from limb to limb several times. That cocky smile he'd give Donovan at the end of a very hands-on lesson, the way he'd strut around as if he owned the studio, everything about the man had ticked Donovan off. He was glad to see Dave go, but sorry for the added trauma Maria would have to work through because of Dave's sick assault.

"That's not all," Beth said, bringing him back. "Before class, I think he saw me when I was changing."

Donovan's face burned as a raging firestorm exploded inside him. His shoulders tightened like cinderblocks. He fisted his hands in his lap, imagining he was strangling Dave. While Beth told him the story, he barely breathed.

"Donovan…" Beth's voice penetrated his thoughts, his rage. "Donovan, you look like you're going to commit murder."

He blinked and refocused on Beth. Taking a deep breath, he forced his shoulders to relax and his hands to unclench. "I'm glad you fired him, because if you hadn't, I would've gone in tomorrow to cripple him and maybe blind him."

"Well…" Beth set aside her beer. "I didn't fire him for what he did to me, but for what he did to Maria. I was so pissed I almost wanted him to make a move on me so I could lay him flat on the sidewalk. And I'm angry at myself for not seeing he posed a threat to my students. I caused this because I turned a blind eye to how he flirted with me."

Donovan shook his head. "This is not your fault. He is the sick creep, not you."

"But I'm supposed to see that. I'm supposed to protect them." Tears welled in her eyes. Her conflict played across her face, drawing her eyebrows together and tilting down the corners of her mouth.

He moved onto the couch beside her, put his arm around her shoulders, and drew her to him. She nestled in to his side. "You can't know everything, Beth, or see the evil in everyone. I know you want to, but you also can't protect everyone."

"In my own studio, I should be able to."

He stroked his finger down her arm. "You stepped in when you needed to and did the right thing. You never could've known Dave would take his sly flirtations this far. He never touched you inappropriately, did he?"

"No. I mean, he never grabbed any of my parts, but his hands did brush."

Hearing her say that made his spine stiffen. He had to inhale and exhale slowly.

"But I always thought it was harmless, only aimed at me, and I could handle it. I was stupid for thinking that. Stupid."

Donovan turned his head and pressed his lips to her temple. "You couldn't have foreseen this."

She didn't argue with him this time, and they fell silent while staring at the TV.

"What are you going to do now?" he asked after a moment.

She let out a sigh. "I need to find a new assistant."

"Any ideas?"

"One." She took a swig of beer. "After this fiasco, it's clear it has to be a woman. I'm not going to risk a male assistant even accidentally brushing a woman inappropriately. And there's only one student who is good enough to ask—Amanda."

Donovan considered Amanda. She was one of Beth's long-time students, always on time and skilled; he'd seen her giving pointers to several students. He nodded. "She'd be a very good assistant."

"That's what I was thinking. Everyone loves her because she's so sweet. I think we'd balance each other out." She grinned at Donovan. "She's the sugar, and I'm the spice."

He threw his head back. "You can be sugar, too," he said with a wink.

****

Wanting to crawl into bed with Beth, Donovan

moved through the first floor, turning off lights. He came to the dining room where his laptop was sitting open on the table. He tapped the mouse pad to see if it was off, and the screen lit up. A website left open filled the screen. The word "adoption" was scrawled across the website's banner. He stared at it a moment.

Is Beth thinking about adoption? She hadn't mentioned it. He lowered the lid and tucked the laptop under his arm. Upstairs, he found Beth sitting on the edge of their king-sized bed, rubbing lotion onto her long, tan legs. He paused a moment to admire her. Watching her complete the simplest task of applying lotion had his chest tightening. She was stunning in her simple beauty—no makeup, pajama shorts, and a tank top.

He stepped up to the bed and sat down next to her. The light aloe scent of the lotion teased his nostrils. He inhaled, drawing the fresh smell into his lungs. "How arc you fccling aftcr your bath?"

Beth squirted more lotion into her palm and caressed the lotion onto her arms. "Much better. On top of the beer, it was just the ticket."

He leaned over and kissed her on the shoulder. "I'm glad." With slow movements, he set the laptop on his lap and eased the lid back up. The screen lit up, and he shifted the laptop so Beth could see it. She stilled in her act of massaging in the lotion. Her cheeks turned pink. She looked at him as if he had caught her red-handed doing something illegal.

"An adoption website?" he asked in a soft voice.

She recapped the lotion and set it on the bedside table. "I was just checking it out."

"Are you thinking about adoption?"

She shrugged but continued to avoid his eye. "It may be our only option."

He set aside the laptop and took her hand. "It's not our only option, because we haven't done everything yet. We've been trying for a few months. Give your body a break. It hasn't happened because it wasn't the time. It'll happen, though, I know it."

She turned to him. "I want it to happen soon."

"I know, and it might. It might happen tonight." He kissed the back of her hand and gazed into her eyes. A slow smirk lifted the corners of her lips. He lifted his eyebrows up and down in a comical show that he knew would make her laugh. "What do you say, Mrs. Goldwyn? Shall we make a baby?"

She linked her arms around his neck. For a moment, she did nothing but return his stare.

Her eyes glistened with unshed emotions. He pressed a hand to the side of her face. His thumb stroked her cheek. She closed her eyes, leaned forward, and framed his face with her hands. Their noses brushed. Their lips touched. But Beth didn't do any more than that. She became still. In that instant, with their bodies sharing the same breath, the emotions bottled so deeply inside her passed to him. He felt what she felt. His throat tightened. His chest constricted. His heartbeat faltered. The punch of her emotion had him squeezing his eyes shut. His wife was hurting. *He* was hurting. For her. With her.

After several seconds, Beth's lips parted, and she kissed him. He kissed her back; gently as if he were kissing butterfly wings. The sensation of her shared emotions on top of the soft kiss was staggering. He moved one hand to cup the back of her head. The joining of their mouths was the most intimate kiss they had experienced yet. Their kiss on their wedding day, though memorable, wasn't even this powerful. This kiss had everything. Their love and pain. Happiness and sadness. Strength and wounds.

Beth continued to kiss him in a way that was almost heartbreaking; yet, it shared a mending emotion. She was giving him all the hurt she'd experienced, and by doing that, she was healing. He was healing her by accepting her burden, by embracing it with both arms and turning it into something beautiful. Each time their lips meshed and their tongues touched, there was more love, more happiness, more strength.

Less pain. Less sadness. Less wounds.

She shifted so her legs were on either side of him and eased back onto the bed, drawing him down on top of her. He didn't break their kiss until she did. She lifted her head to kiss his forehead. Her mouth drifted across his face, kissing his temples and cheeks. When she stopped, he opened his eyes to see a sweet smile on her swollen lips.

"Before we went to San Francisco, the thought of having kids put me into a panic because I didn't think I had the mothering gene. Raising a child from birth to adulthood was a scary thought. How could I do it?" Her fingertips skimmed down his temple to his jaw. "All of that changed the more I fell in love with you, the more I envisioned a life with you. I imagined our wedding and our honeymoon." Her gaze lowered, and he pressed his lips to her forehead. Neither of them foresaw the disaster that would strike on their honeymoon, nearly killing them. "I want a baby because I love you so much. I can't think of another way to show how amazing our love is than by creating another human being. Our children will have the most beautiful parts of us. And carrying a baby for nine months would only make me love you more, because the creation of our love would be growing beneath my heart, a heart that beats for you."

Tears leaked from the corners of her eyes. He wiped them away with his fingers. His heart pounded in his chest. Tears coated his vision and clogged his vocal cords.

"Yes, Donovan," she said. "We shall make a baby."

Donovan dipped his head and kissed her. He wanted to tell her that holding their baby the moment he or she came into this world was something he thought about a lot. Even just imagining it choked him up. A baby that was part her and part him; the thought of it made him swell with love and pride, and she wasn't even pregnant yet.

He planted a line of kisses down her neck, across her chest, and down her arms. The smell of the lotion she had just applied filled him. He lifted her shirt up her body and dropped it to the ground. Every inch of skin on her torso was lavished with attention until her skin glowed a pretty pink. Then he slipped off her pajama bottoms and showed her thighs, kneecaps, and ankles special attention, causing her to squirm from ticklishness and affection.

There wasn't a spot of skin on her he didn't love—the light scar across her chest, the circle of scarring near her shoulder, the dimples in her cheeks when she smiled, the few freckles on her legs, the soft creases of her elbows and knees, the veins showing through the skin of her wrists, the hollow at her throat. He loved it all.

His hands sought the different textures of her body as he caressed every part of her. The satiny feel of her legs. The velvety touch of her shoulders. The dampness of her palms.

With Beth's help, he stripped out of his clothes. Then she took control. Her mouth tasted the skin of his abs. Her fingers followed the cuts in his torso and teased the hair of his happy trail. As she moved, the ends of her hair skimmed over his chest, activating every nerve-ending. His body was revving to go, but he reined it in the best he could until her exploration was finished.

Poised above him, she looked down at him with flushed cheeks and glittering eyes. He knew she was ready without her having to say anything. Wrapping her in his arms, he switched their positions so she was beneath him. He kissed her once more before sliding into her. As he did, she bit her bottom lip, which was something she did every time, and it never failed to arouse him more than he already was. She locked her legs around him and elevated to meet him. Each thrust was like a prayer, a hope, a wish.

When Beth shook with her ecstasy, Donovan gathered her in his arms and held her. Her heart banged against his. He closed his eyes while drawing in her scent. Slowly, his throat unstuck, and the words he had wanted to express to her earlier finally broke free.

"Five years ago, if someone had asked me if I'd ever have kids, I would've laughed at them. Ryan used to tell me all the time 'Just wait until you find the right woman. When you do, you'll want to be her husband,

and you'll want to have her children.' He was right." Donovan let his fingers tangle with her hair as he spoke. The sound of Beth's breathing was all he could hear when he paused to collect his thoughts.

"After I proposed to you, I imagined what I would want our lives to be like. I saw us in a house like this with a dog and three kids. I saw us together to the very end with a big family. I know we'll have that, Beth."

Her hands clutched his shoulders, but she didn't lift her head off his chest.

"At odd times during the day, I catch myself fantasizing about kissing your pregnant belly and talking to our baby. I want to do those things so badly. I also picture what it would be like to hold our baby for the first time. I can almost imagine the dark eyes looking up at me. Your eyes." He took a deep breath. "It'll happen, Beth. Neither of us would have this passion in us if we weren't destined to be parents."

Several seconds went by before Beth rose and peered into his eyes. "I love you so much."

People who said love was only in the mind didn't have a clue, Donovan decided. He didn't believe it was a mere chemical reaction giving us this "in love" feeling, but that the body and soul could actually love. Not just in the mind, but with every fiber of our physical and spiritual beings. So, when he said, "I love you, too" he meant it with every part of him—mind, heart, and soul.

Beth brought her mouth to his, giving him a quick kiss. When she pulled back, she tilted her head at him and frowned. "Do you think this was wise?"

He frowned back. "What do you mean?"

"Aren't athletes supposed to preserve their energy?

Don't they usually restrict sex before a competition?"

Her question made him grin. "I've never been one to follow rules."

She nudged him. "I'm serious. I don't want you to lose your competition tomorrow because you used up everything tonight."

He put a finger under her chin and stared deep into her eyes. "If we made a baby tonight, I don't give a damn about a trophy."

Chapter Five

Beth woke in the morning feeling wonderful. All the tension she had at the end of the previous day had dissolved in Donovan's arms. She showered and went downstairs with a bounce in her step. Donovan was in the kitchen filling a cup of coffee. She kissed him on the cheek and stole the cup from him with a smile.

"You know," Donovan said. "If you *are* pregnant, you shouldn't be drinking coffee."

She froze with the cup an inch from her lips. She thought about that a moment. "If anything happened last night, it'd just be an egg and sperm right now. Plenty of women drink coffee during this stage before they know for sure they're pregnant. So, I think a cup today is okay." She checked the time on the stove. "I have some time before I need to leave. I can make omelets and hash browns."

"I'll help chop."

They diced red, green, and yellow bell peppers, which they added to minced tomatoes, and then Beth added the mixture to some eggs. She poured it into a pan with shredded cheddar cheese. While the giant omelet cooked, she fried seasoned hash browns with butter. With a little finesse, she flipped the omelet so it could cook on the other side. Once it was a light and fluffy yellow with bits of color from the veggies and the hash browns were golden, she divided the meal onto two plates and took them to the kitchen table.

Across from Donovan, she enjoyed her breakfast. As she ate, she read the headlines for today's newspaper. Fire. Fire. Fire. It seemed as though all of Florida was burning. What would happen if it did? The thought of the homeless people and dead wildlife made a dry lump form in her throat. She swallowed it down with some coffee.

As she took a sip, she studied Donovan. Tonight was his big competition. He didn't seem anxious in the least. He never appeared to be nervous about anything, not even his career. His calm-headedness and quick-thinking were gifts. If she were about to compete against the best monster truck drivers in the world, she'd be jittering with nerves.

"Are you excited for tonight?"

"Sure." He shoved in a forkful of egg and potatoes.

She smirked. "Do you think you're going to win?"

"I don't know. Maybe."

"Are you worried about competing against anyone in particular?"

"Nah. I've beat them all at least once before."

She set down her cup. "You're a tough one to crack, Donovan."

He looked up at her. "Are you trying to?"

"Always." She winked at him. "I'm just trying to gauge your level of excitement."

"Oh, I'm always excited." He grinned at her, hinting at something other than driving.

She shook her head at him. "Cute."

"Thanks."

She chuckled as she got up to drain the last of her coffee and set the cup in the sink. "I guess I'm nervous enough for the both of us."

"Thanks for carrying the burden," he teased.

"Yeah, yeah, yeah." She kissed him goodbye. "I'll see you later."

Her drive from city to city was smokier than it had been the day before. While on the highway, she saw three plumes of smoke on the right and two on the left. Five fires burning within miles of each other. More fires were active in other cities farther way. In Palm Bay, there were ten fires burning alone. That was about an hour drive where she lived now. You couldn't drive anywhere without seeing the sign of a fire. You couldn't even turn. She wondered if someone was taking a joy ride through Central Florida, tossing lit matches from their car window every ten miles or so. Did they pull over to watch each match ignite? Did they relish the sight of the fire growing from a single flame to a brush fire? Or did they just toss and drive with the goal of setting as many fires in the shortest timespan?

There was no way all those fires were caused by the hot sun and the dry ground. But what did someone have to gain from starting the fires? What was the purpose?

She got out of her car outside The Fighting Chance. While standing on the asphalt, she rotated to look at the sky around her. The towers of smoke were closer than yesterday. The wind had also carried the smell of the distance fires to the city, telling her there was no escaping it.

She went into the studio to prep for the day. Most of her classes would be unfazed by the absence of Dave, but the advanced class would be affected. After she had the equipment out, the fridge restocked, and the room sprayed with fragrance, she picked up the phone to call her emergency stand-by instructors. She had used them when she was recuperating from the tsunami and during those times when she had come down with the flu. The first two on the list couldn't make it. The third, her old instructor's assistant, Michelle, was free to jump in.

"Thank you. I really appreciate this."

"No problem. Can I ask why you had to fire your assistant?"

Beth pinched the rim of her nose between her thumb and forefinger. "I'd rather not say."

"I understand. I'll be there twenty minutes before to hear your lesson plan."

"Great. I'll see you then. Thanks again. Bye." She hung up as Corissa entered.

"Hey, Beth."

"Hey, Cor. Michelle will be coming in to help with the last class. Can you call Maria for me to check in on her and see if she's coming in today?"

"Sure."

"Thanks."

The first student for the morning beginner's class arrived as Corissa dialed the phone.

Hours later, while Corissa went out for her hour-long lunch break, Beth occupied the front desk. She had heated up a healthy ravioli in the microwave and took a tossed salad from the fridge. At the front desk, she sat down with her food and a bottle of mineral water. During class, she usually had music playing in the background to help her students get excited and ready to move. Now she turned up that music. Her feet tapped the floor, and her head bobbed to the beat as she ate.

Lunch was always a time for Beth to catch her breath, relax, and replenish her energy. She took this hour seriously every day and didn't waste it. Usually, after she finished eating, she'd use the foot massager in her office to sooth her feet and would even stretch out on the couch to rest her body for twenty minutes. Wanting to do her ritual relaxation before lunch was over, she got up to go to her office.

A knock drew her around when she was halfway across the studio. She was prepared to tell whoever it was that she was closed for another forty minutes, but the young woman staring in at her looked familiar. She headed for the door. The closer she got, she recognized the face she had seen only once before. Brown hair was pulled into a bun, and brown eyes were lined with layers of eyeliner. A pink crescent-shaped scar shone on her cheek. It was April, the hooker attacked by a man named Ramirez, a man Beth helped to catch by going undercover.

She unlocked the door. "Hey, April. How are you?" She gave the woman a small hug.

"I'm good. Better. I was, uh, hoping to take a class or two if your offer still stands for free classes?"

"Of course, my offer stands. Come on in." She waved her hand, allowing April entrance.

"It's a bit early yet, but that could give us time to talk." She relocked the door. "You can have a seat if you want. I'm on my lunch break, but I'm done eating now. I suppose I can get out the equipment for the next class." She always swapped out the used gear for clean ones, which Corissa helped her sanitize between sets.

"I can help," April said.

"Okay. Come on." In the storage closet, she

pointed to a bag of helmets. "Grab this and follow me." She hefted a bag of gloves and carried it to the mat. "Everywhere I set a pair of gloves, put a helmet with them." They laid out the equipment for the second beginners class; neither of them saying anything until April broke the silence.

"I, uh, came here a month after I was released from the hospital. Your assistant said you were on your honeymoon…in Hawaii. Were you there…when the tsunami hit?"

Beth froze with her arm outstretched. She didn't talk about what happened to her own friends; they just knew she survived. She straightened her back to look into April's penetrating eyes. "We were there." She paused. "We were *right* there."

April swallowed. "Oh." She shook her head. "It's okay. I won't ask about it." With a pink fingernail, she tapped her scarred cheek. "I hate having to explain when people see this."

Beth looked at her mutilated cheek. April was so beautiful, but everyone who encountered her probably only saw that scar.

"I came again," April said, drawing her attention. "But you were out."

Beth nodded. "Physical therapy." And because April showed her scar, Beth pointed at the round scar on her shoulder. "I was shot in Hawaii. When I came back, I was recuperating." She set down another pair of gloves and helmet. "You still could've taken the class even though I wasn't here. My assistant would've just confirmed with me that your classes are free."

April shrugged. "I didn't want to be here without you."

A twinge in Beth's heart had her reaching out to touch April's arm. She could sympathize with April's feeling. When she first went to therapy, physical and mental, she wanted Donovan there at her side for support. Beth was April's support.

At the start of the class, Beth introduced April. She had started the custom of announcing new students when she first created The Fighting Chance because she wanted her students to feel a comradery to each other. She wanted them to support one another. But April wasn't expecting it and turned several shades of pink in embarrassment.

"Listen up, everyone. We have a new student today. Her name is April. I met her over a year ago, and she has finally decided to join our family. Let's show her what it means to be a member of The Fighting Chance."

Everyone burst into an applause. Shouts of encouragement lifted.

"Welcome!"

"You go, girl!"

During the lesson, Beth stood at April's side to show her how to get into a ready stance and coached her through blocking and throwing a proper punch.

"Untuck your thumb." Taking April's hand, she pried open her fingers to release her thumb from the hold she had on it. Then she curled April's fingers back into her palm and placed her thumb on the outside. "You don't want your thumb inside your palm, because if you strike something, you'll put pressure here and break your thumb." She mimicked what April had done and pointed at the thumb's joint sticking out of her fist.

"Next, which hand is your dominate hand? Are you

a righty or a lefty?"

"Righty."

"Okay. The correct place to put your left fist is near your chin with your right fist farther away. That way you're protecting your face."

She tapped April's sneakers with her feet. "Spread your feet so they're about a shoulder's width apart and lower your body."

April did as told.

"There you go. Now you're ready to kick some ass." Beth grinned.

Grasping a block of foam, she prompted April to punch to get the hang of the form. After several minutes, she changed tactic and taught April how to block punches. She was about to throw a punch for April to deflect when Corissa hurried onto the mat. "Lori, your husband is on the phone. It's an emergency."

Beth lowered her gloved hands as Lori, a middle-aged woman who had been coming to Beth's class for two years, hurried to the phone on the counter. She wore yellow yoga pants and an over-sized T-shirt. Her dark hair, cut in a pixie style, was flattened to her head with sweat.

As Lori talk to her husband, alarm gave way to sheer terror. "Oh God, oh no."

Lori's voice shook. "I'm coming." The phone clattered onto the counter. Lori threw open the door to one of the cubbies and snatched out her purse. "I have to go." Tears zipped down her cheeks. "There's a fire next to my house."

Those words had Beth's heart dropping to her gallbladder. "We'll pray," she said.

A sob broke from Lori, and then she spun around and rushed out the door.

Beth stared after her and watched the door slowly swing shut. The bells clattered, tugging her from her trance; she realized her students were all staring at her. She lifted her hands again. "Back to the lesson." She took a deep breath. "I'll check in on Lori later for news. For now, let's dedicate the rest of the lesson to Lori. Okay?"

Her students agreed and pushed themselves to do better than Beth had ever seen them do. She was proud of them, proud her students had built such a strong bond that they were like family and worried about each other when they were going through tough times.

At the end of their lesson, Beth spoke to Michelle who arrived moments before. She explained the situation and asked if Michelle would be okay leading the class that would start in thirty minutes with one of her students to assist her. Michelle agreed. Beth called Amanda to tell her what was going on and to ask if she'd be up for assisting another instructor for today. Amanda also agreed.

In the back of Beth's mind, she recalled how she had wanted to speak to Amanda today about becoming her permanent assistant, but now was not the time. She hurried out the door as soon as she got confirmation from both women. She didn't even bother to wipe the sweat off her skin with a towel. She hopped into her car, cranked the air conditioning, and sped out of the parking lot toward an expanding plume of smoke in the distance. Worried thoughts circulated in her head. Lori had two children. Were they there, watching the fire creep closer to their home? Was the house still standing? Did the fire department make it in time? Did Lori?

Living in Florida, evacuating your house due to a fire was as frightening as escaping the path of a hurricane. She remembered running to the end of the road when she a little girl in her pajamas. Her mom ran next to her in her nightgown. They were home alone; her dad was working late as a truck driver at the time, and the lights of an approaching fire brightened the pitch-black sky, scoring the night with yellow and orange flares. Her heart had raced ahead of her. The sound of her slippers scratching against the asphalt was loud in her ears.

They made it to the end of the road and looked toward the dancing lights. The fire was a few blocks away. Tears had popped into Beth's eyes and spilled down her cheeks. While they numbly stared at the fire in the distance, a police car stopped in front of them. The officer told them to pack their cars and leave their house.

Beth had scurried back home, tripping on her slippers. She stuffed clothes and her favorite Barbies into her backpack. She snatched up her blankie, pressed it to her chest, and met her mom in the hall as she took pictures off the walls. They crammed their possessions into the car and drove to a hotel. Beth's dad later joined them. She stayed up late watching the news, hypnotized by the blinking red dots on the map that indicating four fires. One of those fires had been close to her home. Luckily, it was put out two blocks from where she lived, but the fear she had that night had stayed with her.

The closer Beth got to Lori's house, the larger the

smoke cloud grew, which meant the fire was large, spreading far and wide. The smoke was black, and the sky was tinged brown. Around the corner from Lori's house the air was so thick with smoke it was hard to see. She pulled over onto the grass with a few other cars—onlookers. Sliding out of her car, smoke encircled her, stinging her eyes and suffocating her. Not bothering to lock the doors, she jogged toward Clinton Street.

Flames licked the sky. Embers floated several feet in the air above the peaks of burning trees. Ashes shattered against her skin and settled in her hair. She rounded the corner, and her feet skid to a stop. Her mouth dropped open. Her hand cupped her chest. Lori's house was engulfed in flames.

Two firetrucks were parked in the road in front of the house. Thick streams of water shot forth from the trucks toward the inferno. Flames had reached the road and were on either side of the driveway. The entire lot was up in flames, including the oak tree in the front yard that used to have a tire swing hanging from a sturdy branch.

Through the haze, Beth saw Lori's yellow yoga pants. She ran down the road, slipping past firefighters, to her friend. Tears were in her eyes when she stopped next to Lori. Holding back a coughing fit, she touched Lori's arm.

Lori turned. Her eyes were bloodshot from tears and smoke. Her cheeks were wet and streaked with black. "B-Beth."

Beth silently pulled Lori into a hug and stared at the burning structure. Beneath the many layers of orange flames, the lines of the house were barely visible. Heat slammed into the side of her face. It was so intense she thought the waves of heat blasting her could sear her skin. She tugged Lori to the other side of the street, away from the flames, and turned her around so the house was behind her. She rubbed Lori's back as Lori clutched her and sobbed.

Over Lori's shoulder, she saw the house collapse into a burning heap.

****

Beth dragged herself into her house. With Donovan's competition starting at six o'clock, she had been prepared to leave work early, but she hadn't even returned to work after going to Lori's house. She stayed until the firefighters forced them to leave. Then she walked back to her car, her lungs bursting, and drove home. She went straight to the kitchen where she filled a glass of water and chugged it at the sink.

"Rough day?"

She glanced at Donovan as he walked to her. "You can say that."

He kissed her temple. "You smell like smoke."

"Lori's husband called during class." She met his gaze and said two words, "A fire."

Donovan sucked in a breath.

"Her house is gone." Her chest tightened. Tears pressed against the backs of her eyelids. "I saw it fall to the ground." She shook her head. "They have nothing left."

Donovan wrapped his arms around her. She nuzzled her face into the crook of his neck and breathed in his scent. "You don't have to come to my competition tonight," he whispered in her ear. "You can stay home, relax."

"No." She inched back. "I want to see you compete. I'll take a shower and wash my hair. Could you make me a sandwich?"

"Sure. What kind?"

"Peanut butter and jelly."

She lathered her hair and let the rancid bubbles wash down the drain. Smelling better, she dressed in jeans and a neon green T-Shirt with the logo from Donovan's monster truck on the front—a black cobra posing to strike. On the back was the name of his truck—*Venom*.

Donovan grinned when he saw her T-shirt. "Looks good on you."

She tugged the hem and winked. "Thanks."

He stepped up to her, dipped his head, and kissed her below her ear. "Mm. You smell nice." He kissed his way down her neck. The way he savored her clean skin made her moan.

She slung her arms around his neck and pressed her body to his, needing to feel his heat that could burn her on the inside but not the outside, not like the fire that consumed Lori's house. The kiss deepened, scorching her. He lifted her onto the counter. His hands sought the heat beneath her shirt. They fondled her flesh and warmth. Her legs locked around him, and her ankles crossed. She felt like a torch ignited with passion. When Donovan's fingers fiddled with the button of her jeans, she put her hand on his chest and pushed him back. She was panting, and her body was humming. She would've loved to take Donovan into her and forget all about the peanut butter and jelly sandwich sitting a foot away on the counter, but Donovan needed to keep his strength for his competition.

"No," she said. "Use what you're feeling tonight. It'll be good fuel." She pushed him back and hopped off the counter. Donovan groaned as she picked up the plate and took a big bite out of the sandwich. Mouth full, she sauntered out of the kitchen with her button still undone.

Chapter Six

Donovan stood next to *Venom*. He wore a black fire suit with neon green lines and a cobra on his back to match the one on his truck. The front was partially unzipped, revealing the white T-shirt he wore underneath. He inspected each tire thoroughly, making sure there were no cracks or leaks. Inside the cab, he checked the gauges and tugged on the harness to make sure it was secure. He did this before every competition, like a ritual. In his head, he worked down a mental checklist. He made sure the tank was full and the tire pressure was right. Without doing a full internal scan of the engine and every part, he felt the truck was good to go. He jumped out and strode to where Beth squatted next to a tire with a rag in hand as she rubbed the silver clean.

He took the rag from her and tossed it at Mitch. "You're not a grease monkey, Beth."

"Hey, I can get greasy," she protested.

"Mm." He dipped his head and claimed her mouth. "I know," he said against her lips.

She laughed.

"Save that lust for later," Mitch shouted. "Better yet, use it in the competition. You're here to make me money, kid."

Donovan raised a brow at Mitch. "Make you money? You're a funny man."

"Who said Donovan would win?" a deep voice asked.

Donovan turned to see his friends Smith and Gordon approaching. Smith's usual Mohawk was flat against his scalp. He had on a blue fire suit. Gordan's thick beard touched the collar of his white and black fire suit. Both men were grinning from ear to ear.

Donovan clapped their hands, and Beth hugged them.

"You better not be dreaming about my trophy, Goldwyn," Smith said.

"Ha! You boys are going to be choking on my fumes," Gordan claimed.

Donovan smiled. "Ah, friendly competition. Why don't you guys make sure you brought your trucks and not your grandmother's cars?"

"Whatever, man."

"We'll see who's laughing when I leave ya'll in the dust."

Donovan chuckled as his friends left. Horsing around with Smith and Gordon before any competition, big or small, had become a ritual.

He turned back to Beth as a group of girls circled him, blocking her.

"Hey, Donovan." They giggled as they pressed closer. The smell of five different perfumes filled his nose, nauseating him. "Can we get your autograph?"

He signed pictures of himself and passed them back. The final girl flung her blonde hair over her shoulder and pushed out her breasts. "Can you sign *me*?" Her voice oozed seduction.

If he were younger, single, and foolish, he would've signed the woman's breasts and included his phone number, but he wasn't that reckless boy anymore. His eyes didn't even lower to her low-cut T-shirt. "Sorry," he said. "I don't do that."

She pouted with lips that shone from too much gloss. "Then my arm?" She stuck out her arm.

Sighing, mouth set, he took her wrist with two fingers and signed her forearm.

"Thanks." She batted her eyelashes at him.

The five girls left, giggling up a storm.

Grimacing, he looked at Beth. Her eyes were locked on the girls as they left.

"Sorry about that." He wrapped his arms around her waist.

She shook her head. "You don't have to apologize. I've gotten used to women drooling after you at the grocery store, but this is your arena. You're a star here. I'm just going to have to get used to women throwing their goodies at you."

He shifted uncomfortably.

She took the side of his fire suit in her hands and looked up into his face. "I trust you, Donovan."

"Thanks." He pressed his lips to hers.

Mitch stepped up them. "It's almost time."

Donovan nodded, and Beth zipped his suit up the rest of the way. After she snapped the collar into place, he reached behind her neck to undo the necklace she wore. He took off his wedding ring and slide it onto the chain. He closed the clasp and draped the necklace over her head so the ring rested over her heart. Before every competition, he did this. It wasn't good to have metal against your skin in case of a fire, and he liked knowing Beth would hold his promise until he could put it back on his finger.

She handed him his gloves. He slipped his hands in one at a time.

"Hey, sorry I'm late." Thorn came up to them.

Thorn was a good friend of theirs. He had their back when they went to San Francisco searching for Buck, one of Donovan's brother's killers, and came to their rescue in Oahu after the tsunami. If it weren't for him, Donovan wouldn't have known Beth was alive, had been kidnapped, and waited for him to find her.

"Thanks for making it," Donovan said.

"I wouldn't have missed this." He slung his arm around Beth. "Can I buy you a drink?"

Beth nudged him in his side. "Maybe later, boyfriend." She sent Donovan a teasing smile.

Ever since Thorn came into their lives, he never failed to flirt with Beth and push Donovan's buttons. He knew they were close but would never be as close as Beth and Donovan were. Because he knew that, their antics no longer bothered him. Much.

"Just don't get her drunk," Donovan said and climbed into his truck.

Beth stepped onto the rail and leaned in through the opening. She waited for him to buckle the harness into place. She tugged on it as became her custom since the first time she attended one of his competitions. Satisfied he was secure, she lay her hands on either side of his face. "Good luck and be safe." She kissed him, deepening it with a bit of tongue.

"Mm. That'll definitely bring me luck," he said and winked.

When Beth hopped down, he shut the door and placed his helmet on his head. Through the shield that protected his eyes, he saw Thorn escorting Beth to the first row where they'd watch the competition.

Mitch gave him a thumbs-up.

Donovan drove out onto the track to his place next to his competitor. He was in the first race. If he won, he'd move onto the second round to face the driver who won the next race. He'd do this again and again until he was eliminated, or won the tournament.

He couldn't hear the cheers over the rumble of his engine, but a glance at the stands showed rows and rows of people with their fists and beers in the air. He peered back at the track. His hands clutched the steering wheel with a death grip. The truck beside him revved its engine, an intimidation factor, but he paid it no mind. He tuned out the other truck and zeroed in on the stretch of brown dirt in front of him. Nothing could disturb his laser concentration.

When the flag was waved, he slammed his foot down on the gas pedal. His truck lifted off the two front tires and dropped down. Side by side, Donovan moved up a wide ramp, big enough to fit two trucks. He launched into the air first. He kept his eyes on the ground as it came back up. He landed smooth, but his competitor didn't. The other truck swerved and smacked into Donovan's bumper. He ground his teeth and fought to control his truck. When he straightened his wheels, he made a sharp turn, lifting off two tires. Then he shot forward, leaving his competitor in his dust. He made the second lap easily and crossed the finish line with the other truck half a lap back.

The next race was between Smith and another driver known as Flame, because he had set fire to four trucks in past competitions. Donovan watched the race, rooting for his friend, and was glad when Smith won.

The cheering for his friend ended there, because they were up against each other now. He took his place next to Smith's truck, which was fashioned to look like the American Flag. He turned his head and nodded at his friend. Smith nodded back. Although they were competitors, they were buds. They could race each other, root for each other, lose against each other, and have beers together while watching a game.

Donovan shot forward with Smith keeping pace with him. Even when they made their first jump, they were head to head. After the first lap, Donovan knew he'd have to do something to get ahead of Smith. He whipped around a turn, sending up a wave of dirt. His back tires fishtailed, but he controlled it and flattened the gas pedal to the floor. The nose of his truck inched past Smith's bumper. When they leapt off the ramp, he got so much air that he rose higher than Smith's truck. He landed a full-truck's length ahead. With his sights on the finish line, Smith gained on him. The bumper of Smith's truck was a foot from Donovan's when they crossed the finish line.

Two more races took place with Donovan competing against the winner of both. The last side-by-side race before the finale was between Gordan and a first-timer. The arena was split. Half of the fans rooted for the rookie, and the other half rooted for the veteran. Donovan watched Gordan gain the lead in the first lap. For the final jump, something went wrong, though. His truck tipped too far, bringing the nose of the truck toward the ground. Donovan stood as the front of Gordan's truck clipped the ground, tearing off a piece of it. Donovan stared wide-eyed as the truck tipped onto two wheels, rolled onto its back, smoothly got back onto its tires, and continued as though nothing had happened. He cheered with the crowd when Gordan won by a foot.

When Gordan returned to where all the trucks were, Donovan tackled him. "Shit, man, that was a sweet save."

Gordan laughed. "Thanks, but friendship aside, I'm gonna crush you."

Donovan shook his head. "All talk."

He went to the bathroom while his truck was refueled and more air was put into the tires. On his way back, he heard an official announcing the final race for the trophy would be between two veteran racers and crowd favorites.

"Donovan Goldwyn driving *Venom*, the undefeated champ so far in this tournament, and his rival, but good friend, Gordan Morris driving *Bone Crusher*."

The cheers shook the stands.

Donovan climbed back into his seat, put on his five-point harness, and drove onto the field next to Gordan. He gave Gordan a thumbs-up before shutting down everything except his connection to his truck. The flag lowered, and his truck flew off the starting line. He fought with Gordan over the lead. As soon as he got a foot out front, Gordan would take it back and vice versa. Gordan had a head on him when they roared up the ramp, but when they landed, he had gained two more feet.

Shit. Donovan's grip tightened. He pushed his truck to go faster, faster, faster. Around a turn and another turn back to the ramp. He knew how Gordan drove, knew he always took his foot off the gas pedal when he was in the air and put it back on after he landed. It was the reason why he was able to save himself after rolling earlier. But Donovan didn't take his foot off. He didn't even keep it steady as he normally did. No, he put the pedal to the floor, so when he landed, his tires rotated furiously and shot him forward. He passed Gordan. He didn't let up around the turns but kept the pedal to the metal. The final stretch of dirt lay before him. He aimed for it with Gordan behind him and shredded the finish line with his tires.

Excitement blazed through him. He imagined he could hear the crowd roaring. He took his foot off the gas pedal to slow the truck, but the truck didn't slow. Frowning, he pushed on the brake. Nothing. He firmly pushed his foot into the brake, a move that would've caused a quick, uncomfortable stop, but the truck continued at its fast speed.

What the hell is going on?

He forced the wheel to the left, away from Gordan's truck and the stands ahead. He moved around the arena as he pumped the brake. His truck wasn't even registering the brake was being touched. It was as if the brakes were disengaged, broken. He kicked both of his feet into the pedal, driving it into the floor with enough force to snap the plastic. And yet the truck kept going.

The wheel jerked in his hands. *What the fuck?* He wrestled with the steering wheel as it turned on its own. Eyeing the ramp ahead, he tried yanking the wheel, but it was locked in place.

He felt the truck pick up speed.

Impossible.

The gauge on the speedometer moved to dangerous speeds. At this speed, the outcome would be bad. Very,

very bad. He had to stop his truck.

He flicked up the first kill switch that should've deactivated his truck, but nothing happened. He jiggled it up and down. Still nothing. He reached for the second kill switch as his truck zoomed up the ramp. Same thing. He flipped the third and last kill switch and looked up in time for his truck to boost into the air. The height he reached was unimaginable. Just by the feel of how long it took his truck to rise, he knew it was an insane height. Then his truck started to fall, and with such a long way to go, he knew what would happen. His truck tipped.

The ground rushed up to him. He let go of the steering wheel and crossed his arms over his chest. His fingers curled around the straps of his harness. His truck was in a nose dive when it collided into the ground. Crunching metal echoed in his ears. His breath was punched from his chest. The force of the hit sent his body forward, but the harness snapped him back into the seat. A grunt flew from his lips. In the next second, the truck dropped backward onto the hood. The sound of the engine roaring filled his ears, although his foot was off the gas and he had toggled all three kill switches.

After a moment, his truck died, and he knew it was because the official with the kill radio had shut off his truck. Reaching up, he unlatched the head strap. He was about to release the shoulder harness when he heard yelling. He turned his head to see Beth being restrained by a security guard a few yards away. "That's my husband," she shouted.

Beside her, Thorn lifted his badge. "I'd let go of her if I were you."

The security guard freed Beth, and she joined Mitch and the paramedics rushing toward him. He hit the button to release his harness and fell to the roof of his truck. Mitch tore aside the plastic covering the empty window. Donovan started to back out of it head-first. Hands gripped him beneath his shoulders and pulled him out the rest of the way.

"You should've let us stabilize your neck first," he heard a medic say.

He shook his head as he shoved himself into a sitting position, with his back against his truck. "I'm fine," he panted. He ripped the helmet off at the same time Beth slid next to him.

"Oh my God, Donovan." She cradled his face in her hands. "Are you hurt?" Fear reflected in her eyes.

He took a deep breath. "I'm good. I'm good." He wasn't sure why he said it twice, but his body vibrated on its own accord. He couldn't control it. What happened had shaken him so much his limbs were shivering.

"What kind of stunt were you trying to pull, Goldwyn?" Mitch asked.

"It wasn't a stunt," he said, with his voice shaking. "The brakes didn't work. The kill switches didn't work. The steering wheel moved on its own, and the truck picked up speed. I couldn't do a damn thing to stop it."

The paramedics helped him to his feet. With Beth on one side and Mitch on the other, he walked off the track. The crowd cheered, and he waved to reassure him he was okay. What they didn't know was that with each step he took, his legs wanted to give out. He collapsed onto the stretcher and lay down so the medics could wheel him into the ambulance. Beth climbed in after him. She smoothed his hair from his sweaty forehead.

"I'll follow in my car," Thorn said.

Donovan nodded.

At the hospital, he had a full-body scan and X-rays done. None of the scans showed breaks or fractures. He was sore, but he figured that was all he'd have to endure. He was lucky. If his harness hadn't held, if the engine had ejected into his seat, if his legs had been trapped, he could've suffered terrible injuries, or died.

Back in his fire suit, he sat on the edge of the hospital bed as he waited for permission to leave. Mitch was there and so was Thorn. Both men had their arms crossed as they listened to Donovan go over everything again.

"I'm telling you it was like my truck was possessed." He met Thorn's eye. "As if someone else was controlling it."

Thorn's frown deepened. "Weren't you with your truck the whole night?"

Donovan shook his head. "No. Just before the last race, I left to go to the bathroom, but Mitch was there." He looked to his manager.

Mitch lifted his hands. "I was talking to an official before the last race. I didn't even know you left."

"So, someone had the chance to fuck with my truck and nearly get me killed."

Thorn uncrossed his arms and grabbed his cell phone. "I'm going to investigate this with a few of my men, find out if foul play had anything to do with it. Your truck is being held under guard for inspection, but I'll have it brought in to the department for criminal investigation. Whether someone tampered with it or not, we're treating it as though someone did."

"Thanks," Donovan said.

Thorn left, followed by Mitch. The only one who remained was Beth, who had been silent since they arrived. He took her hand and kissed her fingers. "I'm sorry for scaring you."

She looked at him with tired eyes. The fear she felt earlier hadn't entirely vanished. He was about to apologize again when she wrapped her arms about his neck and held onto him. He curled his arms around her. Her body rocked against him. His throat tightened; she was crying. He rubbed her back, hoping to soothe her.

"I'm sorry, Beth. I'm okay. I'm okay. I'm okay." He repeated that as she sobbed.

Several minutes later, she eased back and wiped her face with the back of her hand.

"Why would someone do this?"

"I don't know." He touched her swollen lips with his. "But our Superhero Detective will figure it out."

"I'll tell Thorn you called him that."

Donovan managed a small laugh. "Don't."

"Oh, I think I will." She offered him a weak smile. "No one mentioned it but...you won the race. Congratulations."

He cupped her face with his hands and gave her a long kiss that had her leaning into him. "Thanks," he whispered into her mouth.

Chapter Seven

Beth's churning stomach woke her up from a sound sleep. She sat up in bed and placed her hand on her stomach. It gurgled beneath her palm. Her insides danced, her mouth filled with saliva, and her heart rate elevated. She hurried to the bathroom, dropped to her knees, and flung open the toilet's lid as the first wave hit her. The contents of her stomach flowed into the bowl, splashing unpleasantly. Her throat burned with acid. She couldn't breathe. Her stomach heaved several times, not giving her a break. When it finally settled, she sucked in a breath. Her eyes watered. She sat on the cold tile, shivering as she spit the vile taste from her mouth and made sure her stomach wouldn't revolt.

At the sink, she rinsed out her mouth and took a sip of water to soothe her throat. Her face and neck felt on fire. She wet a small towel and patted her skin. Her limbs shook, and she lowered back onto the tile by the door. The last time she had gotten sick to her stomach she was in college and had the stomach flu. She hoped she wasn't coming down with something. With an investigation on Donovan's truck happening, she couldn't afford to be sick. What if it was malicious? She had to be well to be there for Donovan.

A knock sounded on the door.

"Beth, are you okay? I heard you…"

She grimaced. That was exactly what you wanted

your lover to hear…you hurling your guts out into the porcelain throne.

"I'm fine." She reached up and opened the door.

Donovan's head lowered when he realized she was on the floor. He dropped to his knees. "Are you sure?" He touched her forehead. "You don't feel hot."

"Don't worry about me, Donovan. I'm not the one who was in a car accident last night." She put a hand on his shoulder. "Are you sore, stiff?"

"I'm fine." He brushed aside her concern. "What about you?"

She tried to sweep aside his concern as well. "It's probably just stress."

"Or it's the stomach virus. It's been going around." He took the towel from her, refolded it to get to the cool side, and pressed it to the back of her neck. "Or…" He paused. "Or maybe you're pregnant." The mixture of hope and concern in his eyes made her heart tremble.

She shook her head. "I took a pregnancy test last week. It was negative. And if I miraculously got pregnant the other night, I wouldn't be dealing with morning sickness so soon." She frowned. "Or at least I don't think so."

"You should take another test just to be sure."

Her gaze strayed to the drawer where the loot of pregnancy tests and ovulation tests waited for her to use them. Last week, she had used all seven ovulation sticks in a box to figure out which two days were her peak fertility days. It was the week her fertility doctor said she'd be ovulating. Except, she wasn't. Each time the results said her LH surge was low. She used the pregnancy test in the pack, the final test, and it was negative. They were always negative.

"Sure." She started to push herself off the ground. Donovan caught her arm and brought her to her feet. Her legs felt wobbly, and her stomach was still queasy. She opened the drawer and selected a pregnancy test that was supposed to tell you if you were pregnant five days before your expected period. She waved the box in the air. "Get out of here so I can pee on a stick." She managed a smile though she didn't feel at all chipper.

Donovan excused himself. While she waited the three minutes, she sat on the closed toilet seat with her bath towel wrapped around her shoulders. She couldn't stop herself from stealing peeks at the test every thirty seconds, willing the answer to reveal itself sooner. When it did, she picked it up to show it to Donovan. She was surprised to see him sitting on the edge of their bed, with his hands clasped and his head down. If she had known he was there, waiting, and not downstairs, she would've opened the door right away so they could wait together. She held the strip out to him. He took it and saw the single line. The negative line. She shrugged when he lowered his hand and looked up at her.

"Maybe you should call out sick today, anyway. You might have a bug."

She sat on the bed next to him, with the towel still around her shoulders like a shawl. "I don't want to call out. I lost all that time with my students when I was doing physical therapy. One of my students just lost her home, and I got a brand-new student who waited to come until she knew I was there, because she didn't want to take classes without me."

Donovan frowned. "Who?"

"April." When she didn't see recognition, she elaborated, "The young woman beaten by Ramirez? I had told her to come to my studio to learn to defend herself. She did, but we were in Oahu." She paused as she pushed back the tsunami memories trying to resurface. "She came back when I was out for therapy and still she didn't sign up. She had her first class yesterday, and I don't want to disappoint her by not being there today."

Donovan nodded. "Okay. Then cancel your first class, take it easy, and see how you feel when it's time to leave for your second class. If your stomach feels just a little squeamish, stay home."

She knew that was the best compromise. "I will. I promise."

Donovan cracked open a bottle of sports water and set a sleeve of crackers on the end table next to Beth. "I'm going to the department to check on my truck and see if they've found any answers. If you need me, call. I could get Thorn to give me a police escort."

Beth smiled. "I'll be fine. I'm just going to lay here with my drink and crackers and watch some reruns. If I decide to go in to work, I'll let you know."

He seemed reluctant to leave, and it warmed her. "I mean it, Goldwyn. I'm fine."

"All right." He kissed the top of her head twice before leaving.

She adjusted the hot water bottle on her belly and shifted into the couch cushions to watch her favorite sister-witches.

When the two episodes ended, she took a shower and called Donovan.

He answered with, "Are you okay?"

She laughed. "Yes, I was just calling to say I'm much better, and I'm going in to work. I think it was just everything that happened yesterday and the cheeseburgers we ate when we got home last night."

"Okay, but if you start to feel sick at work—"

"I'll upchuck on the mat in front of my students." She chuckled. "I'll sit down. If that doesn't work, I'll come straight home."

As soon as she convinced Donovan she had her upset stomach handled, she headed out the door. Instead of going straight to work, though, she took a detour to Lori's house. A house wasn't there, though. The whole street had been reduced to ash. Burned two-by-fours in the four corners of Lori's house stood like gnawed bones. There was no green anywhere, not a blade of grass or a leaf on a tree. The oak that had stood tall behind a backdrop of flames yesterday was now a black skeleton.

She parked in front of the ruins and got out of her car. Smoky air swooped around her like transparent, arsenic wings. It was quiet. Wind didn't rustle through leaves, grasshoppers and bugs didn't emit their little creaks, and birds didn't chirp as they hopped from branch to branch. No life. Just death.

There weren't even any other cars on the road, or the one behind it, which she could see without the brush obscuring her vision. Filthy water flooded the foot of the driveway. She jumped over it and walked up the driveway littered with curls of ash. They crumbled like dust beneath her sneakers. At the edge of the house's foundation, she stared at the piles of dead embers. She couldn't even tell where any of the rooms had been.

Squatting, she picked up a piece of charred wood. Black rubbed off onto her hand. She dropped the wood and stood up while wiping her palm against her jean shorts.

Ducking under the caution tape, she stepped into the ruins. Her shoes crunched rubble-like charcoal. Smoke rose off piles. Everything was blackened and slightly damp from the water pumped onto the house by the firefighters. She picked her way with careful steps. Near the center, she found an oven buried in wood. The once-smooth surface had rusted. Several feet away, the fridge lay on its side. The black paint had melted off. Scorch marks covered the dented metal. Nothing else was recognizable.

She tramped through the rubble to the cement pathway leading to the front door. Moving across the yard, her sneakers dug into ash and dirt, covering the wet soles with black flakes and brown grains. She went to the oak and pressed her hand to the blackened tree trunk. Seeing the oak without a speck of green saddened her. Did life lurk beneath the layers of burnt bark? Years from now, would it flourish with color? She hoped so.

On her way to her car, she pulled out her cell phone.

"Hello?" The woman's voice on the other end sounded exhausted.

"Hey, Lori. It's Beth. How are you and your family?"

Lori sniffed. "We're okay. We're staying at my sister's." Her voice shook. "We...we lost everything."

Sobs touched Beth's ears, breaking her heart. What she felt when her childhood home was damaged by Hurricane Sabrina and had to be demolished didn't compare to this woman's agony. Beth had been able to salvage a lot, and now her new home was built on that very lot. But Lori had nothing left. Not a scrap of clothing, picture, or book.

"I'm so sorry, Lori. I…I'm going to start a collection at The Fighting Chance for your family. I'll pass out fliers to everyone. We'll get you your basics and whatever necessities your family needs."

"Th-thank you."

"If there is anything Donovan and I can do, please let us know. And keep us updated on how you guys are doing."

"I will. Thank you. Bye."

"Bye."

Beth hung up with a heavy heart, wishing she could do more. *Maybe I can.* She considered the money in her separate account—apart from their joint account used for mortgage and bills. With her money, she could buy Lori's family a lot of basics.

She turned to her car, wanting to start her shopping spree, and noticed a black sports car stopped at the end of the road. The moment she noticed it, the car sped off with a squeal of tires. Her heart launched into her throat. She put a hand to her chest as her knees weakened. The memory of the black sedan spying on her and ramming into her bumper over a year ago came back to her with such force her stomach lurched.

She ran to the side of the road for cover, and then she realized there were no bushes and fell onto her knees where grass use to be. She threw up what little she had kept down earlier that morning. The rancid smell of burnt wood clogging her nostrils made her gag harder. She forced air between her teeth and coughed when smoke rubbed against her raw throat.

Hands shaking, cold and sweaty, she drove away

from the fire-ravaged neighborhood toward The Fighting Chance. Corissa was already there when she arrived.

"Do you have antacid, or anything to settle an upset stomach?"

Corissa lifted her backpack off the floor to root inside it. "Are you sick?"

"I threw up twice."

Corissa looked as though she wanted to spray Beth from head to toe with disinfectant and bathe herself in hand sanitizer.

"I don't have the flu. I think it's just stress."

Corissa took a travel-size container of antacid out of her backpack and handed it to Beth. She shook five colorful tablets into her palm, popped them into her mouth, and crunched on them as she went to the backroom for a bottle of water. The tablets turned to chalk in her mouth. She swallowed it with a shudder and used water to wash it down. After sitting for ten minutes, she felt ready to teach.

When it was time for lunch, she ate crackers in her car while driving to the store. She had an hour before her next set of classes began. At the store, she filled the cart with one hygiene item each for women, men, and children. She added pillows, pillowcases, and blankets. Then she tossed in a few other goodies like candy, a few books, and two board games. She walked back into her studio with bags weighing her down.

"What's all that?" Corissa asked.

"It's for Lori and her family." She unloaded the bags in the far corner. Under her arm, she had a white poster board. She took it over to the front desk. "We're starting a collection. Can you make a sign for the wall and print out fliers to hand out to everyone as they leave?"

"No problem."

Beth was in the middle of teaching her second beginner's class when Donovan arrived. She looked over as she corrected April's stance and told her to throw another punch. "There you go. Perfect form. I'll be right back." Slipping past April and her other students, she met up with Donovan at the front desk.

Donovan waved at someone behind her.

Beth glanced over her shoulder to see April waving back. Smiling, she stopped in front of Donovan. "Hey, what are you doing here?"

"I'm checking in on my sick wife."

She playfully whacked his arm. "You're making me sound terminal. For the hundredth time, I'm fine. I've been kicking ass all over this blue mat."

His violet eyes fell to slits. "Did you eat anything for lunch?"

"Crackers."

He gave her a stern look.

"I know, I know. I'll have soup and peppermint tea for dinner...upset stomach cures." She decided to change the conversation. "Did you see your truck?"

Donovan's stern expression turned pained. "Yeah." His shoulders lowered. "I'm going to have to replace the entire front end."

"Damn. I'm sorry. Did they find anything?"

He sighed. "Not yet. They're just starting."

"I hope they can find out what happened and why," she said, hating the idea someone had sabotaged her husband's truck to cause him harm. Even death.

Donovan trailed a finger down her arm. "They

will." His gaze shifted. "What's all that?"

She looked toward the bags in the corner. "I'm starting a collection for Lori's family. Everyone is going to try to donate something. New and used."

"And your students brought all of that in today?"

"No. I did." She gave him a skeptical smile. "I bought that during my lunch break with my extra money. I had to do something."

Donovan lifted his hand and touched a stray lock of her hair. "You're amazing."

She shrugged. "I'm just doing what I can."

He smiled. "Are you accepting money donations?"

"Yeah, of course." She frowned as he took out his wallet and located the spare check behind some bills he kept for emergencies.

"We have a lot in savings," he said as he filled it out. "I think we can spare this."

She gawked when she saw it was for one thousand dollars. "Donovan. Are you sure?"

"They have two kids. They need it more than we do."

Donovan's compassion and generosity made her heart swell. She stepped up to him and put her hands on his chest. "I married the best man in the world." Leaning in, she touched her lips to his. "In the galaxy." She kissed him again. "On this side of the universe."

He pulled her to him, held the back of her head, and deepened the kiss.

Applause, hoots, and whistles sounded from behind her. She laughed into the kiss as her students egged them on.

Donovan left before her last class started, although he had threatened to stay during the whole thing until

Chrys Fey

she insisted she felt fine. No weakness, no light headedness. And she had to talk to Amanda today. She couldn't put it off any longer.

Amanda was the first to arrive, as usual, ten minutes early. Beth appreciated her punctual nature. She knew she'd be able to count on Amanda to show up when she needed her. "Hey, Amanda, can we talk a minute?"

Amanda set down her bag. A worried look took over her face. Her smile vanished, and her eyebrows lowered. She swallowed. Her hands fumbled as they smoothed her workout top, a nervous act Beth had seen her do a couple of times before, as if she were making sure to conceal the scar on her abdomen.

Beth smiled to reassure her. "Don't worry. It's good. I wanted to ask you to be my new assistant for the advanced class. You're here every day, before everyone else, and I've used you for demonstrations before. You're also very good with the other students. They trust you. And, right now, trust is important. They need someone they can feel comfortable with. You're a familiar face. Plus, you're a sweetheart. One who can kick ass. So, you're the assistant The Fighting Chance needs. What do you say?"

The entire time Beth spoke, a smile bloomed wider and wider on Amanda's face. Her eyes lit up with the same life Beth saw whenever Amanda was on the mat with her gloves on.

It was the same light that had been in Beth's eyes when she became an assistant to her teacher.

"Yes. Yes, times a hundred. I won't let you down!"

What Amanda did next surprised Beth; Amanda hugged her. Amanda didn't touch anyone unless it was

82

while participating in a lesson. Beth hoped this meant the classes were helping her to rebuild her confidence and comfort level with others.

"I know you won't let me down," Beth said. "There's just one thing to do to make it official." She picked up the employee packet on the front desk and gave it to Amanda with a pen.

Amanda took the pen. She stared at it in her fingers a moment. Then she glanced at the wall of signatures in the back of the studio. Somewhere on that wall, she had signed her name after her first class two years ago. She looked back at Beth. With a grin, she started to fill out the application. In seconds, she had gone from a student to an assistant. From experience, Beth knew that feeling was unforgettable. Without a doubt, she knew she had made the right choice.

****

After she locked up the studio, went home, and showered, she shuffled into the kitchen in her robe and slippers to find Donovan heating up a can of chicken noodle soup on the stove. She couldn't help but smile. His attentiveness when she wasn't feeling well was the sweetest thing she had ever experienced. When she had come home, he kissed her and laid a hand on her forehead to see if she felt hot. She had laughed and batted his hand away, but his gesture warmed her.

When the soup bubbled, he turned off the stove and transferred the soup to a bowl. He delivered it to her at the table. "You're so sweet."

"I told you I'd take care of you when you're sick." He had made that promise when they were in San Francisco, hunting his brother's killer.

"You've taken care of me a lot more than just

when I've been sick," she said, thinking of the aftermath of the trauma she experienced in Oahu. His patience with her had been remarkable. Not many men would've handled her physical limitations and mental pain as he had.

He bent over and kissed the top of her head. "I'd do it all again, for the rest of my life."

She picked up the spoon. "Just as long as your life lasts eighty years or more," she said, and blew on the hot soup. His crash in his monster truck was enough to shake her up, but knowing it could be malicious scared her even more.

He sat down next to her, took her free hand, and brought it to his lips. "Deal."

Chapter Eight

The next morning, Donovan was sitting at the table scanning the newspapers when Beth came up behind him and started to knead his shoulders. Her fingers worked out the kinks in his muscles. He let his eyes close as he enjoyed the impromptu massage. She applied pressure in strokes down his neck and along his spine. After a few minutes, he caught her hand as she massaged his shoulders and arms.

"I'm fine," he said. "My restraints didn't let me move an inch. No whiplash, no strains."

"But you have bruises." Her hands slipped down his chest where bruises marred his skin from where the restrains had dug into him.

"A few bruises and a friction rash. That's it."

She moved around him, carefully sat down on his lap, and looped her arms around his neck. Her face was clean of makeup, and her hair was pulled into a ponytail. She wore her pajamas and robe. The fresh scent of her facewash still clung to her skin. "You worry about me a lot, but you know, you can let me worry about you, too. Your accident was scary. If those restraints hadn't held. If a fire had started. If—"

He cupped her cheeks when her eyes misted and her voice caught. "Ssh." He kissed her soft lips and tasted the fruity flavor of her lip balm. "None of those things happened, and I'm not hurt." He smoothed a hand down her ponytail. "Not much," he corrected when one of her eyebrows lifted. The corner of his mouth tilted up. He shifted his hand to stroke her brow with his thumb. "I'll accept your worry if you accept mine."

She smiled, too. "Those terms aren't so bad. Deal."

****

After breakfast, Donovan went back to the Orlando Police Department to talk to Thorn, who sat behind a desk piled high with files. "Hey."

Thorn looked up and tossed down his pen. "Hey, man." He rubbed a hand over his face and picked up his mug but found it empty. Groaning, he set it down again.

Donovan took the chair across from him. "Long morning?"

Thorn nodded. "And it's shaping up to be a long day. I spent all day yesterday questioning your competition."

"And?"

"Nothing. I couldn't find any leads. None of them claimed to know a thing, and I'm inclined to believe them. I can usually tell when someone lies to me, but they showed genuine shock and concern when I said someone tampered with your truck and caused you to crash. They had no idea who would do it either."

Donovan leaned back in his seat. "I've been thinking about who could've done it."

"Any ideas?"

"Not really. My competition and their managers are the only ones I could think of with motive and means. They all had access to my truck. I can't imagine a fan taking such drastic measures because I beat their favorite driver. It's not like with football where fans from rival teams get into fist fights."

Thorn scratched the stubble on his chin. "I asked if anyone saw someone hanging around your truck who shouldn't have been, but no one was paying attention. There aren't cameras in that area, so there's no way to check."

Donovan juggled his keys in his hand. "No leads, no proof...no justice."

Thorn nodded. "Unfortunately. But we're not done yet. We should get back the results of what they find, or don't find, in your truck in a day or two. We may be able to pull some identifying evidence off that."

Donovan peered at the keys in his hand and fiddled with the one that unlocked the door to his garage. "I'm gonna go to my garage, see if someone snuck in."

Thorn's eyebrows lowered. "If the brakes were cut in your garage, you wouldn't have been able to compete in your first race."

"No, but something was done to my steering. I think it was hijacked by a remote control. That couldn't have been done in the few minutes I left to take a leak. The only other logical explanation is someone got to my truck before the competition. Then cut my brakes when I went to the bathroom."

"Makes sense," Thorn said. "I'd go with you but..." He waved his hand at the three open files spread out in front of him. "Let me know if you find anything suspicious."

"Will do."

****

At the gate blocking the dirt road to his garage, Donovan got out of his truck and inspected the lock and chain. Both were fine. He pulled the chain from the bars and drove through. On the other side of the path, he closed the gates. While clicking the padlock into place, he realized no one had to cut the chain to get through. All they'd have to do was hop the fence and walk the rest of the way. He scanned the dirt, searching for footprints. He couldn't make out any, but that didn't mean someone hadn't climbed over the gate and walked along the grass. If he were sneaking onto private property, it was what he would've done.

At his garage, he parked and knelt in front of the door to closely inspect the lock. Thin lines circled the keyhole. He ran his fingertip over it and felt the scratches in the metal. Someone had picked it and had a hard time of it, too.

"Son-of-a-bitch." He slipped his key in and shoved the garage door open. He snapped on the light. His gaze swept over the oil-spotted concrete for a stray bolt or the colorful pieces of plastic from exposed wires. Nothing.

He stood in front of his tool bench, with hands on hips. When he first set up his garage, he had crafted a wall rack for some of his tools, such as saw blades and a sledge hammer. A wooden tool box he crafted himself when he was in shop class in high school sat on the bench. It held flat heads, screwdrivers, pliers, wrenches, and wire cutters. A man of order, he always put his tools back where they belonged, but his Phillips-head and wire cutters were left on the table as if carelessly thrown there.

He took out his cell phone and called Thorn. "Hey, someone hacked at the lock on my garage door and made a real mess out of it. The same son-of-a-bitch used my own tools to fuck with my truck." The culprit probably disabled the kill switches and planted the device while in the cover of his garage. Knowing that intensified his anger.

Thorn sighed. "Okay. Don't touch anything. I'll be there with a team."

An hour later, investigators were taking pictures of the scratched lock and his tools, dusting for prints, and searching the ground for tracks. Donovan watched all of this with his arms crossed. He couldn't believe someone had broken into his garage. Was nothing safe?

Thorn stepped up beside him. "They found partial tire tracks that don't match yours on the road leading to the gate. They're taking pictures of them so we can try to find out what kind of car we're looking for."

"Will that matter? I mean, it could be anyone in any car. Even if we figure out what sort of tires created the marks, there are probably hundreds of cars with those same tires in Central Florida. How will we know which one is our man? We've had this same problem before, remember?"

When a black Buick had smashed into Beth's car repeatedly, they hadn't been able to find it.

Thorn shrugged. "We may not know."

Donovan let out an aggravated breath. "I don't want to keep dealing with shit like this, Thorn. I'm tired of it, and so is Beth."

"This doesn't have to do with Jackson Storm," Thorn said.

"How do you know?"

"Because we got everyone associated with him."

"That you know of," Donovan said.

Thorn held up a hand and shook his head. "Let's not get ahead of ourselves. We're investigating. If we turn up evidence this was done at the hand of one of Jackson's men, I'll let you know. I'll let you know either way."

Donovan knew he had to take that for what it was worth, but it didn't feel like enough.

"On another note, I know Beth's birthday is tomorrow. I was going to stop in at The Fighting Chance tonight to drop off a gift for her. I figure you're heading there now?"

Donovan had to admit Thorn was a damn good detective. He knew Donovan's intentions without him voicing them. "Yeah. I wanted to tell her about all of this and—"

"Check in because you may not be the only one targeted?" Thorn finished for him.

He nodded.

"All right then. Let's go."

Donovan parked in front of The Fighting Chance and was getting out of his truck as Thorn pulled into the lot. He saluted him before stepping into the studio. The sounds of activity surrounded him—the thumps, thuds, slaps, and noises of people fighting each other. He leaned against the front desk to say hi to Corissa. Thorn joined them a moment later.

"Hey, Corissa," Thorn said. "You killing that degree?"

"Sometimes I feel like it's killing me."

"Well stick it out, kid. Pretty soon you'll be shrinking guys like us." Thorn elbowed Donovan.

"I keep telling her I'll be her first patient," Donovan said.

"And I'll have the appointment right after you."

Corissa laughed. "The two of you would be my

favorite clients."

"But I'd be your number one favorite above Donovan, right?"

Corissa shook her head. "How Beth can stay sane with the two of you, I don't know."

Donovan grinned. "It's a gift."

"Someone needs to bottle it," Thorn added and turned to Beth as she announced the end of the class. "Whoa. Who. Is. That?"

Thorn's wide eyes and slack jaw told Donovan that a beautiful woman was the culprit. He shifted to get a view of Beth standing next to her new assistant. Amanda's hair was tied in a messy bun. She had on a pink top and black yoga pants. Beth wore yellow workout pants and a white top, making them look like the Power Rangers.

"That's Beth's new assistant," Donovan told Thorn's stunned look.

"Since when?" The two words were spoken as if he were breathless.

"Yesterday. Beth fired Dave."

"Good for her," Thorn said without taking his eyes off Amanda.

"Yeah, well, Dave touched a student."

Only now did Thorn stop gaping at Amanda. "What do you mean?"

Donovan met his stare. "He grabbed Maria between her legs."

Thorn closed his eyes. "Son-of-a-bitch." On occasion, Thorn would come to talk to Beth's classes, especially the beginners' classes. He told them about their options if they were ever in a domestically violent situation or in danger of any kind. He provided advice and even spoke to each student one-on-one, if they wanted. Many of them had confided in him about the abuse they experienced. Maria had been one of them. "If Dave were here now, I'd kick his ass."

Donovan understood Thorn's temptation to inflict bodily harm on Dave. He had wanted to do the same. Beth had wanted to do the same. Several students in the class had wanted to do the same. If Dave ever showed up, he'd be on the ground, in pain, within seconds.

"Did Beth crush his nuts?"

Thorn's question made Donovan laugh out loud. "No, but she sure wanted to."

Thorn shook his head. "The strength she must've possessed not to hurt him…"

They looked toward her as she came off the mat. Beth gave Donovan a quick kiss and Thorn a hug. "To what do I owe the pleasure of having my two favorite men here?" Her eyes flashed with humor.

"I wanted to tell you happy birthday," Thorn said.

"Aw. Thanks."

"I have a gift for you in my car. Donovan may not like it, though."

"It better not be a bikini," Donovan said.

Thorn winked.

Beth laughed.

Right then, Amanda called out Beth's name and headed in their direction.

"Oh damn," Thorn muttered under his breath. He looked down and shuffled his feet.

Amanda paused next to Beth. "I'm going to start putting the equipment away."

"Wait up a minute." Beth put her hand on Amanda's arm. "I want to introduce you to our good friend. Amanda, this is Thorn. He's talked to my classes from time to time. Thorn, this is Amanda. She's my new assistant."

Thorn rubbed the palm of his hand on his pants, as if it was damp, and offered it to Amanda. Donovan had never seen Thorn nervous around a woman before. He couldn't believe the man who flirted with Beth, despite her married status, and hunted criminals on the job couldn't face a sexy woman. But Donovan had to admit, Amanda wasn't your typical sexy woman. There was something special about her, as there was about Beth.

"Nice to meet you," Thorn said.

Donovan pushed down the laughter bubbling in his chest. When had he ever heard Thorn be so formal?

"Yeah. You're the detective, right? You spoke to my class a year ago. You gave all of us your card. I…" She licked her lips. "I still have mine."

Thorn had handed out his cards to Beth's students and routinely left a stack on the counter in case any of them needed it. From what Thorn had told Beth and Donovan, those cards had come in handy three times.

Thorn nodded. He was speechless, a rare occurrence. He didn't have so much as one word to say. Donovan wished he could slap Thorn in the back of the head. *What is wrong with you? A beautiful woman is talking to you. Speak, you idiot.*

Amanda looked between the two of them. "Are you brothers?"

Donovan turned to Thorn, who's eyebrows lifted in humor. It was the first thing his face had done since Amanda came over, other than look awestruck.

"Absolutely not," Donovan said.

"Hey, I would be a great brother," Thorn protested.

Donovan considered Thorn a moment. They had met only because Ryan, Donovan's real brother, had been murdered. When he lost Ryan, did he get a substitute brother in Thorn?

A sweet smile crossed Amanda's face, conjuring dimples. "Well, it's nice to meet you." She turned to Beth. "I'm going to clean up." Before she left, she gave Thorn one last glance. Her smile warmed even more. She walked away, and the three of them were left staring after her in bewilderment, but for different reasons.

"Damn," Thorn whispered.

Donovan grinned from ear to ear. "Beth, I think Thorn is smitten."

Beth crossed her arms as she scrutinized her best friend. Her mamma bear instincts were coming out.

This will be entertaining, Donovan thought.

"You." She poked Thorn in the chest with her finger. "You better not do something stupid."

Thorn frowned and rubbed his chest as if she had hurt him. "Define stupid."

"It's not my business to tell you her story, but she's been hurt more than you can guess. She can't take anymore. If you try to pursue something with her, remember that."

Thorn glanced at Amanda as she collected boxing gloves. "I will."

"And if you do something stupid," Donovan said, "you won't just have Beth coming after you. You'd have me, too."

"Let's get something clear." Thorn held up a hand. "I'm not afraid of you, Goldwyn." He pointed at Beth, who still had her hands on her hips. "But I *am* afraid of her."

Thorn's gift to Beth turned out not to be a bikini but a framed picture of the three of them taken a few months ago at one of Donovan's monster truck shows. Beth stood between Donovan and Thorn with one arm around each of them. Right when the picture was taken, Thorn had snuck a kiss on Beth's cheek. Neither of them had said a word about it. This was the first time Donovan had found out about it. It didn't make him mad, though. Seeing Beth's happiness at being able to witness that moment again made him happy, too. But he did feel he'd have to have another talk with Thorn about not kissing Beth.

Chapter Nine

In Beth's dream, she saw snapshots of Donovan. They weren't happy images but all the ones that had terrified her—each moment when he could've died since they met.

His car smashed into a tree. His forehead bashed into the steering wheel.

Concrete tumbling from the sky, hiding Donovan from sight.

A trash can, propelled by a great force of water, crashing into him at the same time as the wave plowed into her, stealing her vision and ripping Donovan from her grasp.

His monster truck lifted in the air and, as if in slow motion, tipped forward. Horrified, she watched it fall straight to the ground, nose-first.

The sound of it slamming into the ground snapped Beth awake. She turned her head and was reassured when she saw Donovan sleeping next to her. She touched her chest where her heart pounded frantically. The images from her dream replayed again and again. He had defied death several times. As if he were a cat with nine lives, she wondered how many lives he had left. She watched him as he slept peacefully and hoped he had hundreds. At the same time, she prayed he wouldn't face situations like those again. Never again. He may be an adrenaline junkie, and he may be tough, but seeing him hurt pained her, just as she knew seeing her hurt pained him. He didn't want her to be in danger, and she wanted the same for him. Except, he raced monster trucks for a living.

By the time her heart rate went back to normal, sunlight streamed through the closed blinds. She looked to their bedside clock. It was almost eight-thirty. She rolled onto her side, facing Donovan. He let out a sound that was half sigh, half groan. A smile touched her lips. She pressed her lips to his temple, his cheek, his jawline. He turned his head. Their noses brushed. Her lips rubbed against his. She didn't care if he had morning breath. And, unfortunately for him, she didn't care if she had morning breath. Her lips molded to his. It was a soft kiss to awaken his senses and pull him out of his dream state.

"That's how I was going to wake you up," he said.

"Beat you to it." She slid onto him, and his arms looped around her, hugging her like a child would hug his favorite teddy bear. She looked down at him. His eyes were still closed. "I might not be very good at it, though, because you're still asleep." Her lips pursed when he didn't stir. "I'll go and let you sleep." She started to push herself off him when his arms flexed, keeping her firmly in place.

"Don't even think about it," he said.

"And yet your eyes are still closed."

"I'm enjoying the feel of you." His eyelids opened, unveiling his violet irises. He looked at her a moment, as if he wasn't sure if she were a dream or real. "Happy Birthday."

She smiled. "Thank you."

"How long have you been awake?"

She shrugged. "A little while." She leaned forward and planted a kiss on his forehead. Then she moved down to his neck. Her nose rubbed against his Adam's apple while she breathed in his scent. The lingering notes of his fresh, green cologne greeted her. Beneath it was the smell of his skin. She inhaled. "I had a dream," she said with her lips against his neck. "About you."

"Oh yeah? What did I do in it? We could repeat it now."

She shook her head. "It wasn't a dream like that." She withdrew and peered into his eyes. "It wasn't a good dream."

His brows lowered. He combed her hair from her face. "What was it about?"

She couldn't tell him while his violet gaze bore into her. She lowered onto him, laying her head on his chest. One of his hands embraced the back of her head. "It was about the moments that have scared me the most." She paused. "Your car accident when we met, the concrete that nearly crushed you, the wave that could've killed us both, and now your monster truck falling and slamming into the ground."

Donovan took a deep breath that lifted up her head. "I've had dreams like that but about you." His other hand stroked her back.

"I'm afraid that one of these days, you're not going to be so lucky."

Silence followed her words as Donovan registered what she meant. "I'm not going to leave you, Beth. I told you, I'm going to die an old man. I've already talked it over with Destiny. She gave me her word."

The corner of Beth's mouth lifted.

"And she promised me *you* won't leave *me* too

98

soon."

His words struck her. She propped herself up on her hands and stared down at him. What she saw in his eyes reminded her of her close encounters that have haunted him. She brought her lips to his and sank into his promise while offering him one in return.

****

"So, what do you want for breakfast?" Donovan asked her later in the kitchen.

"Oh no. The least I can do before we begin the day you planned is make *you* breakfast." She pulled out a griddle. "How do blueberry and chocolate chip pancakes sound?"

"Great."

She mixed fresh blueberries and semi-sweet chocolate chips into pancake batter and poured it onto the hot griddle. She made two large pancakes each and warmed maple syrup. On the table, she set down their plates and two cups of coffee. "Are you going to give me any hints on what we're going to do today?" She cut a triangle out of her stacked pancakes, swiped them over the syrup on the plate, and forked them into her mouth.

Donovan wagged his fork at her. "Not one."

She grumbled under her breath. "You sure know how to keep a secret."

He picked up his cup of coffee and peered at her through the steam. "That's what makes me mysterious. Remember, it was my mystery that hooked you." He winked at her.

She swallowed pancake and pointed the prongs of her fork at him. "Correction. It was the mystery that made me suspicious of you. Do you remember *that*?"

He squinted his eyes. "I vaguely recall you throwing a flashlight at me and trying to bash in my head with a candlestick holder."

She peered through the dining room—which they used for special occasions—at the gold candlestick holders in the middle of the mahogany table. "You mean that candlestick holder?"

He rotated in his chair. "Yes." He turned back around. "But it didn't have a candle in it at the time."

She chuckled. "I believe you're right about that."

They finished breakfast and moved upstairs. "Is there a dress code for this place you're taking me?" She opened one of her dresser drawers and considered the contents—bras and panties. Donovan stepped up behind her.

"All of those would work."

She nudged her elbow back, playfully hitting him in the gut.

"Workout pants, a cotton T-shirt, and this will work." He held up a workout bra by the straps.

She snatched it from his fingers. "Okay. I'll change. You—" She lightly jabbed him in the chest with her finger. "Stay away. I don't want you to delay this with sex." She headed to their bathroom.

"But what if I—"

She cut him off. "Nope." Grinning, she shut the door.

****

Donovan took her to batting cages. It wasn't the surprise she had been expecting, but she could enjoy any sport with Donovan, including golf. He pulled two bats from the steel tool box in the back of his truck and handed one to Beth along with batting gloves. She slipped on the gloves and swung the bat over her shoulder.

Donovan paused. "Damn. You even look sexy with a bat."

She winked at him. "Are you sure you can bat? You're still bruised from your accident."

"Of course, I can. And I can do a lot more, too." He winked back. "I thought smashing a few balls would help us relieve some stress."

Beth twisted her lips to stop her smirk. "You know what would really relieve my stress? Smashing the balls of the person who tried to hurt my husband."

Donovan broke into a wicked grin. "Come on, batter."

In a cage, Donovan set up the machine that would dispense the baseballs and demonstrated how it was done. His bat cracked into the first baseball the machine spat at him. It flew into the net and plopped to the floor.

"Do you want to give it a try?"

"Absolutely."

He stepped aside, and she took his place. She bent her knees, spaced out her hands, and slung the bat over her shoulder. She watched the machine, anticipating the release of the next ball. The ball made its way up. A whoosh sounded as it shot toward her. She saw it coming and swung her bat with all her might. The contact of the bat and the baseball colliding vibrated up her fingers to her shoulders.

Donovan whistled. "If we were on a field, that would've resulted in a home run."

"I was imagining that was the perp's first ball. And this next ball is his second one." She wielded her bat like a weapon and slammed the ball out of the park—

figuratively speaking.

"I had no idea you were good at baseball," Donovan said as he switched off the machine.

She shrugged and put the bat across her shoulders. Her hands dangled off the ends. "I played softball for two years in high school. I was on the varsity team in ninth grade; the only freshmen girl in my school's history to do that."

He tilted his head as he studied her. "Will you ever stop surprising me?"

"I hope not." A slow grin took over her face as she recalled her other school activities.

"What?" Donovan asked.

"In elementary school, I was part of the ping pong club."

Donovan chuckled at that.

"I also ran track," she added. "In middle school, I, uh, had a stint as a cheerleader."

Donovan blinked. "Really?"

She nodded. "Seventh and eighth grades. The second year, I was co-captain."

"I hope you have pictures."

"I might." She walked over to the ball dispenser. "You're up." She switched on the machine. It hummed to life. "And I can still perform the splits," she added.

Donovan's body straightened out of his stance. His bat lowered. He gaped at her, and the ball sliced past him into the net. He flinched and peered behind him. When he looked back at her, she couldn't mask her smirk. *Got him.* And he knew it, too. His eyes gleamed, and he slammed the next ball home.

From behind him, Beth cocked her head to the side and admired the way his butt looked in his khaki pants.

She bit her bottom lip. *Who said women couldn't appreciate a man's backside?* His body twisted as he hit another ball. *Oh yeah.* He resumed his position.

"You're staring at my ass, aren't you?"

While shaking her head, she sighed. "Guilty."

He laid into another ball. "Okay." He faced her. "It's your turn. I want a chance to ogle you."

"Hm." She took his place. Her hands smoothed down her hair, and she flicked her ponytail with a slight shake of her head. She lowered, being sure to sway her hips from side to side, shaking her butt.

Donovan's laughter touched her ear. The corner of her mouth tilted up, and she sank her bat into the ball. She hit two more before trading off with Donovan. They played a couple more rounds, then went to get lunch, which consisted of loaded hot dogs and jalapeno nachos.

Beth finished her hot dog and wiped her mouth with a napkin. "That was a lot of fun. Just what we needed."

"I'm glad, but I still have plans."

"You always do."

His next event on her birthday agenda was an afternoon movie for two at home. On the couch, he put his arm around her, and they watched a new action movie. At the end, she followed Donovan into the kitchen to put her empty cup into the dishwasher.

Donovan checked the time. "You should probably start getting ready so we can make our dinner reservation."

"Reservation?" Her interest piqued. "You're not going to tell me where, are you?"

"That would spoil the surprise."

"A reservation sounds fancy," she said, wondering what she should wear.

"Would you like me to pick out your dress?" he offered. "I can't guarantee we'd make it in time for our reservation, though."

She smiled. "No, I think I can manage. Just as long as I don't need diamonds."

"Baby, whatever you decide to wear will be perfect."

"Okay. I'll go get ready." She walked to the entrance of the kitchen but came to a stop as an idea came to light. Her foot lifted, and she glided the bottom of her sock over the smooth tile. *This would work.* Before her students came to her studio for classes, she liked to tumble over the mat and execute the flips and splits she had done as a cheerleader long ago. She only ever did it for fun and to stay flexible, but she'd do it for Donovan.

She faced him. He was adding dish detergent to the cubby in the dishwasher's door. She waited for him to close it and turn it on. "Donovan."

He turned.

"Just one thing before I go." She cleared her throat. Then she let her legs slide apart and her body sink to a perfect front split. Bending forward, she reached her hands down her right leg and rested her forehead on her thigh. She turned her head to Donovan. His eyes were wide. His mouth had fallen open, and his right hand supported him on the counter.

Enjoying his reaction, she sat up, lifted slightly on the tile, and shifted her body so she was in a side split with both of her legs extending to the left and right of her torso. She held this pose a moment while watching

Donovan. His mouth closed and opened again as if he wanted to say something. She rose and curled her legs under her so she could get to her feet.

She shrugged a shoulder when Donovan's amazed gaze met hers. "That's all," she said and left the kitchen, leaving Donovan behind in his stunned state.

She showered, blow-dried her hair, curled the ends, and did her makeup. In their walk-in closet, she examined the few dresses she owned. She selected a hanger and pulled out a sky-blue sleeveless dress that went great with her tan. She slipped it up her body and zipped it as far as she could. The dress stopped just below her knees, showing off her toned calves. She slipped into the white heels she preferred with the dress and peered at herself in the full-length mirror. The dress showcased her nice arms and curves. Consequently, it also revealed every one of her scars. The pale scratch across her chest she could deal with, but not the one scar below her collar bone where new skin had grown over a hole.

Sighing, she went back to her dresses and picked a red dress with a sweetheart neckline and two-inch straps. In front of the mirror, she held it up to her body and tilted her head. It was a pretty dress. She wore it on their first Valentine's date as a couple. And she brought it out only for Valentine's Day, as a tradition. It was the only dress she had with straps thick enough to cover her scar. Donovan liked it because the bodice formed to her and the short skirt swished around her hips, but the blue dress she had on was his all-time favorite. She lowered her arm, letting the skirt of the red dress puddled on the floor. The blue dress was like a second-skin with a slit up the side that she liked to tease Donovan with while crossing her legs.

Since Donovan was doing all of this for her, she wanted to do something for him. She hung the red dress back in its place and resumed her position before the mirror. Her lips scrunched to the side as she glared at her scar. There was only one thing she could do. She arranged a few curls over her shoulder, placing them to cover the scar. But would it cover from the back? She twisted to peer over her shoulder at her reflection and jumped when she saw Donovan. He leaned against one shoulder at the entrance. His arms and ankles were crossed as he studied her. He wore gray dress pants and a black button up-shirt. He looked delicious.

"How long have you been standing there?"

"Long enough."

She turned away. The entrance to the closet wasn't visible in the mirror. *Damn.*

The sound of movement came to her, and his refection appeared behind her. "Why do you do that?" he asked.

"Do what?"

His hand reached around and swept her hair off her shoulder. "That."

"Why do you think? To cover it." She went to pull her hair back into place, but he brushed her hair onto her opposite shoulder. "Donovan."

He wrapped his arms around her waist, lowered his head, and trailed kisses from her neck and down along her shoulder. "You don't need to hide anything," he said. "Remember what I told you about this scar?" His finger followed the pale line across her chest.

"Yes." She swallowed. "You said that you think about...licking it all the time, but Donovan, this scar—"

she pointed to her shoulder "—isn't the same. This is from a gunshot wound that nearly took my life. It's not a good memory. It's ugly, and I hate it. There's no way you can feel the same way about this scar."

He turned her around, cupped her face with his hands, and drew her into a tender kiss.

When he eased back, his heart was in his eyes. "I love every inch, every millimeter, of your body, including this scar." He pressed his lips to it.

Tears bit the backs of Beth's eyes. The warmth of his lips seeped into her scar, into her heart. The scar was a part of her now, and Donovan had accepted it. She believed him when he said he loved everything about her, even the parts of herself she hated.

"This scar is a part of you now. Please don't hide it…not from me." He kissed her again.

This one was longer, deeper. He cradled the back of her head with one hand while the other hand drew her closer, so their bodies molded. She clutched his shoulders. Their tongues glided and tasted. Their lips sucked and enjoyed. Her head began to spin as if she was intoxicated, drunk on his kiss.

He pulled away but not completely. He continued to touch her lips with his feather-light kisses. When he moved his lips out of reach, he maneuvered her hair off her shoulder so it lay against her back. Then he took a step back and scanned her from head to toe.

"This is the woman I love. Every part of her." His gaze met hers. "Don't hide even the smallest fraction from me. Please."

She lowered her head and took a shuttering breath. Her chest ached from his tenderness. She hadn't known she was hurting him by concealing her scars. But she understood how he felt. If he tried to shroud a part of him from her, she'd be heartbroken, too.

She looked back at him and shook her head. "I won't. Not anymore."

He picked up her hand and pressed a kiss to it. "Thank you." With his other hand, he stroked her cheek. "Are you ready?"

She pressed her hand to his. "I will be once you zip my dress up the rest of the way."

Chapter Ten

Donovan took Beth's hand and tucked it in the crook of his arm. She laughed at the gesture. He led her into an elegant restaurant and told the maître d' the info for their reservation. She checked her tablet. "Great. Right this way." She took them to a table with a white tablecloth and flickering candles that floated in a crystal dish of water. Donovan pulled out the chair for Beth. As she sat down and crossed her legs, the slit in her dress parted to expose her smooth thigh. His abdomen clenched. He hadn't forgotten about the super sexy splits she had performed in their kitchen. When he took his chair, the maître d' handed them the menus, and then he went back to the front desk.

"Donovan." Beth clutched the menu in her hands. "This place is very…"

"I know, just don't look at the prices. Get what you want." He detected a hint of anxiety in her stiff posture. She opened the menu, and her eyes widened. Telling her not to look at the prices was equivalent to telling someone afraid of heights not to look down, he realized. He reached across the table to take her menu. "I can order for you."

"No. No, I'll find something." She resumed studying the options. Amused, Donovan saw the whites of her eyes get bigger, and her cheeks become pinker. He knew she was trying to find the cheapest entrée and wasn't having much luck.

"Beth, I know what you like. I can order for you."

She looked at him. "Normally, I'd hate someone ordering for me, but you've been doing such an amazing job all day that I'll let you order for me this once." She set aside her menu with visible relief on her face. The pink of her cheeks faded, and her eyebrows lowered.

He glanced over his menu. The waiter approached the moment he set his menu aside. "The lobster linguini for my wife, and the halibut for me."

"Very good. Would you like to see the wine list?"

"Yes, thank you." He scanned the wines and discreetly pointed to a price. "We'll have your recommended wine pairing." Donovan didn't know much about wine, but his mother had taught him well, hoping he'd find a girl worth her lessons. And he had.

The waiter nodded and left with their menus tucked under his arm.

"Donovan, you know I would've been happy with something simple," Beth said under her breath.

"I know. You're easy to please, which is one of the things I love about you. You indulge by buying a bag of French fries." He smiled. "But I like to do things like this for you. I don't get to do it often." He reached across the table and took her hand. His thumb rubbed her knuckles. "Let me spoil my wife."

She sighed. "If you insist." Her smile and lowered shoulders told him she was surrendering to the idea.

"Enjoy it," he urged.

She nodded. Her eyes twinkled in the candlelight. "I will."

The waiter presented a bottle of chardonnay.

Donovan tasted the pale gold wine and gave a nod of approval, so the waiter poured Beth a glass.

"Thank you," she said and picked up the glass by the stem. She stole a sip. "Mm. It's perfect." She set the glass down. "What you ordered for me is perfect, too. You weren't kidding when you said you know what I like."

"I pay attention."

Beth lowered her voice. "Do you know something else I like?" Her gaze went from sparkling to smoldering. "You."

Donovan suddenly wished they weren't at a restaurant but at home. "Now that I already knew."

"Did you?" Her teeth flashed at him.

Do we really need to eat? He pushed down that thought. They'd need food to do what he had planned for later. While they waited for their food to come, they chatted, whispered, laughed, and flirted as if they were alone in the restaurant. When their meal arrived, they fell into a comfortable silence.

"That was delicious." Beth set her utensils on her plate. Sighing, she sat back. "This was lovely, Donovan. Thank you."

"You deserved it."

Although he knew she had been reluctant to order, he could see she was content. He didn't know if he would be able to bring her back here, as she'd probably tell him it was an unnecessary indulgence, but he hoped to repeat this for all their important anniversary milestones. Especially since, upon Beth's request, their one-year anniversary was spent at home with tacos and cheap beer.

"Do you want to order dessert?"

"No, I'm stuffed. Besides, we can find dessert at home."

Her words ignited a spark of lust inside him. Beth's body was like a decadent buffet of the best desserts—every curve, dip, and inch.

"I better ask for the check then."

She nodded. "You should."

During the ride home, Donovan clasped Beth's hand and kept raising it to his mouth to kiss it. Her fingers grazed his lips. He felt the hard warmth of her infinity engagement ring and wedding band. Seeing them on her finger still brought him pleasure. On their one-year anniversary, he had offered to get her a diamond engagement ring, even a tiny one, which would've been more her style, but she had refused. *I have you, and I have this home. Those are more precious to me than a precious gem*, she had told him. And the infinity knot meant more than a diamond of any cut or clarity.

He pulled into the driveway, unlocked the front door, and escorted Beth to their bedroom. His mouth sought hers immediately. His hands cupped her butt, and he pressed into her. Hunger burned through him. This ravenousness hunger was purely sexual and only his wife would sate that appetite. His hand curled around her hip, and his fingers crept toward the slit in her dress. Warm silk appeared at his fingers. Just when he was about to nudge it aside, Beth's hand grasped his wrist. She inched back. Her face was flushed. Her eyes were glazed with lust.

"Not yet," she panted. "I have a surprise for you. Take off my dress."

Her order had his libido roaring. "You don't have

to tell me twice." He reached around her and whisked the zipper down her back. Gazing into her eyes, he helped slip the dress off her curves. Once the fabric left the shape of her hips, it tumbled to her feet. Underneath, she wore a white strapless panty set with lace and sheer fabric that did nothing to cover her. The bottom of the chemise stopped short. Too short. Red, silk panties peeked between her legs.

His mouth went dry. He couldn't tear his gaze away.

"Do you remember that store I went to when I needed that undercover costume? *Virgin No More?*" Boy, did he. Her purchases had been fuzzy handcuffs, intimate oil, and blindfolds. "I went there last week to buy this. I put it in a Walmart bag so the surprise wouldn't be spoiled." She smiled. "I wanted to do something for you."

He swallowed. His gaze trailed back down her scantily clad body. The chemise looked so good on her. Part of him wanted to peel it off her body, and the other part wanted to enjoy her in it. That side won. "I don't think I can take that off you."

"Then don't." Her words were soft, enticing.

His stare settled on the red, silk triangle. "Well, I'll remove one piece." He brought her close and nibbled on her earlobe. "Just one piece."

Cradling her in his arms, he maneuvered her onto the bed. His hands caressed lace and silk and flesh as his tongue twisted and stroked hers. The longer he tasted, the more he felt, the harder he became. Blood hollered in his eardrums and scorched his veins. He needed to feel Beth, sink into her, join her. His fingers pinched the straps of her panties and slipped them to

Chrys Fey

her ankles. The heels she wore were still strapped to her feet. He didn't want to take them off either, so he worked the panties off her heels. Then he parted her thighs and settled between them. She locked her arms around his neck, drawing him closer. Between their bodies, he undid his pants and entered her with a quick thrust.

Beth purred, and he groaned. With his head buried in the crook of her neck, he breathed in the sweet scent of her hair. It made him feel high. He put his mouth to her neck and sucked and nipped and enjoyed. Each moan that Beth made vibrated against his lips.

He pushed them to the brink of ecstasy, and they dove off the cliff together. Donovan fell onto his side, so he wouldn't crush Beth beneath him. After a filling dinner and great sex, he finally felt sated. Neither of them spoke until they caught their breaths.

Beth looked down. "You didn't take off my shoes?"

He shook his head. "Nope." Smirking, he turned his head to her. "I don't get to see you in heels much. And with that on…" He let his words trail off as he gazed at the chemise and the points of her nipples pressed against the flimsy fabric.

"You're lucky I didn't poke holes through the mattress," she said.

"It would've been worth it."

"Well, I'm going to take them off now and put my underwear back on."

Donovan grinned as she did just that. He held out his hand when she finished. "Beth, your birthday isn't over yet." She took his hand and lowered onto the edge of the bed. "I have one more thing for you." He

114

indicated the drawer in the nightstand on his side of the bed. "Open it."

She slid open the draw, revealing a flat, square jewelry box. She glanced at him before taking out the box. The lid made a soft creaking sound as she lifted it. Two pieces of silver lay on the inside. She covered her mouth. The gesture was of surprise and delight. She peered at him. Her eyes glistened with a sheen of happy tears.

"I thought your bracelet could use a couple more charms," he explained.

She moved her fingers from her lips. "A shell and a heart." Her voice was choked up. She lowered the box to her knee. Her bracelet, with the single hurricane charm, jingled. "You really do know me."

Donovan picked up her hand and kissed the space beneath her wedding band. "Of course, I do."

****

Donovan's cell phone pulled him awake. He rolled over, away from Beth's soft, supple body, and reached toward the nightstand. His hand slapped the wood surface until it collided with his phone. He snatched it up, swiped his finger over the glossy surface, and brought the phone to his ear, nearly dropping it on his face in the process. "What," he snapped.

"Donovan, sorry to call so late, but I got the report back about your truck."

He sat up, suddenly awake.

Beth clicked on the bedside lamp and put her hand on his arm. Her hair was mused. "Who is it?"

He held up a finger. "What does it say?"

Thorn let out a breath; Donovan braced for the news.

115

"Your brakes were cut, as we figured. More disturbing, all the kill switches were deactivated, and a little gadget was placed beneath your steering wheel that allowed someone within a one-mile radius to take full control of the steering. You were right, Goldwyn. Someone did hijack your truck."

Chapter Eleven

Someone had been in the stands, maybe right behind her, with a remote-control device that let him steer Donovan's truck toward the highest ramp, toward what he thought would've been Donovan's death. The thought sickened and enraged Beth. Why would someone do such a thing? Donovan said Thorn didn't think any of the other drivers had anything to do with it, and Donovan didn't think a fan was responsible. So, who would do it? Who was sadistic enough to steer a man's truck and initiate a dangerous crash?

She thought of the usual suspects: Jackson Storm and Buck.

Both men were locked up, never to get free. After Jackson had issued a kill order on them, he was stricken of phone and visitor privileges. He saw no one. Not even other prisoners. And the men who had tried to follow his order had been taken care of in Oahu. For over a year, they hadn't received a death threat. Beth had thought it was over, but it was always when you let your guard down that the enemy struck.

A new threat was out there, watching them, waiting to make the next move.

She went into the kitchen for a glass of orange juice. Donovan sat at the table with a cup of coffee and the newspaper in his hands. She glanced at the front page as she passed. A picture of a woman running with a calico cat in her arms was posted above the fold with a backdrop of flames behind her. Beneath it was another picture of trees ablaze and firefighters trying to push back the fire.

She took out the carton of orange juice, filled a glass, and sat across from Donovan.

He lowered the paper. "Good morning."

She smiled. "Morning."

"I'm sorry about the call last night. It sort-of ruined your birthday."

She shook her head. "No, it didn't. Besides, my birthday was over by then. The real ending was quite satisfying." She winked and took a sip of the sweet, tangy juice. "What are you going to do about your truck now?"

"I ordered the parts that need replacing and had it towed to my mechanic. He'll be looking it over again to see if there's anything the department's investigative team missed?"

"Like what?" she asked.

Donovan shrugged. "Like something they didn't realize wasn't supposed to be there. Or should be there."

Beth nodded. She was glad he was having it looked at again by a man he trusted. "I'm gonna sit on the porch for a while."

"All right. Enjoy your time with her."

Beth smiled as she headed toward the sliding glass door in the back of the house. When she was little, she had spent every Sunday morning on the porch with her mom, who would paint while Beth watched, and then they'd snack on fruit, chocolate, and scones. It was their special Sunday morning, mother-daughter bonding time. Beth started doing it again after moving into this grand house. Although her mom wouldn't be standing in front of a canvas, Beth still felt her presence on those calm mornings on the porch.

She unlocked the door and stepped out with her glass in hand. Her favorite outdoor chair with chestnut armrests and a yellow cushion waited for her across the way. She took a few steps before coming to a halt. Something was stuck into the right armrest. Metal gleamed. She took a small step forward and another and another until she realized what it was—a knife.

Her feet stopped moving. She stared at the knife. Her heart banged against her chest, vibrating her T-shirt with its vicious beats. Something white was pinned to the wood beneath the blade. She had to see what it was. Forcing herself to keep moving, she stepped up to the chair. The glass fell from her hand. Glass and orange juice crashed into the tile, splashing her bare feet.

A piece of paper was stabbed to the armrest with a message scrawled in what looked like blood, a message for her—*Happy Birthday!*

"D-Donovan." Her voice was weak, nothing more than a breath. She filled her lungs and shouted, "Donovan!"

A moment later, Donovan threw the sliding glass door open and hurried to her. She pointed at the blade, the blood, the birthday wish.

"God dammit," he cursed.

His hand caught hers and pulled her away from the chair. He brought her into the kitchen and sat her down at the table. He snatched the towel hanging over the side of the sink, and while kneeling at her feet, cleaned the sticky juice from her skin. When her legs were dry, he picked up the house phone on the counter.

"Thorn, we have a problem. You need to get here ASAP."

Beth waited for Thorn to arrive. She stayed at the table with her hands clasped. Every time she blinked, she saw the message in the blackness beneath her eyelids. What did it mean? Who would leave that for her? They had apprehended all the people in Jackson Storm's drug ring. Or had they? Were there people out there flying under the radar, waiting to carry out his orders?

Thorn arrived ahead of the CSI team. He went straight to the porch to inspect the message before joining Beth and Donovan in the kitchen. She got up, poured a cup of coffee, and handed it to him.

"Thanks." He accepted the cup. The steam rose to his face. His eyebrows were drawn, and his eyes were penetrating. "Are you okay?"

"I don't know." She took her seat again. "I think I went into shock when I saw it, but I'm better now. Just tell me your theories and if it could be linked, in anyway, to what happened to Donovan's truck."

"We won't know anything unless prints can be found on the knife's handle and on the tools from Donovan's garage."

Across the table, Donovan shifted. Beth's gaze was drawn to the movement. He wasn't looking at her but was staring off into space with a hard glare.

"What is it?"

His gaze ticked to her. "The display is sadistic," he started slowly with a deep tone. "But the message is personal, intimate. Only someone from your past, with passion toward you, would leave a message like that."

Beth frowned. "Who would do that?"

"Your ex."

Imagining her ex in his sleek suits, with his combed-back hair, dipping a finger in blood, or even ketchup, and writing a note with it was laughable. He had been the sort of child who hated getting messy. "Last I heard, he was happily banging his blond psychic slut. Why in the world would he care about me or my birthday?"

Donovan and Thorn exchanged glances.

She eyed Thorn. "What are you keeping from me?" When neither of them answered right away, she shouted, "Tell me."

Donovan sighed. "He's no longer with the psychic. His coworkers say he's been obsessed with getting you back."

Beth peered between them. "How do you know that?"

Thorn spoke up. "I looked into him when we were in San Fran."

She shook her head. "Why?" It didn't make sense. He hadn't been a threat. The threat had been Buck and Jackson Storm.

"Because I asked him to," Donovan admitted.

She stared at him. "I ask again...why?"

"Damn it, because I'm protective of you. I needed to know if he would be a threat to us, and he proved to be one."

"No, he proved to be a prick who talks too much. He always has been. If you knew him at all, you'd know how ridiculous it sounds that he'd do something like this."

"People change."

Beth considered his clenched jaw and fisted hands. "I feel like I'm missing a piece of the puzzle. What haven't you said?"

He met her gaze. "When we came back from California, I confronted him and told him to never come near you, say your name, or think about you."

She gaped at him. Donovan was usually a smart man, but sometimes his love could make him do stupid things. "Did you even once think that doing that could make things worse?"

He didn't reply, but he didn't need to.

Thorn cleared his throat. "Let's get back to why I'm here. Someone is targeting the two of you. We don't know who yet, and we don't know why. I'm going to need both of you to come up with a grudge list of anyone you could think of who might have a grudge against you, big or small. Doesn't matter if you think it's petty. Anything can set someone off."

"Thorn." Beth spoke slowly. "Do you realize I'm a self-defense instructor? I help people in domestically violent situations. If any one of their spouses or exes found out about me, I'd be a target for revenge. As a matter of fact, some have found out and have confronted me before."

"What?" Donovan's voice was a blend of shock and anger, and she realized she should've kept that tidbit to herself. She couldn't erase the words hanging in the air now.

She swallowed. "I've been threatened by a few men whose wives or girlfriends I taught. They blamed me when their spouse got up the courage to leave."

"What sort of threats?" Thorn asked.

"We're talking about wife beaters. There's only

one threat they know—bodily harm."

"Why didn't you ever tell me this?" Donovan wanted to know.

The way he looked at her made her feel as though she betrayed him, but she felt he had been disloyal, too. He had confronted Craig over two years ago and hadn't told her about it until now, when something happened that could be a repercussion. "Because nothing has happened since we've been together," she said. "And those situations were taken care of by the police. I never saw any of them again."

"That's doesn't mean they forgot about you," he said in a low voice.

"I agree with Donovan."

Beth turned her attention to Thorn.

"I'm going to need the names of all of your clients who are or were in domestically violent relationships," he said.

She blinked. "That's more than half of my students, and I've been open for seven years. I'm not going to be able to remember all of them." She rubbed her eyes. "But I can print out my complete client list. From that I can star the ones I know would qualify."

"That'll help," Thorn said.

With a sigh, she got up and retrieved two pieces of paper and two pens. She handed one of each to Donovan. Their grudge lists weren't going to be short, she knew that. When you added the pages of clients from her job, Thorn would have his work cut out for him, looking into and questioning all of them.

To the top of her list, she put Jackson Storm, followed by all his minions as well as Buck. After that, she added Cruz Ramirez, the man she helped Thorn apprehend when she went undercover as a prostitute. She glanced at Donovan's list and saw the same names topped his; these men were their main threats. They'd always be at the forefront of their minds. To make Donovan happy, she included Craig. Then she added her most recent grudge: Dave. She tapped her pen to the table as she considered who else could hold a grudge against her.

When the CSI team came, Beth set her list aside. From a distance, she watched them bag the knife and note while investigators dusted the chair's armrests and the screen door for prints. They pulled off several, but Beth felt certain they would be Donovan's fingerprints, or her own. When they finished, they left, leaving behind an uneasiness that clung to Beth like skin. She stared at her favorite chair with a stab wound and a layer of white residue over the wood. Never would she be able to sit there in relaxation again. Never would she be able to escape to the porch to feel her mother's presence, because now the only presence she would feel was a psycho's.

"I'm gonna go," Thorn said. "I have a lot of cases waiting for me. Two of which are yours." He rubbed Beth's arm. "We'll figure out who's doing this. Trust the system." He faced Donovan. "And you...don't do anything stupid. We don't know who did this, so don't go to Craig's house and cause trouble." He moved closer and lowered his voice, but Beth could still hear his final words. "Stay with your wife." With that, he followed the CSI team out the door.

Beth sighed as she looked at the chair, ruined forever by a creep who wanted to scare her. And scare her he did. She hated that she could be so rattled by a knife after all she had been through, but she suspected that was also the reason why she had been so easily shaken by it. Someone had been on their property, on their porch, feet away from their bedroom. And if the message was written in blood, whose blood was it?

Although he wasn't in her peripheral vision, she knew Donovan stood behind her, watching her. "Could you help me move the chair to the curb? I don't want it anymore."

"Sure."

Together, they carried the chair to the end of the driveway and put it next to their trash cans. Someone would pick it up, not knowing the story behind the one-inch long cut in the armrest. That was for the better.

Inside the house, Donovan locked the front door and put in the code for the alarm system; they'd be staying in for the rest of the day. "I think we've been stupid."

She arched a brow at him. "How so?"

"We don't have security cameras here. I don't even have them at my garage. After we risked our lives to get the security footage from my brother's house after Hurricane Sabrina, I should've thought more like him. He had the cameras installed for a reason, and they ended up helping me prove my innocence. We've been dealing with the same men he had, worse men, and we never figured it would be smart to add cameras as a precaution. If we did, we would know who's doing this."

"We thought it was over," she said.

"And that's how we were stupid a second time."

Donovan's statement was exactly what she had thought that morning, before she found the knife and bloody note. They had been stupid. They got too comfortable. But were they supposed to live on pins and needles their whole lives because of what they went through in the past? What kind of life would that be?

"One day, Donovan, this will be over. I have to believe that."

He wrapped his arms around her and put his head in the crook of her neck. His lips touched her skin, warming her. "I know, but that time isn't now." He sighed. "I'm sorry for seeking Craig out and not telling you. If I hadn't, we may not be in this situation."

"If you're right that this is Craig, he may have done this sooner-or-later, without your provocation but—" she shook her head "—I still can't see him doing this. He would cringe whenever he got something sticky on his hands. And he would grow faint at the sight of blood. This doesn't make sense."

Donovan stroked his hands through her hair. "Maybe I'm wrong. It wouldn't be the first time. Let's do something that goes against my nature and listen to Thorn. We'll wait for any information the investigators get and let Thorn do what he does best."

She chuckled. "I think he'd appreciate that. We've been a pain in his ass for too long."

Donovan smirked back. Then his smile faded. "So, what do you think about getting security cameras set up?"

"Can we get them by tonight?" She let out a slow breath. "I'd feel better if we had them in place before we crawled into bed."

Lines appeared at the corners of Donovan's eyes as he studied her. She knew he saw fear.

She couldn't mask it. Not now. Not after their

home had been breached. Not after seeing her friend's house burn to the ground. She had no fear-masking powers left.

"I'll get right on it."

Donovan called the man who had installed Ryan's security cameras to equip their property with interior and exterior cameras. He used the same technique that had stumped Chewy and Buck when they disabled the outdoor cameras, thinking it shut down all of them, but because the cameras inside had their own system, they were left running. Beth hoped that whoever was targeting them now would be as inexperienced with security systems as Chewy and Buck had been. That night, she felt safer knowing that if anyone came close, they would be recorded and Thorn would be able to catch them.

Chapter Twelve

Early the next morning, Donovan contacted the security tech for a second job and called a locksmith. He met them at his garage where cameras were set up and new locks were put on the door. Neither would stop someone from breaking into the garage in the future, but he'd be able to catch the asshole's face. He almost wished whoever was responsible would make that mistake so he'd be able to nail the bastard and do away with him once and for all.

He drove home wondering who that person could be. He considered Craig but just wasn't convinced. It frightened him more that it could be someone not even on his radar, as opposed to a creepy ex-fiancé; he hated that someone he didn't expect could be causing havoc in their lives. Every criminal they had ever faced was now behind bars, from the dirty cops in Jackson Storm's drug ring to the criminals who acted on Jackson's behalf after he was locked up in maximum security. Maybe a lone man, who had lain low, resurfaced to enact vengeance in his boss's name. Based off their past experiences with these men, they'd stop at nothing to complete their mission. Beth had nearly died because of their determination.

He passed lawn after lawn of brown grass. Everything was dry. Too dry. A single ember would set everything ablaze. Ash from a nearby fire floated from the sky and shattered against his windshield.

At home, he parked next to Beth's beat-up car. He had offered to buy her a better used car, but she had declined. As long as the engine didn't crap out, she preferred cars with character. He suspected it also had to do with the fact her cars never lasted long and, in her mind, paying for a new car that could get bashed in by someone trying to kill her would be a waste.

The driveway was speckled with ashes. The lawn had huge patches of dead grass. The palm tree in the front was brown. He knew how vulnerable his home was with the ashes falling from the sky. He could just hope the ashes had time to cool before touching the roofs, trees, and lawns in their neighborhood.

Beth was watching the mid-day news when he came in. "Another fire broke out near us, and two more in Palm Bay," she said as he came in.

"I know. Ashes are coming down pretty heavy. I'm going to make sure our gutters are clear of debris. Can you turn on the sprinklers?"

"Sure." She turned off the TV and followed him out the door. It took a good hour, but he picked every last leaf clear and flushed the gutters with water for good measure. While he did that, Beth pulled down the dead branches from the palm tree and used loppers to cut away as much brush as she could that hung close to their house. When they were done, they were sweaty and hungry. Side by side, they worked on sandwiches. Beth slathered mayo on slices of bread and cut tomato; Donovan layered cuts of turkey and pieces of Romaine lettuce. They had just finished eating their late lunch when there was a knock at the door.

Beth dusted off her hands. "I'll go see who it is."

He peered over his shoulder as she looked through the peephole.

"It's our favorite detective," she said and unlocked the door.

Thorn stepped in and kissed Beth on the cheek. "I heard that and appreciate it, but I'm afraid I'll be your least favorite detective soon."

"Not possible," Beth said and walked into the kitchen. "Do you want a sandwich?"

"No, I'm good."

She pointed to a stack of papers on the counter as she went to the sink to rinse off their plates. "Our grudge lists are complete. Or as complete as we can get them anyway. I printed out my client list and starred the ones I thought could fit."

Thorn picked up the papers and flipped through them. "Damn, Beth. There's ten or more stars on every page."

Beth leaned against the counter and shrugged. "I told you it would be a lot. My job is to help these women, not turn them away. I wouldn't be a good self-defense instructor if I did."

Thorn set the stack on the table. "I'll have my team look at these. I, uh, have a couple of things to tell you." His tone told Donovan that neither of these things were going to be good.

Donovan glanced toward Beth, who looked at him at the same time. She crossed her arms over her chest, a defensive stance. In his chair, Donovan's spinal column shifted as he braced himself. "What is it?"

"Well, I went to talk to Craig." Thorn's gaze met Donovan's. "I questioned him about his whereabouts between the morning of Beth's birthday and Sunday morning when the note was found. He said he was out of town for a business trip. I checked, and his boss confirmed a weekend business conference in Jacksonville." His eyes shifted toward Beth. "He also claims not to know where you live."

Donovan shook his head as anger radiated through his system. "That's a load of crap. She lives on the same lot where she has lived most of her life."

"Yes, but if he's checked, he would've seen that the house was demolished and the land put up for sale."

"And if he's been stalking her, he easily could've followed her here and seen her."

Aggravation flashed across Thorn's face. "I'm telling you he has a sound alibi. He didn't get back until Sunday night. I talked to his coworkers and the hotel. They all confirmed this. He's not the one responsible for what's been happening. Someone else is."

That was what Donovan hated. He wanted it to be Craig. Not just so he could nail the prick for his disgusting ways, but so the problem would be dealt with quickly. Yes, he wanted Craig to be the culprit for an easy way out of this mess, but that wasn't going to happen.

Thorn shifted his feet. "The other thing I wanted to tell you…" He looked uneasy. Donovan clenched his hands into fists, as if he could hold onto his control.

"The results came back on the knife. No fingerprints." He paused. "And the blood wasn't human. It was pig's blood."

Donovan frowned at that. There weren't many places you could get a pig in these parts. They didn't roam wild, and there weren't any farms close by. Someone had to have killed a pig, collected the blood in a bucket or something, and brought it to their porch to leave their sick message. And when did they accomplish this? While they were out celebrating Beth's birthday, while they were making love, or while they slept soundly in bed?

Out of the corner of his eye he saw Beth whirl around. The sound of her gagging met his ears. He turned his head to see her throw up in the sink. He jumped to his feet as Beth twisted the faucet and let water flow. In a few strides, he was at her side. He took her shoulders in his hands and tried to look at her face, but her head was dipped low as she braced her hands on the counter.

She breathed slowly between her teeth.

"Beth?"

She shook her head. With a shaky hand, she collected water into her palm, brought it to her lips, and swished out her mouth. Then she flipped the switch for the garbage disposal. The loud whirling sound filled the kitchen. After a moment, she turned off the disposal and faucet. When she faced him, he saw all the color had drained from her face. Beads of sweat dotted her brow.

"Pig's blood," she whispered. "Not a good thing to think about when your stomach's out of whack."

"You've been sick?" Thorn stood a few steps away. Concern dominated his face.

Donovan had thought she was better. Was she keeping an illness from him?

"It's nothing," she said. "But I do think I'll sit down." She went to the table and dropped into a chair. She didn't look like his indestructible self-defense instructor anymore, but more like a porcelain doll that could shatter into a trillion pieces.

"I'll get out of your hair. Take care of yourself, Beth."

She gave him a weak smile. "I will."

For the rest of the day, Donovan stole peeks at Beth. Her color came back, and she ate as if nothing was wrong. After dinner, they went for a walk. Hand in hand, they strolled around the block. Wildflowers sprouted in the tangle of overgrown grass along the woods. Beth stopped to pluck a few. One of them had long, white, triangle-like petals.

"This one was my favorite when I was little," she said when she came back with a handful. "Every time I took a walk with my mom, I would pick every one of these I saw, because I thought they looked like stars. Back then, we were just about the only house on the block. Well, except for the Franks." She pointed at the house at the end of the road. "They moved in a few years after we did. A few more families came, but it wasn't until I left to live in my own apartment that the neighborhood really built up. I'm just glad there's a few lots yet to be plowed. I like seeing the trees. I'd really hate it if we were side-by-side houses."

As they were walking past the lot next to their house, Donovan admired the pine trees. He wondered how much the lot would cost. They could buy it and never worry about losing this bit of nature and the privacy it provided.

Beth kicked a stone in the road. It rolled to a stop several feet away. When they reached it, she kicked it again. Donovan chuckled at the innocent fun in the action.

"Are you making fun of me?" she asked.

He shook his head. "No. You're just incredibly cute."

"What? Because I'm kicking a stone?"

"Exactly because you're kicking a stone."

She lowered her head. Pink touched her cheeks. "I used to kick a rock around the entire block back to my house when I was little." She shrugged. "It's a habit."

"Like I said, it's cute. You can do it with our kids."

Her hand flexed on his. She stopped and turned to him with her boutique of flowers, which he suspected were really weeds, but he didn't have the heart to tell her so. A sweet smile was on her lips, and a twinkle was in her eyes.

"I like it when you talk about our future kids. I seem to recall when the mention of our future made you squirm."

He thought back to his uncertainty about what he wanted when they went to San Francisco. It was after the quake when he realized he wanted it all with Beth—an engagement ring, a wedding, a marriage, a home, and some babies.

"I was an idiot then."

She laughed. "When you took me to Michigan to meet your mom and grandma, they asked me about our relationship. Your grandma even asked if the sex was good."

Donovan stopped breathing. He stared at Beth with wide eyes. "Please tell me you're kidding." He couldn't believe his grandmother would ask a woman she just met such an embarrassing, not to mention intimate, question about her grandson. Then again, she was a spunky one. When the time came, Grandma Lily had given him his first box of condoms—much to his horror. He gave them to a friend and asked Ryan to buy him another box. He couldn't use the condoms his grandma had bought; he would've had nightmares afterward.

Beth threw back her head in laughter. "I'm not kidding. When she asked, I nearly chocked. But I think she was just really trying to get at what you meant to me."

Horrified, Donovan rubbed his hand over his face. "Leave it to my grandma to use sex to do that. Gosh that even sounds wrong."

Beth laughed again. "You're impossibly cute when you're embarrassed. I don't get to see that much." She kissed his cheek. "I hope I get to see you embarrassed more often."

"You will. Just wait for when you're pregnant and she starts talking about my sperm." He could imagine his grandma inspecting her first great-grandson while she changed his diaper and her winking at him when she saw the baby's fresh circumcision. "Oh God."

Beth doubled over. "This is great. We need to have a baby just so I can witness this."

Donovan gave her a soft whack on her butt. "Just you wait. You'll be the one who will be pregnant. Just think about the things she can say or do to embarrass you."

Beth's laugher came to a halt as she considered this. All the humor fled from her face. "Shit."

Now it was Donovan's turn to grin. "Exactly." He put his arm around her shoulder. "We'll be in the same boat, Mrs. Goldwyn."

She elbowed him. "But we'll have life vests on in case we have to jump ship."

"Why of course."

****

The air wasn't choked with smoke the next morning, so Beth went on a run with Donovan. The sky was a soft gray with the sun barely above the horizon. Most of the houses they passed were still shut tight as the people inside dreamed. They ran side by side, gently pushing each other. Their shoes made a steady rhythm, two beats blending into one.

Beth glanced over at Donovan. He was shirtless and in basketball shorts. His arm muscles bulged as he swayed his arms back and forth with perfect form. He had an amazingly fit body, and it was hers to enjoy. Smiling, she pushed a little harder, getting a few strides ahead of Donovan.

"Hey, where do you think you're going?" He caught up to her and edged a little farther.

She ran with him to their stop sign where she came to a stop and put her hands to her knees to catch her breath. When she looked up at him, panting beside her, she laughed. He tilted his head to her. "What's so funny?" he asked.

"Nothing. It's just that this was one of my relationship goals with—" She stopped when he glared at her. "Before," she amended.

"So, Craig didn't like to run?"

"Please, he only ran on a treadmill with a mirror in front of him."

Donovan shook his head. "I can't picture you with a guy like that."

Beth thought about it. "Actually, neither can I, but he weaseled his way in. Somehow."

He twirled her ponytail around his finger. "I like

the part where you kicked his ass right out of your life."

She smirked. "So do I." She poked Donovan in the ribs. "Race you home." And she took off running.

"Cheater!"

Her feet pounded up the driveway and the walkway to the front door. She spun around on the welcome mat as Donovan came up behind her. His arms locked around her waist, and his body pressed into hers. The smell of his sweat teased her nostrils. "You're sweaty," she said.

He put his mouth to her throat. "We get sweaty together all the time," he muttered,

She let him lavish attention on the sensitive spot below her ear. "I have to shower before work."

"Shower for two?"

"If we take a shower together, we'll do more than shower."

Donovan chuckled. "That's the point." His mouth trailed down to her breasts.

"If we do that, on top of this run, I'll be too exhausted to go into work."

"That'd be a bonus."

She pushed him back. "Sorry, cowboy. Not happening." She entered the house and headed for the stairs.

"You sure know how to break my heart."

Beth shot a look over her shoulder as she started up the stairs. Donovan still stood on the welcome mat, as if he had forgotten how to walk. She blew him a kiss and swayed her hips just a little more on her way to the second floor.

She came back down twenty minutes later in paint-splattered workout clothes. Passing the sliding glass door, she tried not to look, but she couldn't stop herself. She paused in front of the glass. Her favorite chair was no longer there, and everything appeared normal. No messages.

No knives. No blood.

The fact someone had been on their porch, so close to being inside their home, rattled her. It reminded her of the time, six months before their wedding, when someone had broken into their apartment during a freak lightning storm. The only thing that had gone missing was a picture of Beth and Donovan. It had been on their refrigerator, beneath two magnets. Even after moving, it never showed up. And no prints were found.

Was it possible for a crime that occurred two years ago to be linked to the crime that happened here two days ago? Unlikely, but not impossible.

She hurried into the kitchen where Donovan was pouring milk into a bowl of cereal. "What if the guy who broke into our apartment and took our picture did this?" She pointed toward the porch.

Donovan set down his bowl. "I hadn't thought of that. If it is the same person, it sucks that nothing was uncovered. We have no leads."

She let out a breath. "I know." It had been a good revelation, but it didn't help them in knowing who that culprit was.

She got down her own bowl and fixed herself cereal. At the kitchen table, she sat across from Donovan. "What are your plans for today with your truck temporarily out of commission?"

"I have a meeting with my sponsor. They're curious about the truck and the investigation and are looking into a hood latch protector and other ways to prevent tampering."

"That's good." She never wanted anything like this to happen again. Watching Donovan make a successful high jump was one thing. It was exhilarating. She'd cheer just as loud as anyone. But watching his truck fall nose-first was another. She had felt helpless.

"I'm sure my team's not happy about the repairs."

"That's not your fault, though. They should happy they still have their driver."

"They are. I got a lot of texts making sure I wasn't dead or paralyzed." He smirked. "They sure made it clear they didn't want another driver. I felt loved."

Beth laughed. "That's because my man is the best." She winked at him.

"Despite the crash, a lot of people are thinking the same thing. Apparently, several companies want to help us advertise. Advertisers mean money. I sure didn't do it as a stunt, but it seems everyone loved it. Mitch says it's because no one had ever seen me crash like that. Or crash period. It got me noticed." He shook his head. "I would think the opposite would work, but who am I to question what gets fans and advertisers hyped?"

She didn't like that everyone was excited about his crash. It could've been worse. It could've been deadly. Perhaps the fact it was the highest any truck had ever risen, and he had survived, was what thrilled everyone. What would happen if he landed that jump perfectly? She didn't want to know, because attempting to go that high again, or even higher, could result in countless injuries.

"Donovan, you better not try to jump that high again."

"Don't worry. I won't."

Satisfied with his promise, although she knew that didn't eliminate him from attempting to jump past the world record mark, she left for work. At The Fighting Chance, Beth had several minutes to herself. Corissa wouldn't be there for another twenty minutes, and since she had run before work, she didn't have to get a warm-up in before her first class. She sat in the chair behind the front desk, with nothing to do but think. And she could only think about the bloody knife she had found. Who would leave that for her to find? Who would want to scare her?

She considered the possibilities. A bloody knife and a birthday note were personal, as Donovan pointed out. And for it to happen now had to be a sign. She'd had two birthdays since Jackson Storm was arrested, so she had to believe this crime wasn't connected to him. What had happened recently? Who had she pissed off before her birthday?

One name came to mind. *Dave.*

Anger simmered inside her, bubbling to the surface until her breathing quickened. Her hand lashed out, and she picked up the phone. Her finger punched in Dave's phone number as she seethed. The ring tone only aggravated her more.

"Calling to hire me back?" Dave's voice made her hand clench around the phone.

"In your dreams," she spat. "I hired Amanda to be my new assistant."

"Amanda? The girl who can't even look people in the eye?" He laughed. "You've got to be kidding."

"Amanda has more skill in self-defense than you ever did."

"Please. She doesn't like to touch people. How is

she supposed to teach? Does she wear oven mitts?" His laughter grew louder.

Beth ground her teeth. "Let's just say she doesn't touch them in places she shouldn't."

There was a fleeting moment of silence on the other end.

"You're lucky all I did was touch Maria."

Beth's jaw unhinged. She got to her feet, as if he was in front of her and she could knee him in the groin until his manhood was beyond use. "You're a sick son-of-a-bitch. You came to my house on Saturday, didn't you? You were pissed that you got caught sexually assaulting someone, pissed that I fired your scumbag ass, so you slaughtered a pig to leave a bloody knife on my porch. What else did you do to the pig, Dave? You're a pig, yourself. Did killing it get you off? Did writing 'Happy Birthday' on a note make you giddy? Did sneaking onto my property give you a rush? If you did it, I promise you you're going to go down."

"I didn't do that, you lunatic. A detective was already here. I have an alibi."

"I hope it's a good one," she hissed.

"I was job hunting all day Saturday. So, I have you to thank for my alibi. If you hadn't fired me, I would've been home all day. Alone. Luckily, I have a paper trail for all the places I went to inquiring about job openings and submitting applications."

"I hope you didn't put down The Fighting Chance on your resume, because if potential employers call me, you can bet I'll tell them you're a threat to their female clientele and staff. And if I ever hear you're working at another studio or gym, I will have a one-on-one meeting with your boss. Maria has filed a complaint against you. The police will be investigating, so good luck trying to get another job in this line of work. I'll make it my personal mission to make sure the only job you ever get is as a pest control worker killing cockroaches, or worse." She slammed the phone down before he could reply. Needing to blow off some steam, she looked forward to her first class. Too bad Dave wasn't her assistant anymore; she usually took out her frustrations on him.

****

That evening, Beth came home, showered, and changed into cotton pajamas. After her day, she just wanted to laze on the couch. Her bare feet padded into the kitchen. She had to figure out dinner, though. That was the thing about being a wife; she didn't always want to cook, or even think about what to have for dinner. She opened the drawer next to the refrigerator and inspected the menus for local takeout. She was debating between Thai food or deli sandwiches when Donovan came home.

"Talking to sponsors and advertisers can be more draining than wrestling with a beast of a truck," Donovan grumbled as he came into the kitchen.

"I'm drained, too, so you won't fault me for ordering take out, will you?"

He kissed her temple. "I love take out."

"Break the tie." She held up the two menus.

He peered over her shoulder at the options. "Deli subs sound simple. I need simple right now."

She dropped the Thai menu back into the drawer. "Subs it is." She called in their usual order, requested delivery, and then shuffled down the driveway to check the mail. Through the tree line, she could see a wisp of smoke stretching toward the sky. Although it appeared close, she knew it could be miles away. The sight of it still filled her with dread.

She paused in front of the mailbox and pulled down the plastic door. Something long and black tumbled out and fell at her feet. She looked down. A scream flew from her lips. A black snake lay on the road, inches from her toes. She hopped back. Chills of disgust rolled through her. She hustled up the driveway, shaking her arms and legs as if she could dispel the morbid image seared into her mind.

Chapter Thirteen

Donovan heard Beth's scream. He looked out the kitchen window to see her hurrying up the driveway, looking as though she were doing a strange dance. He opened the door.

She waved her arms and jumped from foot to foot. "Gross, gross, gross."

"What's wrong?" Try as he might, he couldn't stop the corners of his mouth from lifting.

"It's not funny!" She smacked his arm several times while hopping up and down. "A black snake just fell out of the mailbox."

He looked toward the mailbox. A black wavy line was still on the road. "Did you kill it?"

"That would entail touching it, so no, I didn't kill it!"

"Okay." He rubbed her arm. "I'll go check it out."

Beth was afraid of snakes. Although black racers were harmless, that wouldn't stop her from freaking out over glimpsing the tail of one slithering away in the grass. As he walked down the driveway, he was aware of Beth creeping close behind him. He made sure to keep his laughter from breaking loose.

He stood in front of the mailbox and studied the snake. It wasn't moving. He bent over to get a closer look. "It's dead."

"Why would it go into our mailbox to die? And

how could it get in there? It was closed."

He glanced at her. She was several feet up the driveway, not wanting to get any closer to the serpent. "It didn't. Someone cut the head off."

"Ew."

"And put it in our mailbox."

"You mean the snake's body, right?"

He shook his head. Inside their mailbox was the severed snake's head. "I mean both."

Beth took two giant steps back. "That's sick."

He nodded. "We need to call Thorn." In their house, he picked up his cell phone.

Thorn answered on the second ring. "Whenever my phone rings, I always expect it to be you or Beth, making my day more complicated than it already is." He sighed. "What happened?"

"Someone put a dead snake in our mailbox. Its head was severed and included as a little present."

A hissing sound sounded on the other end. "Did Beth see it?" He also knew about her fear.

"She was the one who opened the mailbox. The damn thing fell out at her feet."

"Damn it. I'll be right over."

Thorn arrived shortly after he ended their call. Investigators took pictures of the snake on the ground and the head inside the mailbox. They even bagged both body parts and swabbed the inside where the snake's blood had collected.

When an investigator came over to dust it for prints, Beth said, "Just take the mailbox."

They all looked at her.

"Seriously. I don't want to ever touch that thing again, so take the whole fucking box."

After collecting their samples, they pried off the box and put it into a large evidence bag. Then they left. What sort of work they could do with a dead snake, Donovan didn't know, but he was glad it was gone.

"So…" Thorn stood with the two of them by the front door. "Are we thinking this is related to the knife on the porch?"

"I think it is," Beth muttered. She sat on a white porch chair. "I'm the one who's afraid of snakes, which isn't exactly a secret." She looked up at them. "You might want to start with Dave. I called him while I was at work and sort of threatened him."

She looked at Donovan. "I guess I had no right to get mad at you for threatening Craig when I can't even take my own advice." She addressed Thorn again. "It didn't end pretty. He told me I was lucky that all he did was touch Maria, which set me off. I told him I'd make sure he'd never work in my line of business again."

Thorn let out a deep breath. "I'll question him, but—" He looked back and forth at the eaves. "Didn't you get a security system set up with cameras?"

Donovan's eyes widened. He had already forgotten about the camera. There was one in each corner of the house, facing opposite directions. Surely, one of them had caught the perp's face. The three of them crowded in front of his laptop as they studied the feed from that day. Donovan rewound from the point that he had stopped the recording. No one had come close to the mailbox all day, and the mail truck had driven right past it.

"It's a good thing we didn't have any mail today," Beth said. "The poor mail woman would've had a heart attack."

Donovan had the same thought. Their mail woman was sweet. He'd never want her to get that sort of rude surprise.

He continued to rewind the feed straight through into the previous night.

"Stop." Thorn pointed to the screen. "I saw something."

He played the footage, and they all leaned forward. According to the time, at three o'clock in the morning, a dark vehicle had pulled up to their mailbox. The pitch-black window on the passenger's side rolled down, and a person's upper body emerged in the glow from their motion-sensitive lights. The man wore a black ski-mask over his face. He pulled the dead snake from a bag and stuffed it and its head into the opening. He fiddled with it just a little before quickly putting the lid into place. The moment he was done, the car sped off.

Donovan craned his neck, but from that angle, he couldn't even catch a glimpse of white on the license plate. He input the CD from the other camera, hoping that angle would give them a clear view. It did, except a black square completely covered the license plate.

Thorn cursed. "They're smart. They probably covered their plate with black paper or duct tape before coming down the street, and then they uncovered it before getting back onto the main road."

That didn't make sense to Donovan. "Why would they do that?"

"They could've seen the home security van out front when you were having the cameras installed."

"Which means they're watching us?" Beth asked.

"Yeah."

Donovan sat back in his chair and stared at the frozen frame on his laptop. It didn't reveal anything, but seeing the man put the dead snake in the mailbox and fool with it before leaving got Donovan thinking. The culprit had made sure it would fall out when the door was lowered. He wanted it to fall out for bigger impact. Something coming at you was more frightening than merely seeing something immobile. It was a fear tactic as much as a warning or threat.

Putting a dead animal or serpent on someone's property jived with what many stalkers had done for decades; they enjoyed it. So, it could be another sick message for Beth. Or not.

A knock at the door made him tense.

"Our food," Beth said. "I'll pay for it." She returned a couple of minutes later with a bag. "Thorn, do you like California clubs?"

"What's not to like?"

"I'll split my sandwich with you," she offered. "I've sort of lost my appetite."

While they ate, Donovan went over everything that had happened recently. While the bloody knife and dead snake seemed to fit, and both appeared to be targeted at Beth, he felt as though he was missing something. He mulled it over as he consumed his sandwich.

He got up to throw away the wrappings for his sandwich and caught sight of his keys on the counter. The only keychain he had was a piece of merchandise, metal designed to look like his truck. It was silver with the exact black and neon green paint job his truck had. On the side, the black cobra was visible.

He whirled around. "What if the snake was meant

for me?" He lifted the keychain. "My symbol is a snake. A black snake."

****

Tuesday morning, Donovan and Beth took the day off to handle a few errands. They went to the hardware store to pick out a new mailbox. He couldn't fault Beth for not wanting the old one. If it had been crawling with spiders, he wouldn't want to go near it either, even if the spiders were long gone. Although it wasn't spiders, the thought of a dead snake in their mailbox didn't exactly make him want to skip to check the mail.

"How about this one?" Beth indicated at a black, steel mailbox. Behind the door was a mail slot with a key lock. "It's pricey, but it'll stop people from putting undesirable stuff in it."

"Actually, it stops them from taking out our mail. They could still fit…undesirable stuff into the slot."

"But getting a snake through that would be hard."

"Good point."

They paid for their new mailbox before heading to Donovan's mechanic's garage. The sound of drills and the smell of car oil overwhelmed his senses when he entered the garage with Beth. Those sounds and smells, which could give many people headaches, relaxed him. He had worked as a mechanic when he was in high school. The knowledge he gained had helped him greatly in his monster truck business.

"Hey, Scotty." He walked up to a man in a grease-stained T-shirt and trashed jeans. Donovan had met Scotty when he moved down to Florida as a young twenty-something looking for a life, not just parties and fist fights. After Ryan took Donovan to a monster truck show and he realized what he wanted to do, he and

Scotty had spent weeks formulating ideas for his truck. Scotty was his go-to man. The only one he trusted with his truck.

Scotty turned. "Hey, Goldwyn. Is this your wife?" He wiped his hands on a dirty rag and held one out to Beth. "I don't think I've had the pleasure."

Beth shook his hand. "It's nice to meet you, Scotty. Donovan says you're the best mechanic in Florida."

Scotty rolled up the rag and snapped it near Donovan's hip. "He better say that."

Donovan chuckled. "Yeah, whatever. So, how's my truck?"

"The parts came in today. I removed the hood. There's something I want to show you."

They followed him to the back of the garage where Donovan's monster truck was parked. The engine was exposed, and the bumper was gone. It looked sad, like a patient with his stomach opened on the operating table, revealing all his intestines. Instead of bringing them to the truck, Scotty turned to the wall where the crumpled hood was propped up.

"Take a look at the corner there." Scotty pointed to the bottom. "I put this hood on myself and know for a fact that neither of us put that there."

Curious, Donovan squatted in front of it. Painted on the metallic underbelly of the hood was a snake head. He frowned at it. The image didn't match the logo on the side of his truck. "It's not a cobra."

Beth joined him. She reached out a hand. Her finger touched the snake's image. Then she snatched her hand back as if the metal had shocked her. "It's a viper."

That single word brought the walls down around

Donovan. His head snapped around. "What?"

"It's just like his tattoo," she said. Her voice was barely audible over the racket of the other mechanics going about their jobs. She peered at him. "He's the one behind your accident and the bloody message—Viper."

****

Viper was the drug dealer Beth met when she went undercover, hoping to find out Buck's whereabouts. What she did led to the Orlando SWAT team breaking down the door to his house and arresting him, and all his buddies who had been there getting high. She hadn't put his name on her grudge list. She hadn't even considered him. Her heart rate escalated as she thought about his sneer, the gold canine tooth, and the platinum gun clamped in his hand as he stared her down. How could she have forgotten about him and his black eyes that pierced straight through her, making her fear that he saw through her disguise?

More remarkable than the fact she had forgotten about him was that she wasn't afraid. She was angry. Out of all the criminals she faced, including murderers, a marijuana drug dealer was the one who snuck in under their radar. She realized she hadn't thought about him because she thought he was out of the picture, locked behind bars, but his sentence wouldn't have lasted forever. Eventually, he would've been released. And she knew that a criminal behind bars could be as dangerous as one who was free. Jackson Storm had proven that.

She sat on a stool and glared at the snake. Viper, or one of his weed buddies, had broken into Donovan's garage, tampered with his truck, and left that snake as a calling card. The snake in the mailbox was no doubt his doing as well. He wanted them to know who was responsible. What troubled her more was the fact he knew who Donovan was. Beth had dressed up as a cocaine addict going through withdrawal, and the name she had given him was Felicia. How had he figured out her identity to know to go after Donovan?

The moment she asked herself that question, she knew the answer—Buck. They were at the same prison. Over the course of the last two years, they could've seen each other and talked about their arrests—both of which she had had a hand in.

"The two of you are making my days into never-ending headaches," Thorn announced when he found them in the garage. "What do you have for me?"

Donovan pointed at the snake image. "A suspect."

Thorn squatted to look at it. "I don't get it."

"It's an exact replica of Viper's tattoo," Beth said.

Thorn's shoulders pulled back. He stared at if for several seconds before getting to his feet and facing them. "It is the same."

Donovan cursed.

"The question is whether we are dealing with him or someone acting in his name? I'm going to make a call." Thorn stepped outside with his cell phone to his ear.

Beth glanced at Donovan. His body was tense as he paced in front of the crumpled hood. She worried for him, because his worry for her could become so great, terrifyingly so. Whenever that happened, he did extreme things, like going to prison to pry a confession from a murderer, or knocking on her ex's door to issue a threat.

"Donovan, you're not breathing."

"Am I supposed to be?"

She was about to reply when Thorn shouted, "Is this a joke? Why wasn't I notified?"

"That doesn't sound good," she said.

"No, it doesn't," Donovan agreed.

A few minutes later, Thorn stormed back inside. "Viper escaped," he snapped. "He was on work release, and the first chance he got, he split."

Beth swallowed. So, they weren't dealing with Viper's friends or buyers. They were dealing with him, the man who had an arsenal of guns and bullets in his house. The man with cold eyes. The man she tricked and who was arrested the same night.

"What did they say when you asked why you weren't notified?" Donovan asked.

"They said the cops in the area were notified, citizens received emergency phone calls, something was in the paper, and a news bulletin was put out on all news stations, but with all of the fire coverage, it probably went unnoticed by many."

"Like us," Beth said. She eyed the snake defacing a piece of her husband's monster truck. Viper was the most well-known drug dealer in Central Florida. He didn't sell the big drugs and wasn't a part of Jackson Storm's drug ring, but he was known for his intimidation as well as his potent marijuana. Everyone knew him as Viper. If the news reported his real name, would anyone have realized who he was? Beth didn't even know his real name.

She looked at Thorn. "What's his real name?"

"Keon Roberts."

No, she wouldn't have recognized that name.

"What do we do now?" Donovan asked.

"Sit tight. Wait for him to come out, and he will."

Yes, he would. They always did.

"He's not after Donovan," she said with her gaze still on the hood.

"What do you mean?" Donovan asked. "He fucked with my truck to kill me."

Beth looked at him. "Remember how Jackson's men used me to get to you?"

His jaw ticked. They had kidnapped her, used her for bait, shot her, and beat her. All because they wanted Donovan to come running.

"Well, now Viper's using you to get to me," she continued. "He'll take you out only to hurt me." Her eyes ticked back to the hood. "I was the one who went undercover." Thorn had asked Beth to go undercover because Viper would've recognized a cop. Beth was a normal civilian, and she tricked him; something that had never been done before.

She turned back to the men staring at her. "He wants *me* to pay. Not you. Me."

Donovan had been right. The bloody birthday message had been from someone in her past, just not who he expected. He also said it was intimate; vengeance could be very intimate. Viper wanted her dead. There was passion in that—the worst kind.

She wasn't going to let another criminal scare her, though. Never again. She had spent too much time afraid of Jackson Storm and his goons. They took from her—blood, security, sanity—moments of her life that should've been bursting with joy. Never again would a single one of them accomplish that. Not even Viper.

No, she wasn't frightened. She was pissed.

Viper had gotten under her skin once—for a few

minutes after she was face to face with him—but she never lost a wink of sleep over him. She wouldn't let him steal her sleep now. Or her security, sanity, or happiness. And definitely not her blood. Or Donovan's. If Viper thought she was weak, he had another thing coming.

After one of Jackson's men shot Donovan and he lay at her feet on the soft sand of Waikiki Beach, she had shed her fear and threatened the man with every fiber of her being.

You don't think I'm a threat? You don't know the meaning of the word. If you don't kill me, I will become a threat bigger than Jackson Storm. I've studied stalkers, wife beaters, and murderers, and I will use that knowledge to hunt you down and kill you. So shoot me or be a hunted bitch.

Now she was sending those same words to Viper. She hoped he heard them loud and clear, because she was issuing a challenge, which she planned to win.

Chapter Fourteen

"I want to talk to Buck."

Beth's request stunned Donovan. He turned to face her. On the stool, her glare was pinned on the snake. Thorn stood beside him. He was also gaping at Beth.

"What?"

Her gaze left the snake and met his. "I want to talk to Buck," she repeated but slower.

"Out of the question," Thorn said.

She sent her icy stare in Thorn's direction. "When Donovan asked to see Buck, you took him. When he asked to be taken to maximum security to talk to Jackson Storm, you did that, too. Well, now, I'm asking. Buck is the only one who could've given Viper information. I want to talk to him."

"And what do you want to talk with him about?" Thorn asked.

"I want to know what he told Viper. We could try to ask him what Viper has in store for us."

Donovan faced Thorn, who was their only mediator and the man who could grant Beth's wish. Donovan wanted him to see how a confrontation between the two of them would be a bad thing, especially for Beth. "I don't want her to talk to him."

"Didn't I once ask you not to make decisions for me?" Beth spat. Her face was tight, and her gaze was hard.

156

"I'm not," he snapped back. "I'm hoping Thorn will understand I don't want you to step foot into that prison, to see Buck and hear the things I heard when I spoke to him and Jackson." Doing that didn't change anything, but it had haunted him.

"You found out about the kill order. If we go now, we could find out what Viper's plans are. Knowing that could work in our favor. We'd be able to prepare." She looked to Thorn.

He shook his head at them. "Knowing that Viper's only connection to you is Buck, it makes sense to talk to him." He turned cautious eyes on Beth. "But I don't want you to go either."

Relief rushed through Donovan. *At least Thorn has my back on this.*

"If the two of you think you're going to go and leave me behind, think again," Beth said. "The two of you have done this too many times, and it needs to stop. We're in this together. We have been since San Fran. So, unless you go alone, Thorn, I'm coming, too."

Thorn shrugged at Donovan. That gesture made Donovan's relief go up in flames. "It might be better if the three of us go together," Thorn said. "We'd be a united front. And Beth wouldn't be alone."

Donovan ground his teeth. Thorn knew that last part would seal the deal for Donovan. The last time they went to the prison and talked to Buck and Jackson Storm, he had been frantic, thinking Jackson's murderous goons had gotten to Beth while he had been gone. He could still hear Jackson's threat word for word.

At least they weren't going to see Jackson. Never again did Donovan want to experience that fear. The only way to ensure nothing happened to Beth while they questioned Buck was to have her there with them.

"Fine," he said. "We go together."

"Great." Beth got off the stool. "Let's go now while I'm still mad." She walked past them to the exit.

Donovan and Thorn stared after her.

"This is going to be good," Thorn said and then hustled to catch up with her.

Donovan stayed in place a moment longer, with his hands in his pockets. Only one thought came to his mind—*Shit.*

****

Donovan took up the rear as Thorn led them to a secure room where they'd be able to talk to Buck. Beth walked in front of him. No, she marched. Her shoulders were pulled back, and her chin was high—a woman on a mission. He had seen her like this before, but not in a while. The threat of Jackson's men had truly gotten to her, but this new threat was bringing back her feistiness in full swing.

The room was empty when they gained access to it. Three chairs occupied one side of a table. A single chair took up residency on the other side. Beth sat between him and Thorn. He stole glances at her while they waited for Buck. Her hands were clasped on the table. She stared straight ahead, breathing in and out as if to keep herself in check. Normally, he'd be the one with clenched fists.

A few minutes later, the door opened. Two guards led Buck into the room. Donovan looked over his shoulder. Buck's long, greasy hair was pulled into a ponytail. His face was shadowed with thick stubble. His eyes, from the deep pits of his eye sockets, lit with amusement.

"Another visit from little boy Goldwyn and his two-bit cop."

The guards pushed Buck into the chair across from Beth. His gaze found her. "Now this I did not expect." He sneered at Donovan and returned his look to Beth. "Looks like the two of you managed to tie the knot. Congratulations."

Donovan ground his teeth and spoke with a clenched jaw. His plan to be calm wasn't working out so well. "You don't talk to her."

"Ah, but since she's here, I think I will. And the fact that the last time you were here because of her makes me wonder..." He looked at each of them. "What mess have you gotten into now?"

"The mess you created for us, right?" Beth's voice had an edge to it that said she wouldn't take any bullshit. "Despite being surprised by my presence, you know exactly why we're here."

She sat forward. "You and Viper picked up your partnership while incarcerated, didn't you? Reminisced about your take downs and the common link in both— us. Or more specifically...me. What did you tell Viper, and what did he tell you?"

Buck smirked. "We discussed many things. It's hard to keep track."

It was the same crap Buck spun when Donovan and Thorn questioned him before. Buck could sure talk, and it annoyed the hell out of Donovan. Last time, Thorn had threatened Buck by telling him that a knife would get slipped to an inmate with a vendetta against Buck, but he doubted that would work a second time. He was hoping Thorn had more leverage against Buck when

Beth rose halfway out of her chair. With her hands on the table, she bore down on Buck.

"That bullshit may work on these two, but not with me."

Donovan reached over and put a hand on her thigh. She lowered back into her chair; her back was as stiff as concrete.

"Out of the three of us, the one you don't want to piss off is Beth," Thorn said. He leaned forward. "Remember those privileges I gave you? The ones you've been enjoying? Those have been officially revoked. From now on, you're going to be met with restrictions." He sat back, and Donovan had a feeling he was going to dish out a piece of information that would get Buck to cooperate. "Not telling us what we need to know will only make matters worse for you. We have evidence of your partnership with Viper inside and outside of these walls. We know you gave him information that helped him to escape and carry out his plans. Whatever he does on the outside will be on your head—big or small. What he does will be added to your rap sheet with you as an accomplice, which will lengthen your sentence. And if you're ever up for parole, you can bet the three of us will be there to testify to keep your ass behind bars. Every time, we'll be there. Every damn time. You won't be getting out."

Buck looked up at the ceiling. Silence filled the room.

Donovan stole a glance at Thorn, who shrugged. Beth didn't acknowledge either of them. She was glaring at Buck, unflinchingly.

Finally, Buck sighed. "Viper told me about a brunette who worked with the cops to bring him down.

It didn't take much to connect his brunette with the one who helped to nail me." He winked at Beth.

Anger flashed searing hot through Donovan's veins.

"With Donovan's full name, Viper had all he needed, but it was so kind of you to tell me Beth's name the last time you came to visit me." He sneered at Donovan and tapped his temple. "Not very smart."

"What did Viper say he'd do?" Thorn asked.

Buck's grin doubled. "Get even." He met Beth's watchful stare. "With you."

Donovan's trimmed fingernails cut into his palms as his fists tightened.

"Then he can come for me," Beth growled, surprising Donovan. "The three of us took down Jackson's men, neutralizing the most powerful criminals in the States. You and Viper are lowly in comparison. We'll take down Viper, eliminating any little power you *think* you have. You'll be nothing, and you'll have nothing but time to think about how you failed. Again and again." She rose, pushing back her chair.

Donovan recognized her exit and got to his feet. She knocked on the door. The guard outside opened the door, but Beth paused at the exit. "I hope you enjoy your incarceration."

Marveling at his wife's strength, Donovan followed her out of the room.

Thorn walked beside him. "We should've brought her last time," Thorn mumbled.

No kidding.

In his truck, Donovan peeked at Beth in the passenger's seat. Her display had reminded him of

161

when she had tackled Buck before he could bash in Donovan's skull with a sharp rock. Beth had always been tough, even when suffering through the aftermath of the tsunami and her kidnapping. No, especially then. But he hadn't seen her at this caliber since before their wedding. Part of him was proud. And yet, he was concerned, too. He didn't want to her to become reckless. That was his job, and hers was to keep him level-headed.

"What was that back there?" he asked.

Beth shrugged. "I was sending a message." She paused. "If we can't stop these criminals from coming after us, then we should welcome them. Maybe this time, they'll fall into our trap."

"And what would our trap be?"

"Us."

At a red light, Donovan met her intense expression. He didn't have a good feeling about that look on her face. Or her tone. Or her statement. *Us.*

"Once Viper comes, Thorn can do his thing," she said.

"So, you want us to be bait again?"

They were bait before, and he had been rewarded with a bullet. Sure, he had been wearing a Kevlar vest, but it still hurt like hell. He didn't want to relive that. And he didn't want this time to turn out worse.

"Well, we're so good at it." she said.

"That's not a good thing."

"But if it works…"

Donovan sighed. He was as fed up as she was at being targeted by criminals. More than anything, he wanted this to end, but they needed to be smart. "If Viper comes to our property now, we'll know it."

"And when he does, what do we do then?" she asked.

There were only two things they could do in that situation, what anyone would do during a home invasion, and it was what she trained people to do.

"We call Thorn," he said. "And then we defend ourselves."

****

Beth was thankful when her stomach behaved itself during the next few days. Whatever had plagued her was gone, which was good. She needed all her strength to beat Viper and whoever he had behind him. She had Donovan, Thorn, and the entire Orlando Police Department on her side. She liked her odds.

When she told Donovan she wanted a gun, he backed her up. Years before, she had gotten her gun license but had never purchased one, so they went to a gun shop recommended by Thorn. They handled a few guns and bought one each. Afterward, they headed to the gun cages to test out their new pieces.

Donovan stood in the booth next to her, wearing protective eyeglasses and earmuffs. "Do you want to make this interesting?"

She arched a brow beneath her own protective eyewear. "How so?"

"The person with the best shots picks dinner, and the loser buys?"

"I like that bet. You're on." She picked up her gun, placed her left hand under her right, took her stance, and aimed at her target. She took a deep breath, let it out, and squeezed the trigger. The pop and slight kick-back surprised her. It had been a long time since she had shot a gun, but she realized it was like riding a bike.

It didn't take much to get back into the groove of comfortably popping bullets. She released another. As she set free the other bullets in the magazine, she counted them. Each one she imagined sinking into Viper's chest. When she had one bullet left, she elevated the gun, adjusted her aim, and let it fly.

Feeling good about her shots, she turned the level to bring her target forth. She pulled it down and examined it. All the shots were clustered in the center, but the last one had hit the target smack dab in the middle of its forehead. She stepped back to show it to Donovan. He held up his at the same time.

She pursed her lips. "I think I won."

"No way," Donovan objected.

"Yes, way. Most of yours are in the center like mine, but what's this?" She pointed to a hole a couple of inches off the mark. "A lung shot?"

"That was my first shot. I had to make adjustments."

She rolled her eyes. "I still won."

Not wanting to accept defeat, Donovan said, "Let's ask a pro."

Beth waved her hand, inviting him to lead the way. Donovan took her target and asked the man at the counter which one had the best kill shots. The man studied the targets and pointed. "This one."

Beth grinned. "I want sushi."

****

On Saturday, Beth and Donovan loaded the back of Donovan's truck with all the donations that had accumulated at The Fighting Chance for Lori's family. Four large garbage bags were filled to the top with clothing, bedding, and children's toys. Six boxes were packed with non-perishable food items, drinks, and books. A manila envelope in Beth's purse contained the money donations that had been collected inside a giant cheese puff snack container. Along with the bills and checks was a card. All her students signed it, wishing Lori and her family well and telling her how much she was missed in class.

With a tarp secured over the goods, they drove to Lori's sister's house in Merritt Island. Beth was brimming with excitement. She couldn't wait to present the truck-load of gifts to her long-time student and friend.

The feminine voice from Beth's phone told them to make a right. They soon found themselves in front of a single-story three-bedroom house. No toys littered the front yard, as they usually did at Lori's house where a basketball could always be found in the ditch and bicycles lay in the grass next to the driveway. A pang struck Beth in the middle of her heart. She climbed out of the truck and walked to the door as Donovan removed the tarp off the truck's bed. She rang the doorbell and waited. After a moment, Lori opened the door with her two kids surrounding her.

"Beth!" The kid's jumped up and down when they saw her.

"Beth." Lori looked surprised. "What are you doing here?"

"Special delivery," she said with a smile. "Come on. I have something to show you."

Lori stepped outside. Sophie and Glenn followed their mom.

"This is for you and your family, from everyone at The Fighting Chance," Beth said with a sweep of her hand at the truck's bed.

Lori stared at the bags and boxes with her mouth open.

"There's food, clothing, other necessities, and..." She looked at Sophie and Glenn. "Toys."

The T word had Sophie squealing in delight and Glenn jumping up and down chanting, "Yes."

Donovan lowered the tailgate and helped Sophie and Glenn up so they could raid the bags. He pointed to one of the bags with a wink. They dove at it and ripped it open. Sophie dug through the contents and pulled out a Barbie doll and then another and another. She piled them in her arms. "Look, Mom." She had a family of ten Barbies cradled in her arms, all different colors with varying hair styles.

Beth looked at her friend. Tears were streaming down Lori's cheeks. She reached out and rubbed Lori's arm. "Are you okay?"

Lori nodded. "Seeing them smile like that..." Her voice caught. "You did this for us?"

"Everyone pitched in." Beth shifted her purse and pulled out the manila envelope. "There's also this."

With shaking hands, Lori opened it. Her breath caught when she saw the contents. "Oh my." She hugged the envelope to her chest.

"I didn't count it, but I'm sure there's more than enough for a security deposit on a house and the first month's rent. When you move into a new place, Donovan and I have a few furniture pieces in storage you can have, such as his bachelor couch, a dinner table, and a coffee table. We'll haul them over on moving day."

Lori gawked at her. "I don't know what to say."

Donovan hopped down from the truck where he was helping the kids rummage for the best toys. Glenn now had gigantic Hulk mitts on his hands and was banging them together with glee. Donovan put a hand on Lori's shoulder. "You don't have to say anything. We're glad to help."

"Thank you." Lori threw her arms around them. "Thank you both!"

****

Sophie and Glenn played with a few of their new toys in the living room as the adults moved the boxes and bags into the garage. Lori stood in awe while staring at the loot taking up an entire corner of the garage.

"You're going to have a lot of fun going through all of this with your family," Beth said.

"I just can't believe it," Lori whispered.

"Believe it," Donovan said gently. "It's all yours."

"Enjoy it," Beth added.

They left to the sound of kids playing excitedly and Lori crying on the phone, telling her husband what had happened.

In the truck, Donovan couldn't help but smile as they drove away. After his accident, the knife found on the porch, and discovering Viper was the cause for all of it, it was nice to experience some joy, and to be the one bringing that happiness to someone else was a great feeling. He'll remember the sparkle in Sophie's and Glenn's eyes when they pulled out the toys, and the shock on Lori's face when she saw the money, for years to come.

"That was amazing," Donovan said.

Beth squeezed his arm. "I know. It makes me wish

we could do the same thing for all of the other families who lost their homes."

"Well, maybe we could. I heard on the news a fund was started. People from across the nation have been donating to it. We could use our professional avenues to raise awareness to bring in more donations to the fund."

"That's a great idea. Corissa and Amanda could help me make phone calls to my work acquaintances and past students."

"And I'll talk to my truck pals and everyone I know in the industry."

Beth tapped her legs in an excited beat. "We should be able to raise a sizeable donation." She fell silent a moment. "I always wished we could've done more for Oahu after the tsunami."

"Me, too."

Donovan followed the road back home. When they rounded a curve, changing their direction, a deep brown plume of smoke appeared in the distance, exactly where they were headed. He swallowed hard. The sight sent shivers racing down his spine. An icy hand gripped his throat. That smoke looked far more menacing than any of the smoking towers that had dominated the sky for weeks. He pushed down this irrational fear and continued to drive.

Beside him, Beth had fallen silent.

They were miles from home, but the closer they got, the closer and darker the smoke plume became. It stretched across the sky, carried by the wind, like a leaping lion.

Donovan stared at it, and he knew their current nightmare was happening.

"Beth, it looks like it's right next to our house."

Chapter Fifteen

Beth's heart clenched at the sight of the smoke stacks, as if a fist had driven through her chest and was squeezing the meaty human drum, paralyzing it. She gripped the door handle. The faster Donovan drove and the closer they got to home, to those tiers of billowing, dark smoke, the more anxious she became. Donovan's words replayed in her head.

It looks like it's right next to our house.

Her heart woke from its coma and punched her ribcage like a boxer attacking a speed bag. Perspiration dampened her underarms and slicked her palms. *Please, God, no. I can't lose my home again.*

The smoke stack was soon right in front of them, right where their home was located. Donovan turned down their street, and the tower of smoke loomed above them. Fire consumed the empty lot next to their house. Flames ate their way up the bark spines of pine trees. Orange flickers slithered along the length of the branches, reaching toward the roof. The fire was descending upon their forever home as a raiding army would race toward a city with swords drawn.

Donovan floored it down the street and brought the truck to a jerking stop in the driveway. He jumped out of the truck without taking the key out of the ignition. Beth shoved the door open and stumbled out onto the driveway.

"Call the fire department, pack some clothes. I'm getting the hose." Donovan raced toward the fire and slipped around the side of the house.

Beth dug her keys out of her purse and ran to the door. Her hand shook as she unlocked it. The heat of the fire beat against her. The rancid smell of burning nature clogged her nostrils. After two failed attempts, she grasped the key with both hands and managed to get it into the hole. She threw the door open, not even bothering to shut it again, and let the smoke roll in after her as she dashed up the stairs. In her bedroom, she grabbed the portable landline headset and jabbed 9-1-1. While she waited for the operator to answer, she hurried to the closet. She yanked down two duffle bags from the top shelf. They fell to the ground. Out the window, she could see red, orange, and yellow flickering sparks drifting in the breeze.

"9-1-1, what's your emergency?"

"There's a fire right next to my house," Beth panted as she rattled off their address.

"We've received calls about it. Firetrucks were dispatched. They should be there soon."

"Hurry," Beth told her. "Tell them to hurry." The fire was nearly at their doorstep. If they took too long, there wouldn't be a house left to save. Their entire neighborhood would be gone.

"Try to stay calm, ma'am. Help is on the way."

Beth hung up and dropped the phone on the carpet. She ripped clothes of the hangers and tossed them into the duffle bags. Now was not the time to worry about wrinkles. If they lost everything, at least they'd have clothing, wrinkled or not. She shoved in the contents from their drawers—underwear and socks—until she could barely zip the bags shut.

Donovan stood at the edge of their property, spraying the flames burning the pine trees and creeping along the grass, when she ran back outside to her car. The trunk was blanketed with soft dove-gray ashes. When she opened it, they slid back and fell through the crack into the trunk. She hefted the duffle bags inside and dashed back into the house. In a large white garbage bag, she stuffed in their bed comforter and two pillows. Then she snatched a backpack from the closet. Before she left the closet, she grabbed one last thing that hung at the very back—her wedding dress. She wasn't an overly sentimental woman, but she didn't want her dress to become ashes. After depositing the garment bag with the bedding, she hurried to the filing cabinet that contained all their important papers and family photos. She tucked the folders into the backpack.

Outside, she found Donovan had brought out their ladder. She craned her neck to look for him and found him standing on the roof, near the edge, attacking the fire with their garden hose.

Adding the garment bag, bedding, and backpack to the trunk, she slammed it shut and went back into the house. In the kitchen, she unplugged their expensive coffee maker and the world's best blender, according to her anyway. Cradling the appliances, one in each arm, she rushed back to the front door. On her way out, she saw the one item she treasured the most inside the house. She quickly set the coffee maker and blender on the floor behind the driver's seat and ran back into the house one last time. From above the mantelpiece, she brought down the artwork of a Florida beach her mother had painted. The same painting had survived

Hurricane Sabrina. It would also survive this fire.

Once the painting was safely in the backseat, she shouted up to Donovan, "I got what I could think of. I want to help you."

"Good. Drain the pool."

With a nod, she sprinted to the backyard to their above-ground pool. They had bought it to cool down during the summer until they could start the process of putting in an in-ground, screened-in pool. The pool was close to where the fire was spreading, which meant the water would wet the grass and help slow the progress.

She pushed down on the inflated ring. Water flowed over her hands and splashed against her sneakers. At the rate the water was moving, the pool would take too long to drain. She pushed down harder. Suddenly, the plastic wall caved in and water gushed forth, like an ocean wave, and crashed into Beth. The force of it knocked her off her feet. Chlorine water washed over her head and shoved down her shoulders. A mouthful of the disgusting water flowed down her throat. The water sent her rolling over the grass as if she were a foam noodle. She fought against it and managed to stop the momentum at the edge of their property. Her feet were inches from flames. She scooted away even as water continued to push at her back. Water moved around her, past her, and doused the flames with a hiss.

She got to her feet, gasping and dripping from head to toe. Turning back to the pool, she saw there was only a foot of water remaining.

"Are you okay?"

She looked up. Donovan stood at the edge of the roof, still spraying the fire, but his head was turned to her. "I'm fine," she shouted.

Donovan nodded before turning back to his task. She resumed her job of draining the pool. After she released the rubber cap, holding the air inside the inflated ring, she stepped on it to let the last of the water free. She worked her way around the pool to soak all the ground she could. When less than an inch remained, she paused, with her heart pounding, to look at the fire. It was a wall forging toward them. Past the brush surrounding their house, flames had completely engulfed the trees. They stood like fiery giants.

The sound of nature burning, the cracks and creaks and pops, rose up all around her and joined the roar of the fire. As she watched, transfixed, burning branches broke off the trees and fell to the ground. Sparks shot up. More sparks swayed in the air, letting the wind take them wherever it pleased. Those hot embers fell all over their yard and the roof of their house.

Beth sprang into action. She unwound the hose at the back of the house—Donovan had the side hose for the front yard—turned on the water and ran as far as it would allow her. She wet the brush at the edge of their property until water dripped off their leaves. As she went, she swept the spray back and forth along the grass. Once every square foot was damp, she attached the hose to the sprinkler head to keep the grass wet.

Racing back to the front yard, she prayed she wouldn't see fire spreading along the lawn or feasting on the patch of woods across the street. When she reached the driveway, she was relieved to see the fire hadn't gone that far yet, but it had devoured the lot all the way to the edge of the road.

"Beth!"

She looked up. Donovan was hosing down the roof

to keep it from catching fire.

"Drive the cars to the end of the street. Just in case."

Just in case. Those words made her panic. Donovan meant to drive the cars to safety in case they had to get out of there fast and their efforts failed, in case the fire continued to spread and their house went up in flames. If they lost everything, they could run to their vehicles and flee from the burning neighborhood.

Just in case.

She climbed into Donovan's truck, put it into gear, and with a squeal of tires, flew out of the driveway. At the stop sign, she shoved the truck into park, yanked out the keys, and locked the doors. She had to run back to get her car. Her lungs were burning with smoke and a lack of oxygen. Her legs shook with each stride. Approaching her house, the fire looked massive. She feared they wouldn't be able to stop it; that no one and nothing could end its fiery terror.

While driving her car to the end of the street, with the flames flashing at her in the rearview mirror, she imagined the fire sweeping across the city, following them down the highway. Nowhere they'd go would be safe. It'd be right behind them, frying everything to a crisp wherever they went, until the world was an inferno.

She got out of her car to hear sirens shaking the air. The urgent horn of fire trucks wailed as they tried to get to them. She turned toward the end of the road and saw a crowd of onlookers staring at the fire knocking at her door, staring at her. Anger flared inside her. How could they gawk and not help? How dare they watch as she loses the home she wanted to build a family in? How dare they?

"What is the matter with you?" she yelled at them, with her throat tight and raw. She wanted to tell them to help or go home, but right at that moment, the fire trucks came.

****

The heat radiating off the trees reminded Donovan of the heat he felt in the San Francisco condo, alight by a gas leak. At the moment, he couldn't decide which one scared him more, because he was still in the midst of this blazing disaster.

His feet slipped on the slick shingles. He quickly caught his footing and continued to hose down the roof from corner to corner. He returned to the side where the fire scorched. Flames reached toward the roof. He shot a stream of water at those flames, but it had no effect on it, as if the water was nothing more than a strand of spit.

A burning branch broke off the pine tree a mere foot away. It crashed into the ground below, sending embers into the air. The grass caught fire near their house.

"Shit." Donovan directed the spray at the fiery branch. He held his breath as he doused it, waiting for the fire to go out, not sure if it would actually go out, but it did. Donovan felt a bit of relief. He watered the charred grass. A burst of flames made him jump as a pile of pine needles caught fire. Dozens of pinecones that had dropped in the past couple of months started to explode with pops and flying sparks. Florida's wildlife was a natural kindling for hungry fires—palmetto bushes, tall grass, Spanish moss, and pine needles.

Donovan showered the dry grass at the end of their property. No way in hell did he want to lose the house he built for Beth, where they dreamed of raising their kids and having sleepovers with their grandkids. Before he climbed down, he added another gallon or two of water to that side of the roof to eliminate the threat of it going up in flames. The gutters filled with water. With the roof dripping wet, he descended the ladder. He was spraying the front yard when the fire trucks arrived.

Dropping the hose, he said a silent thank you. He shut off the water as the firefighters evacuated their trucks. He got out of their way and headed to the end of the driveway, looking for Beth. Smoke was thick, like a heavy fog. Looking toward the end of the road where Beth had driven the cars, he couldn't see her or anything else, because the wind had moved all the smoke there, creating a curtain.

He cupped his hands around his mouth. "Beth?"

He turned in the opposite direction. Fire burned along the street, licking the asphalt with its orange tongues. The flames were as tall as him and seemed to be gyrating against an invisible barrier, trying to break through it. As he watched, the unthinkable happened. A ribbon of fire broke off and leapt into the middle of the street. The flame bounced along the asphalt to the other side where it ignited. He ran to the burning grass, but that flame had a mission. It spread quickly, aiming for the dry brush a foot away. When he reached it, he stomped on the flames with his sneakers. He wasn't fast enough, though. The brush burst into flames, and those flames were slithering up a tree trunk. He had nothing to put it out with, so he ran back to the firefighters.

"Hey, it jumped the street!" He pointed. In the short time it took him to get to the firefighters, the fire had doubled in size.

"We got it," a firefighter said, but none of them went to extinguish it, because they were all too busy battling the fire threatening his home.

Two fire trucks were parked between the burning lot and his house. From ladders, firefighters used the fat hoses to send strong currents into the ravenous inferno consuming all the vegetation. Black smoke rose above the trees. An overcast of dirty, brown fog hid the sun. The light from the fire reflected in the brown sky, giving it the illusion that it too was on fire. Ashes continued to fall. They dotted the ground like morbid snowflakes and collected on his shoulders.

He took a deep breath but coughed it back out again. The air was choked with the stench of burning wood and dirt. He switched to shallow breaths. Each inhale made him inwardly wince at the filth entering his body. Not even breathing with his mouth would help any. The same amount of smoke would still fill his lungs.

A wind stirred the smoke and blew it into his eyes, making them water. He squeezed his eyes shut against the harassment. All around him were the sounds of dying nature and firefighters attacking it with everything they had. A loud rumble prompted him to open his eyes. A red truck with six large tires and a metal guard wrapped around the front came down the street. Standing in the back, with a hose ready, was a firefighter in a beige and yellow suit.

Donovan knew exactly what that vehicle was—a brush truck. The job of a brush truck was to go where no other vehicle could. It zoomed up the front yard, shredding the lawn and leaving behind two thick tire tracks. He chased after it into the backyard where it plowed through charred brush into the blazing woods. The firefighter in the back turned on the hose. A puff of whitish-brown smoke expanded from the ground and rose to the sky. Donovan watched the truck until billows of smoke swallowed it. He couldn't see the yellow stripes on the firefighter's suit or the red paint on the brush truck.

He turned around to see the fire rapidly eating its way through the woods. Already, it had devoured half of the lot behind their home. He had a feeling this beast would never get its fill, not even after it burned their house down or when all of Central Florida was a pile of ash. This fiery monster would continue until someone stopped it.

He prayed the good men and women of the fire department, who had been trying to defeat the fire outbreaks across the state, would be victorious with this blaze and all the others. He also hoped the culprit responsible would be found and locked up forever. Countless people had lost their homes, pets, and loved ones to this arson. *No more,* he thought. *Not in this neighborhood. Not here.*

A horn made him jump. He spun around to see a firetruck squeezing past his house, barreling toward him. He ran out of the way and stood in front of the porch, out of their way and away from the flames. The firetruck parked sideways in front of the burning lot. The hose was turned on, and water shot out of it.

He paced back and forth as he watched the firefighters do everything they could to control the blaze, to stop it in its tracks, but it pushed forward.

A flame touched a tangle of vines. In seconds, they ignited. The fire snaked up the vines to the top of the pine tree where the green bristles caught. The whole left side of the tree was burning while the right side was untouched. Slowly, though, the flames crept around the trunk and found their way to the other half, and then the tree was a torch.

He lifted his T-shirt over his mouth and nose and took a deep breath. He smelled his deodorant, sweat, and smoke. He kept an eye on the fire.

A ball of fire leapt off a tree and plopped onto the yard. He flinched, ready to run to it, but the flames didn't spread. After a moment, the ball of fire fizzled out. He smiled; Beth had done a good job soaking the ground.

Another flaming sphere, and another, and another, flew off the burning trees and scattered in the grass. The ones near the edge died with a puff of smoke, but a few had landed in the middle of the yard, and those weren't going out. He rushed to them as the flames crawled away from the burning blobs. He reached the closest one and stomped it out. Then he hurried to the others. The last one had spread to about a foot in circumference by the time he got to it. He studied the heart of it where a skeleton of something lay burnt and withered.

After a moment, he realized what it had been—a pinecone. The pinecones were becoming bombs, and the fire was throwing them like grenades.

Cursing, Donovan rushed to the backyard hose Beth had used. He yanked it from the sprinkler head and started to defend the yard, now dotted with black orbs. He wasn't going to let this fire defeat him. If the fire wanted a war, it had one. He stood on guard, soaking the balls of fires as they fell. Briefly, he thought of what their water bill would be next month, but it didn't matter. Using water was necessary to protect his home. He'd risk a huge water bill if he could save his house for Beth and their future.

The fire was implementing all its troops, though, and all its weapons. No matter what the firefighters did, they couldn't beat it. Before Donovan knew it, the whole back lot was compromised and advanced on the woods behind their neighbor.

Donovan stepped back as the brush truck burst out of the smoky woods to the left and zoomed across the lawn to the neighbor's backyard. It flattened the bushes and disappeared into the brush. He knew it would try to cut the fire off, to make it surrender. The firetruck sent a continuous flow of water at the fire and kept it from climbing closer.

The fire was massive, as tall as the trees, and it stretched across their entire backyard like a wall. He didn't know how the firefighters could ever make it fall to its knees, but he knew that, if they kept it back, it would eventually run out of fuel and die.

He wanted that to happen sooner rather than later.

A gust of wind, fire's best alley, blew into Donovan. Smoke swooped around him. The flames bent and lunged, but before they could leap or rush forward like soldiers in battle, the wind settled and the fire calmed. Donovan thought the fire's tactic had failed, but then he heard a yell. He whirled around to see a firefighter being thrown to the ground by his friends. Flames were attacking his sleeve. The other firefighters used their gloved hands to beat it off. They kept the firefighter down as one of them spoke into a portable radio.

Donovan swallowed. A firefighter had been burned.

Chapter Sixteen

Beth was walking back home when she heard someone call out to her. "Beth, please, help!" She turned to see her long-time neighbor, Mrs. Caraway, carrying a blue cat carrier down the driveway. She wore a long, flowery nightgown and white slippers.

Beth jogged up the driveway to her. "Mrs. Caraway, are you okay?"

"I couldn't get my Misty. Felix is in the carrier, but I'm afraid if I open it to put Misty in, Felix will get out."

Beth put her hand on the carrier. "No, leave it closed. Put Felix in the backseat and sit in your car. I'll get Misty and put her in the car with you so you can leave." She hurried past marigolds and lilies, their fragrance overpowered by the smell of smoke. She opened the pale-yellow door and stepped into Mrs. Caraway's house.

A haze lingered in the air, tainting the usual lavender potpourri scent. Old stripped wallpaper covered most of the walls. The rest were painted peach. Beth recalled visiting Mrs. Caraway with her mom after Mr. Caraway passed away. Beth would pluck at the keys on the Baby Grand piano, nibble on licorice, and play with Mrs. Caraway's cats. Back then, it was Emma and Sugar, two long-haired orange tabbies. Not much had changed, except for the cats.

She made kissing noises with her lips, the universal call for all cats. "Misty, come here."

Walking through the house, she checked in corners and behind furniture. In the living room, she got down on all fours to peek under the couch. Misty stared at her with wide, green eyes from where she sat in a frightened huddle.

"Hi, Misty. It's okay, sweet girl." She reached out her hand to let Misty sniff her fingers, but the feline didn't budge, not even to take a whiff of her scent, which was probably overwhelmed by the smell of smoke anyway.

"Come on, Misty." Her voice was soft and high, the sort of tone she'd use to talk to a scared child. Lying flat on her stomach, she scooted farther under the couch. Her fingers brushed Misty's calico coat. Misty shifted away.

"Oh, come on, Misty." She pursed her lips at the skeptical cat. "I'll be right back." She got to her feet and went into the kitchen. Mrs. Caraway and Beth's mom would sit in there at the small, chestnut table, sipping jasmine tea and nibbling on cookies while they talked.

On the beige linoleum tile, in the corner of the kitchen, was a yellow plastic dish of cat kibble. She picked it up and gave it a shake. When she was little, Emma and Sugar used to come running after she shook their food dish. Misty, however, wasn't taking the bait. She carried the bowl into the living room and got down on her belly again.

"Look, Misty." She put the bowl under the couch. "I've got your food."

Misty didn't care, though.

Beth sighed. "I wouldn't want to come out either." Except, she couldn't leave Misty in there. If the house burned down with Misty inside, Mrs. Caraway would be heartbroken, and Beth would feel at fault. "Maybe your mom has something more tempting."

Back in the kitchen, she quickly hunted through the white cabinets and the food pantry for cat treats. She found a bag of hairball control treats in the cheese compartment in the refrigerator. Smiling, she snatched it and hurried back to the couch. She gave the bag a shake and saw Misty's ears perk up.

"Look what I've got, Misty." She peeled open the bag, shook out a handful, and laid one in front of Misty's nose. The feline couldn't resist the crunchy treat with a soft center. She gobbled it down. Feeling a bit triumphant, Beth set out more in a straight line all the way to the coffee table. She didn't have to wait long before Misty emerged and ate all the treats.

"There you go." She stroked Misty's back. Purrs touched her ears. "Okay, time to go." She picked up Misty and held her close. "This next part will scare you, but we just have to get to the car, okay?" She scratched Misty's neck before reaching for the door handle.

Trying to walk quickly, but not too fast to frighten the cat, was tricky. She made shooshing noises, as if she were comforting a baby, and fluffed the fur on Misty's chest with her fingers, hoping the contact would soothe her. At Mrs. Caraway's car, she slowly lowered her right hand to open the back door. Her plan was to gently toss the cat inside and shut the door before she could escape. She pulled on the door handle and had the door cracked open when Misty panicked. The cat fought her. Claws pierced through her T-shirt and sliced the skin on her stomach. Beth attempted to keep her hold on the lashing cat, but Misty let out a yowl and ran her nails up Beth's arm. She let out a startled cry and instinctively released Misty, who darted across the lawn and into the woods. In her fear, Misty ran right to the thing she should've been running from—the fire.

"Misty!" Mrs. Caraway climbed out of her car.

Ignoring the sting of the two scratches leaking blood down her arm, she grabbed Mrs. Caraway's hand. "Misty will be fine," she said, praying she was speaking the truth. "It's not safe for you here, though. You should take Felix somewhere until the fire is out."

"What about Misty?" she said, her eyes filling with tears.

"I'll keep an eye out for her. I can even leave out some food."

"There's a spare key under the lady bug by the front door. If she comes back, please let her in."

Beth hugged her. "I will. I promise." She stayed on the driveway, cradling her arm, while Mrs. Caraway drove away. Forcing down her sorrow, she extracted the spare key from under the ladybug garden stone and locked the door.

Wincing, she blotted the scratches on her arm with the underside of her T-shirt. Dark lines were left behind on the cotton fibers.

On her way home, a black racer snake hastily slithered across the road. She paused to watch it make its journey. A tear slipped down her cheek when she realized it was fleeing from the fire. All the wildlife that lived in the woods around them were losing their habitats and possibly their lives.

A siren cut through the ruckus of the firetrucks, burning brush, and Beth's thoughts. She sprang out of the way to let an ambulance pass and was surprised to see it come to a halt in front of her house. "Donovan." Worry had her sprinting home. She got there after the paramedics had wheeled a gurney onto the road and carried a backboard to the backyard.

At the end of the driveway, she lifted her head and eyed the rooftop, searching for Donovan, but he wasn't there. She stood anxiously near the ambulance, afraid Donovan had slipped and fallen off the roof, or had gotten burned.

While she waited for the paramedics to return, she stared at the scene unfolding around her. So much smoke rose from behind her house that she didn't have to look to know the fire had dominated the woods surrounding their property. Firefighters ran back and forth. Hoses were on full blast. Everywhere was a frantic rush to save their house and the other houses in the neighborhood. Would they be successful? Would they beat this outbreak of fires?

Another firetruck came and parked beside the truck tackling the flames next to their house. The new truck aimed its efforts at the fire on the other side of the street. Beth hadn't even known the fire had spread that far. Seeing it now instilled more fear in her. Fire was almost on all sides of their house, bearing down on it, closing in one burnt branch and blade of grass at a time.

The paramedics appeared out of the smoky cloud carrying the backboard with the assistance of two firefighters. Beth stopped breathing. If Donovan was strapped to the backboard, she would spring into the ambulance after him. She loved their home, but she loved Donovan more. She wouldn't let him get taken to the hospital alone. Even if he was unconscious, she would want to be with him, to hold his hand, to kiss him, and to pray. When she saw a firefighter on that backboard, she felt a mixture of relief and horror. The fire was winning.

The medics and firefighters set the backboard on the gurney. From where she stood, Beth caught a glimpse of charred rubber and red flesh. She covered her mouth. The gurney was loaded into the back of the ambulance; the doors slammed shut and off it went, sirens blaring. She watched it go, becoming distorted by the thick smoke the farther it went, until it turned the corner out of sight.

She stood in the same spot, rooted, unable to move. She didn't know what to do now. Fire was everywhere. Whatever the firefighters did, it didn't seem to make a difference.

The red and white lights atop the firetrucks danced in circles, bathing her and her house in colors. Smoke cocooned everything in its foggy grasp, even her lungs. She coughed as she looked for Donovan among the people rushing back and forth from her backyard to the front yard—firefighters and police officers. She wondered if he was back there, helping in whatever way he could. It was definitely something he'd do, even if they told him to back off. Donovan wasn't the type to sit back. If he loved someone, or something, he'd fight.

She took a step but froze when she heard a shout come out of a radio near her.

"The brush truck broke down. We need assistance!"

From a few paces away, the fire chief pointed and

roared orders into his radio.

Strong hands grabbed Beth's shoulders and nearly lifted her off the ground as they ushered her to the side. She stumbled into the ditch and spun around to see a truck burst out of the woods directly behind where she had been standing. A branch was caught in the guard in the front of the truck, and it was on fire.

The truck sped onto the street and paused next to the chief. While the driver shared a quick word with the chief, a firefighter yanked the burning branch out of the guard and tossed it to the ground. After a handful of seconds, the truck lurched forward and floored it across their once-groomed lawn to the backyard. From where she stood, she could see clear to the back and was able to keep an eye on the brush truck as it slipped into the woods.

Her heart clenched in her chest. She grasped her hands and bounced on the balls of her feet. *Don't let the fire take them. Please, let them get out safely. Let them all get out.*

Flames rolled over the clearing, closing off the pathway.

A stream of water fell onto the flames. White smoke erupted from the ground.

Beth chewed on her bottom lip. She chanted the word "hurry" in her head to the firefighter with the hose and the ones in the brush trucks. *Hurry.*

More fire spread through the clearing, blocking their way out.

She took a step forward, as her fear pushed her to move. Although she knew she could do nothing, she had to do something other than stand there uselessly. The booming voice of the fire chief filled her ear canals. He was demanding to know their status, but a reply wasn't coming. The concern he felt for his men wrapped around Beth and made her realize, more than ever, the danger of the situation. A firefighter had already been burned. More could parish within the flaming woods. They were putting their lives on the line to save people's houses, belongings, and ways of living. They were truly heroes, and the fire chief was scared for them. Beth was scared for them.

Hurry. Hurry. Hurry.

She was praying with all her might when a brush truck leapt out of the burning woods and swerved before coming to a complete stop. *Where is the other one?* She glanced toward the fire chief who hadn't stopped shouting into his radio. Static broke from the speaker when he waited for an answer. The emission broke, and a voice said, "We're here!" And the second brush truck erupted from the flames.

****

Donovan lifted the hose to his head to let the water flow over his head and wash away the sweat on his face. Then he brought it to his mouth for a quick drink. Sitting with his back against the concrete, he stared at the battle taking place between firefighters and the brush fire. The flames had taken possession of the entire woods behind their house, the woods Beth had said she used to explore when she was a kid.

He recalled the memories she had shared with him when they first moved in and the tour she had taken him on. She had led him through a winding path in the woods lined by palmetto bushes with inch-long teeth on their branches.

He could hear her voice as if she stood beside him.

"One time, when I got lost in here, I pushed through all of the palmetto bushes to get to our backyard. By the time I made it, my arm was cut up, and I was bawling. My mom had to bandage my arm with pieces of fresh aloe, gauze, and elastic wrap."

Deep in the woods, in a beam of sunlight, was an igloo-shaped structure made of pine needles—Beth's childhood fort. She had said she would go to her fort and play house for hours. "Now I don't have to pretend," she had said and kissed him.

Now the fort that held such sweet memories of her childhood was nothing but a pile of ash. Donovan let out a sigh. First, Beth had lost the home she grew up in because of Hurricane Sabrina. Now the woods she had played in were up in smoke. He didn't want to see anymore, but he did want to see Beth's face. Pulling himself to a stand, he dropped the hose and left behind a scorched lawn to see the same situation in the front as in the back.

He followed the tire marks in the grass to the mailbox that had been run over by a firetruck. The black, metal box had burst open, envelopes spewed from the opening. He collected the mail and stuck it in his back pocket.

The fire that had started in the lot next to theirs was burning down. Bare, blackened trees could be seen through the last flickering flames. It was the fire in the back and the one on the other side of the street that were blazing in full force. At the edge of the road, he turned at the sound of a deep rumble and saw a bulldozer. Curious, he stood back while it plowed through the woods, lifting out everything in its way and replacing it with nothing but dirt.

Dirt wasn't good fuel for fire. It couldn't ignite; so with all the brush gone, the fire should be stopped in its tracks. The firefighters should be able to conquer it.

Should. With this fire, there was no way to know for sure.

The bulldozer deposited the ripped-out brush in the middle of the next street over, hopefully out of the reach of the dancing flames. When it was done, it lumbered off, maybe to take down more sections of woods in danger of burning.

Donovan scanned the smoky surroundings. Beth should've been back by now. He hadn't caught a glimpse of her anywhere and was worried about how she was handling seeing her home threatened. Again. He moved along the road, dodging firefighters and their tools.

"Beth?" Squinting, he tried to peer through the smoky haze for a figure he recognized. "Beth?" He raised his voice as he called for her. "Beth!"

"I'm here."

Beth came from the other end of the firetruck and ran into his arms. He embraced her, folding her into his body. Though his face was in the crook of her neck, he couldn't smell the sweetness of her shampoo or the soap on her skin. All he could smell was burnt wood and hot dirt. But she felt good in his arms, like home. Even if their house became a pile of charred rubble, he'd still be able to find a home in Beth, wherever they went. By the way she clutched him, he knew she felt the same way about him.

She inched back and looked at him. Black smears were under her nose from breathing in so much smoke. He swiped at the streaks with his thumbs. Then he noticed the blood. He took her arm as he examined the long scratches. "What happened?"

"I was trying to get Mrs. Caraway's cat, Misty to the car when she freaked and ran toward the fire." Tears formed in her eyes.

"It's okay. You tried. Misty will be okay."

"I said the same thing to Mrs. Caraway, but we don't know that. Misty is a house cat. She's probably terrified and doesn't know where to go."

She looked over her shoulder at their house. "What do we do now?"

"I don't think there's anything we can do."

She shook her head. "I can't accept that."

Hell, he didn't want to accept it either. The two of them were fighters for the people and things they loved, especially each other, which meant sitting back wasn't their forte. They preferred action.

"How far do you think this fire has gone? Or where it started?" she asked.

He shrugged. "I have no idea, but we can check." He nudged his chin at the firefighters. "They don't need us. Let's go." Taking her hand, he started toward the end of the road where their vehicles were parked. So far, the fire hadn't reached that part of their street, on either side. He was grateful for that. The people who lived in those houses were good people; they had children and pets. Beth had known them for years.

After they had moved in to the rebuilt house as a newly-wed couple, they held a barbeque with the neighbors. Seeing Beth with the people she grew up with, and getting to know them himself, had been fun. They barbequed chicken and burgers, which they served with corn-on-the-cob, potato salad, fruit salad, iced-tea, lemonade, and beer. From a branch on a tree in the backyard, they had hung a piñata for the kids to attack to get to the candy and little toys inside it. The night had ended with sparklers and s'mores from a clay fire pit. Having smiling faces around them and listening to laughter had helped them after their Oahu ordeal.

Donovan wanted to have more barbeques like that, but if the fire stole their neighbors' houses, they would be homeless and would have to rent somewhere until they could rebuild. Some people, he knew, had to move out of state after natural disasters took their homes, because they had to live where their support system was located. Occasionally, they wanted to get away from the state where the disaster happened, not wanting to go through another one. He knew how they felt.

At the end of the road, he saw a crowd of people he had never lain eyes on watching the spectacle. He imagined it was like passing a car crash, you can't help but look. Since fires had been threatening so much of their state all month, seeing one of the beasts up close was a magnificent thing to behold—as long as it wasn't at your front door.

"Those people were there when I drove the cars down," Beth said. "Looks like there's more. Gosh, they make me so mad. They're just sitting back and watching people's lives change, and they don't give a damn."

Donovan could understand her anger. After Hurricane Sabrina, the state came together to heal from the storm. The same occurred in California after the quake. In Oahu, the survivors of the tsunami had banded together to help the island. But with fires, it was different. Neighbors came to the aid of neighbors, but if someone wasn't directly impacted by a fire, they didn't feel obligated to lend a hand. They wanted to see it but not be in the shoes of the people scrambling to save their homes.

"They're just doing what people do." He climbed into the driver's seat of his truck while Beth hurried to the passenger's side. He created a path in the crowd of onlookers and made a left turn to the street behind theirs.

"Keep a lookout for Misty," Beth said.

He scanned the road and the woods for a shuddering feline but couldn't spot one. The lots between the few houses on this street were untouched, except for the one directly behind their house. That lot had flames taller than him. Another firetruck was posted there, draining water from its tank. He maneuvered around it to the other side and slowly drove along the edge of the road, with his eyes on the fire. Beth was silent behind him, also staring.

Near the end of the street, black stumps became visible. Everything was smoking—piles of ashes, trees, and the ground itself. Although it looked dead, he knew there was still life beneath the smoking heaps and charred bark. The trees would grow new bark, branches, and leaves. Grass would poke through the ashes, and bushes would fill it again. Not immediately, but over a few years, it would flourish into the woods it had been yesterday.

The black bareness went on for another lot and then turned back to green. Donovan eased the truck to a stop and put it into park. He got out and stood a few feet from the stark difference between burnt and lush greenery. Beyond the green lot was a house that had just missed the terror.

Beth joined him. He pointed at the line that divided where the fire had been and hadn't been. The wind pushed against his side, ruffling his hair. "It started somewhere over here and the wind pushed it."

"It started so close to our home." She turned to him. "They've been saying these fires have been started by arsonists." She shook her head. "They've also been saying they appear to be random, but someone could've tossed a match right here to bring this fire to life, a couple of lots from our house."

He knew what she was saying. Her line of thinking was his own. What if this wasn't an accident? What if they were being targeted, and this fire was their enemy's weapon?

He took Beth's hand. "Well, if someone did this, they made a big mistake, because we have the whole city on our side."

Looking back toward the firetruck and raging fire, he had the sudden desire to get back to the action, not to fight it but to be near it. "Let's get back."

He drove around the corner, back to their street, and passed the areas left untouched. When they came to one of their neighbor's houses on the opposite side of the street, they saw their neighbor tackling flames that were spreading across his lawn. Flames were creeping toward the shrubs along the front of his house and the palm tree offering the front porch shade. Dale had a wet towel and was frantically slapping it at the flames, but there was too many for him to handle.

Donovan shoved the truck into park. "I'm going to help him. Check on the house." He jumped out of the truck without waiting for an answer from Beth. A second soaking-wet towel sat on the driveway waiting to be used. He didn't say a word but snatched up the towel and worked side-by-side with Dale to put out those flames.

Chapter Seventeen

Beth couldn't get a word out before Donovan
sprang out of his truck and rushed to their neighbor's
rescue. He had left the door open, letting the smoke fill
the cab, and the engine running. She unbuckled her
seatbelt—a habit although they only went around the
block—and stepped onto the road. With her hand on the
door, she watched Donovan pick up a wet towel and
dive into the job. Doing this sort of thing was so
Donovan. He liked to help people in need, even when
he was in great need. He put others before himself
without a thought. That heroism was one of the many
reasons she loved him. Knowing he would be okay, she
took his place behind the wheel and parked the truck
back by the stop sign.

While passing Mrs. Caraway's house at the end of
the road, Beth saw flames feasting on Mrs. Caraway's
pink, flowering tree. As a child, Beth would lie under
that tree and let the pink petals fall around her,
pretending they were fairies. Now those fairy petals
were falling to the grass, burnt. She raced across the
lawn. Crisp petals rained down on her. She turned on
the garden hose, compressed the handle, and pointed
the beaded streams at the burning tree. Flaming petals
came off the branches. She watched the wind carry
them. They landed in the grass, on the driveway, and
drifted over her head. She ducked as they got close. The

ones that landed in the grass fizzled out once the petals dissolved. A few ignited the grass. She continued to spray the tree, because if she didn't extinguish it fast, the flames would send off more fiery petals into the wind. Those petals could set fire to other properties, other segments of woods. If that happened, they'd all be surrounded by it. Trapped. And the firefighters wouldn't have enough hands to go around.

The flames in the grass weren't as big of a threat. Not yet.

She aimed the hose's spray higher on the tree's canopy. The water shot loose petals and doused the flames on the branches, but other branches were stilling blazing.

A flare-up in her peripheral vision caught her attention. She turned her head to see her shirt sleeve had caught fire. Gasping, she dropped the hose and patted her shoulder with her bare hand. The flames didn't burn her, but her heart was ticking so violently that she had to bend forward with her hands on her knees to catch her breath.

The hose lay at her feet. Drops of water dripped from the wet nozzle. She picked it up with shaking hands and was extra careful of the petals that swirled around her like hornets. When the flames were finally gone, leaving parts of the tree black, she attacked the burning grass. Then she sprayed down the rest of the tree and the ground around it where crisp petals had landed; they looked like cremated insects. Before turning off the hose, she walked along the edge of Mrs. Caraway's property, spraying the woods. She hoped it would be enough to keep the fire back, at least until the firefighters could get to it.

She hung up the hose and jogged back to her own house. Standing there was her neighbor Karen. Karen's house was the one right next door. They shared the same woods and saw each other when they came home or went to get the mail. When Hurricane Sabrina had ripped off Beth's screened-in porch, it had slammed into Karen's house.

Beth hurried to her. "Karen."

Karen spun around and grabbed Beth's arm. "Oh, Beth, I can't believe this is happening. It doesn't feel real."

Beth knew the feeling. Ever since Donovan had said it looked like the smokestacks were next to their house, she had felt as if she were in a dream.

Guilt ripped through her. She hadn't called Karen. Or pounded on any of her neighbor's doors to let them know about the fire. All her actions, since she had jumped out of Donovan's truck to gather a few possessions and call for help, hadn't felt like her own. The one thing she remembered doing for Karen was trying to reach as much of her backyard as she could with the reach of their hose. Everything had happened so fast.

"I tried to wet as much of your backyard as I could with my hose, but I should've called you. I'm so sorry."

Karen put her arms around Beth. "It's okay. I'm just glad our houses are still standing."

Beth nodded. She was grateful for that, too. So far, no one's house had been touched. "Do you need my help getting stuff out of your home?"

"I grabbed a few things already. I was running around in circles in there because I could barely think." She gave Beth an embarrassed smile. "I actually brought out a bag of potatoes. And a reporter from the newspaper came up to me and asked me my name." She covered her face with her hands. "He got a picture of me doing that."

Despite the chaos, Beth gave a small laugh. "I brought out our coffeemaker and blender."

Karen laughed, too. Then her smile faded. "If I could, I'd put a giant bag around my whole house and carry it out of here."

Beth nodded. "So would I."

They turned back to look at their endangered homes. Neither of them said anything for several moments. They just held each other.

"Excuse me?"

Beth turned to see a man with a note pad and pen. He had a camera around his neck. "Is that your home?"

"Yes, it is."

"Can I ask you a few questions?"

"Sure, but don't use my full name or put my address in your paper." She had heard about a young woman, a victim to these fires, whose address had been put in the newspaper along with her picture, and because of that, a prison inmate had written her a letter. Beth didn't want the same thing happening to her, especially since there were a few inmates who would very much like her address, if they didn't already have it.

The reporter asked her questions, and she told him everything that had happened up to that point. As she spoke, her gaze kept drifting toward her house and the fire. She didn't want to take her eyes off it for too long.

"You said you saw the smokestacks on your way home and your husband knew it was here. What was the first thing that went through your head when you realized he was right?"

Beth peered at her home. The fear she had felt at the moment was still with her. Her thought then continued to echo in the back of her mind now.

"No," she said. "No…"

The reporter thanked her for her time and backed away. She watched him snap pictures of her house and the firefighters running back and forth.

Karen put her hand on Beth's arm. "I'm going to my car to call my husband again. He's in Tampa and is trying to get back. I know he's worried."

Beth nodded. "Okay. I'll be here, or somewhere around here, when you get back."

"Thanks, Beth."

Beth glanced toward the opposite end of the street, wondering about her own husband. Donovan was taking a long time to get back. The smoke was still thick, obscuring her vision, but she could see a figure stuck in that smoke and moving toward her. She smiled, thinking it was Donovan, but the closer it got, the more she realized it wasn't him. The way the figure walked wasn't right. This man swayed back and forth. His pants were baggy and low on his hips. His arms were buff; his torso was lean. Nothing about this figure was her husband. Nothing.

A burst of wind blew past. It whipped Beth's hair and swept away the smoke, clearing the road. Her heart caught in her throat when the figure became visible. Dark skin. A shiny bald head and black beard. Black pants held up by a silver belt buckle and a gray wife beater tank top. She didn't have to see his tattoo to know it was Viper.

Her eyes lowered to the silver gun in his hand. It was just like the one she had seen him with before. The bullets in that gun—each and every one—had her name written on them.

He continued to walk toward her. Only the length of a firetruck separated them.

She was rooted in place—unable to move, to dodge, to go for cover.

His lips spread in a sneer that showed impossibly white teeth. One of those teeth was gold. She couldn't see it, but she could visualize the sneer he had given her when they were face to face. Even given the distance between them, she knew the one he wore now was the same. The first time she saw it, ice had laced her spine. His smile had spoken volumes then, menacing, like a hyena's grin. Now it called to her through the haze, telling her she was in deep shit. She was his mouse, and vipers like to swallow their mice whole.

The gun at his side elevated.

She slowly lifted her hands. Would he shoot her if her hands were in the air, if he saw she was unarmed? Of course, he would. That answer came to her, and yet, she still couldn't unstick her feet from the road. Viper would shoot her dead right where she stood. The gunshot would get lost in the commotion going on around them, and no one would realize she was shot until someone saw her lying in the road, bleeding.

"Ma'am?"

She whirled and came face to face with the fire chief, a burly man with nutmeg skin and a black mustache. His presence at that moment was the answer to her unspoken prayers. She felt sure Viper wouldn't shoot her with a witness beside her, especially not the fire chief.

"Are you the homeowner?" He pointed at her house.

"Yes, I am. Is something wrong?" Something was very wrong. A criminal was on the scene with a gun and a death sentence for her. She debated telling him this, but he had so much to handle already. What more could he do about Viper? Not much. She needed a cop.

"Everything is okay," he said, and she wished he were right. "We have the fire in the back contained."

A small dose of relief surged through her. At least her home was safe. With that flash of relief came more anxiety. Had Viper set the fire to smoke her out? Had he set it up as a cover to kill her out in the open? Was he setting the fires across Central Florida, or was he a copycat?

She swallowed, but her mouth was dry and her throat was full of smoke. "Thank you," she told the fire chief. "Thank you so much."

He stepped away, and she looked back toward where Viper had been. He wasn't there now. She turned in a full circle, scanning the faces and searching the smoke for him, but he was gone. Except, he wouldn't be gone for long.

She raced up her driveway and dove into her house. Heart pounding, she spun the deadbolt and bolted up the stairs. The house phone was on the floor where she left it after calling 9-1-1. Now, she needed help for an all new reason. She snatched it up and jabbed the buttons. She paced back and forth while she waited for the ringing to end.

"This is Thorn."

She froze. "Thorn, there's a fire at our house, and

Viper is here. He's *here!*"

"Fuck. Where's Donovan?"

"I don't know. He was helping a neighbor."

"Find him fast and get out of there. You can't stay. I'm on my way, and I'm bringing reinforcements." The line cut off before she could thank him.

In the next moment, she was pounding down the stairs. She threw open the door, slammed it shut at her back, and ran through the firefighters to the end of the driveway. Her gaze ticked back and forth. Viper wasn't hiding in the smoke, at least from what she could tell, so she took off into it toward Dale's house, the last place she had seen Donovan. She needed to find him before Viper did. Deep down, she was afraid he already had found Donovan and that was why her husband hadn't come back to her yet. Viper would've shot down Donovan, and even innocent Dale, to get to her. He wouldn't care about them as long as he got his end goal—her. She pushed the thought out of her head, not wanting to believe Donovan was dead.

****

The moment Donovan smacked out one section of flaming grass, another section had caught fire. After beating out several flames, the wet towel he had was dry, burnt, and holey. He tossed the ragged towel on the sidewalk and started to stomp on the flames. As he kicked dirt from Dale's garden onto the flames, more inched toward the shrubs.

The two men worked side by side, pointing at areas for the other to get to quickly. Dale with the hose and Donovan with his boots attacked the flames that continued to hop over from the woods. Every once in a while, they raced to the backyard to check on it, but the fire hadn't ventured that far yet. By the time they got the fire extinguished and doused the flames closest to the yard, the entire front lawn was crisp.

They collapsed onto the sidewalk, panting. Sweat slithered down Donovan's spine. It was a hot April day, with the temperature higher than usual for that time of year. That was one reason the fires were sparking up easily and thriving so well. Donovan took the sleeve of his shirt and swiped it across his face. A peek at his watch told him it was five o'clock. The sun would be setting in another two hours. When it did, firefighting would be even more difficult.

Donovan stayed with Dale, monitoring the fire with him until more help could arrive. The crackling sounds of fire devouring wood was so loud it was the only thing Donovan could hear. And with the fire so close, it felt even hotter. He couldn't stop sweat from pouring down his face. With the hose in hand, he marched up and down Dale's lawn, feeling the heat of the blaze against his skin. Whenever the fire edged closer, he'd blast it with water, but soon he wouldn't be able to keep it at bay, even with Dale's help. The fire was expanding and gradually dominating the lot next to Dale's house. The fire wanted to push on, to take more, eat more, destroy more; Dale's property would be the first thing it would target. The only thing they had working for them was the wind was blowing away from Dale's house, but that wouldn't stop the fire. Oh no, it would move with or without the wind's sway.

The sound of a car driving past drew Donovan back to the front yard, but by the time he got there, the car had passed. He looked to the right to see taillights disappearing in the smoke. The red lights blinked out.

Donovan turned away from the street to join Dale. They were exhausted by the time the firetruck came to take over their efforts. He left Dale in the capable hands of the firefights and headed back to his house, back to Beth. His steps were slow, and his feet dragged. This day was crawling. He wanted it to be over, so he could hold Beth on the couch and know their home, their lives, were safe. He walked through the smoke and past the steaming remnants of where the fire had been.

Drilling and beating and grinding filled his eardrums, collided against his temple, and planted the first seed of a headache. Sighing, he lifted his shirt and mopped his face with it. Wishing for clean air to breathe, a cool shower, a cold beer, and Beth, he trudged on, but a shout made him come to a stop in the middle of the road. He couldn't tell what the man had yelled, but anger vibrated off his deep tone. Wondering if it was the fire chief issuing commands, he picked up his pace again. If something was wrong, he wanted to know.

Halfway home, he saw red taillights flash on. Frowning, he headed for the car. With each step he took, the smoke thinned, and he could make out the backend of a black sports car.

"Get in the fucking car!"

The order made Donovan's heart plunge to his colon. He jogged forward, frightened for a reason he couldn't explain.

The form of a man took shape. He had his arm extended and was pointing something at someone else. This other person was a little shorter, shapely. Female. She had her hands lifted on either side of her head. Donovan's heart rate doubled. That feminine figure belonged to his wife.

"I don't have a problem killing you now, but I don't want to do it this close to so many pigs and firefighters. Get. In."

Beth took a hesitant step forward. Viper pointed the gun at her temple. She flinched away from it and shifted to the opened car door. Horrified, Donovan watched her slip into the backseat. Viper followed her, with his gun leading the way. The door slammed shut behind him, locking Beth inside that vehicle with a gun in her face and criminals surrounding her.

Donovan ran with everything he had in him. "Beth!"

The car peeled off with squealing tires. In seconds, it vanished in the swirling smoke, but Donovan didn't stop running. Couldn't. That was the love of his life being taken away from him. He had vowed never to let that happen again after Oahu, but it was happening again—right in front of him.

"Beth!"

Chapter Eighteen

Viper was in front of her.

"Hey, bitch," he said. "Remember me?"

She tried to calm her body as it screamed, *Fight! Run!*

"No," she said, her voice hoarse. "Who are you? What do you want?"

Viper laughed at her questions. "Nice try, Felicia," he said, using the name she had given him when she was undercover. "Or should I call you Beth?" He jabbed the gun at her, not giving her a chance to respond. "Get in the fucking car!"

She didn't move.

He took a step closer so she could see his gold canine tooth. "I don't have a problem killing you now, but I don't want to do it this close to so many pigs and firefighters. Get. In."

She inched to the car.

Viper followed her movements. The gun never once left her head. She ducked into the car and slid as far away from Viper as she could, pressing herself into the other door. Two other men were in the car, sitting in the front seats. The driver had dreadlocks, and the man in the passenger's seat had a small afro, but she didn't care as much about them as she did about Viper. He angled his body and pointed the gun at her temple.

"Drive."

The car sped off.

"Beth!" Hearing Donovan's voice shouting her name made her heart break. She looked over her shoulder and caught a glimpse of Donovan running toward them before the smoke swallowed him. Overcome with fear, she faced the front and saw the car zoom past the firetrucks, the cop cars, and her house. They were taking her away from everything she knew and loved, the place she needed to be. Her palms and underarms dampened. Her heart banged against her chest and all her pressure points, making her feel like she'd explode into a million pieces.

The car zipped around the corner, almost hitting some of the people who had congregated there. She had no idea where Viper was taking her. He could just be looking for a quiet neighborhood where he could pull her out of the car, force her onto her knees, and pop the bullet in her head, execution style. Or he could be taking her somewhere special he had picked out, a house or shack out in the boonies where he could keep her for a while, forcing her to take drugs and do other things she didn't want to think about.

After the terror she experienced in Oahu, she never wanted to be someone's prisoner again. She couldn't be trapped in another closet, bleeding and starving and hoping. She would rather kill herself than to go through the trauma again. Yet, the idea of taking herself out made her think of Donovan. How could she do that to him? Leave him forever when she knew he'd do anything and everything to get her back?

Donovan would risk himself if it meant she'd live. She couldn't let him do that.

She looked out the window as her body shook. No,

she wouldn't let Donovan risk himself for her. Nor would she let Viper torment her.

Streets blurred as the car raced out of the neighborhood, aiming for the main road. She thought about the lessons she'd taught her students. She had coached them on what to do if someone had a knife to their throat, grabbed their arm, and wrapped their arms around their middle. She had told them to run in a zigzag if someone was shooting at them and to look for a toggle switch, button, or wire to pull if they were ever put in a trunk. They could also kick out a taillight or push down the backseat to escape through the car. But not once did she ever tell them what to do if they were trapped inside a car with a gun pointed at them.

There was only one thing she could do.

Her eyes lowered to the buttons for the door and window. Her hands were gripping the handle, just inches from the lock; she doubted they had the sense to flip the child lock. She had one way out—the door her body was pressed into.

Viper probably thought she was too frightened of a loaded gun to attempt escaping. No, she didn't want to get shot, but she was a self-defense instructor, damn it. Escaping was what she encouraged her students to do. *"Do whatever you can to get free. If a man is sexually assaulting you, scratch him, bite him, pee on him. Do whatever you have to do to save your life."*

She also told them not to let fear hold them back. *"Don't let your fear paralyze you from trying. Even if he has a weapon, fight back. Look for your own weapon. Hit him and run."*

She had no weapon other than her own hands and feet, and she couldn't pee on him, but she sure as hell had a way out. Even if he shot her, it was a risk she'd have to take—for Donovan. Everything she was doing from here on out, it wasn't for her but for the man she loved. Running with a gunshot wound wasn't impossible. All she could do was hope the bullet wouldn't hit her in the back or strike a major organ or artery.

The car fishtailed around a corner, ignoring the stop sign, and pulled out in front of an oncoming car. A horn blared at them. She felt the car pick up speed, passing the legal speed limit.

Beth knew her neighborhood well. Just up the road was a red light, and the road was congested with after-work traffic. She could never pass that light before it turned red, and she doubted they would be able to accomplish the same, not even going over the speed limit.

She eyed the green light ahead. Her hands, slick with sweat, were flat against her stiff jeans. Her clothes had dried a while ago but were now rough against her skin. She dug her fingernails into the fabric, into her leg.

The light turned yellow then red. Cars ahead were stopping, but the car she was in didn't slow. Her throat tightened. Would Viper's man swerve into the other lane to pass the light?

Suddenly, the driver slammed on the brake, and she flew forward, hitting the back of the seat in front of her. She pushed off it and saw that Viper had also lost his balance. Before the car came to a full stop, she took the opportunity in front of her. In one movement, she flipped the lock and shoved open the door. Then she threw her body outside. Gravity seemed to hold her suspended in the air. But in the next heartbeat, her body punched the ground, taking the breath from her lungs and leaving her shocked. She came back to her senses as her body rolled over the grass. It was like a slap to the face to get her to breathe again. She gasped and sucked down as much oxygen as she could. When her body stopped bumping along the ground, she was lying on her back. She didn't wait for a gunshot or a shout or squealing tires. She shot to her feet and bolted into the woods.

Her sneakers sank into piles of pine needles and got tangled in vines, but she yanked them free and made her way through the low branches that slapped her head. The pine trees grew thick, so close to each other the brush around them were knotted up in each other, making it difficult for her to pass. She wrestled her way through the tangled mess to the other side. She stumbled down a ditch, crossed the road in three strides, and dove into the woods across the way.

The sound of a car made its way to her through the trees and bushes. She stopped behind a tree and tried to figure out which way the car was headed, but she couldn't pinpoint where it was. She peered around the tree she leaned against and checked over her shoulder, but she couldn't see through the thickness of leaves.

She stepped around the tree and pushed on to the other side. She still had to cross a main road and pass two blocks before she would reach her neighborhood.

A few feet from the edge of the woods, she caught sight of the black car. She fell backward and landed on a pinecone. Biting her bottom lip to keep from crying out, she pried a crushed pinecone out from under her. Setting it aside, she peeked through the thick shrub hiding her from their eyes. The car cruised past and made a left turn; they were slowly heading back to her neighborhood. Well, she'd just have to follow them, out of their line of sight.

She hurried out of the woods and made her way to the stop sign. Hands clutching the metal post of the stop sign, she edged closer, peering left and right for the black car. There was no sign of the car, so she sprinted across the main road to the street on the other side. She cut across someone's lawn to the other side of their house. Crawling on all fours, she snuck past windows to get to the back. Once there, she inched her head around the corner to see the road. She flinched back when the black car idled by, heading in the direction she needed to go. The moment it was gone, she started to dash across the dry grass to the woods.

She passed a birdbath and ducked under a bird house hanging low on a tree branch. At the halfway point, the sound of tires spinning on the asphalt pierced the air. Her feet became immobile. She was like a deer caught in headlights when the car reversed and screeched to a halt. The back window rolled down, and Viper leered at her. He pointed his gun through the opening. She uprooted her feet from the ground and took off as the gun popped.

The woods were only a few paces away, but it seemed much farther. As she leapt over a log, an ant pile in front of her exploded. She dodged the gray sand flying out in all directions and hurried into the woods. Instead of running straight through it, she made a right and followed the woods to the next house over. Running backyard to backyard, she managed to lose the black car, or at least she thought she did.

Breathless, she propped herself against a tool shed, her gaze ticked from left to right, on the lookout for Viper. After a few precious moments to catch her breath, she went on the run again. She stayed in the woods, hunkered behind a bush. Her ears strained for the sound of an engine until she was sure the coast was clear.

The smoke was getting thicker and stronger the closer she got to home. She had three more streets to cross. Three. Just three.

Glancing from side to side, she stepped out of the woods.

"There she is!"

She spun to see one of Viper's men pointing at her. He had a gun in his hand and was running toward her. She twisted around. The second man was coming at her from the other end of the street. He, too, had a gun.

She didn't debate what to do. Surrendering was not an option, because right there, three streets away from the action, was far enough for them to shoot her dead. She launched forward. Gunshots sounded. Her chest tightened. A spark lit at her feet from a bullet hitting the asphalt. She didn't falter. She forced her legs to pump faster, faster than her heartrate. In seconds, she was in the woods, shredding bushes with her body. The men's shouts and gunshots were behind her.

The only thought in her head was to escape. No prayers. No regrets. She just had the need to lose them and get to safety.

She paused behind a tree. Bark ripped off it on both sides, inches from her shoulders and hips. Flinching, she dropped to her knees and crawled as low to the ground as she could to the closest cover. When she reached a shield of palmetto bushes taller than her, she sprang to her feet and ran through the bushes with inch-long teeth. Getting cut up was a risk she'd have to take. Cuts were preferable to gunshot wounds.

The shouts and curses of the men trying to shove through the palmetto bushes echoed through the woods. She didn't peek over her shoulder to see how close they were. Having run track, she knew that if runners peered over their shoulders at their competition, their pace slowed. She couldn't afford to slow down. Not even a fraction.

Her legs pumped. Her lungs burned. She lifted her elbows above the tops of the bushes as she barrowed through them. The thorns tugged at her shirt and poked through her jeans. The sting of them slicing into her flesh made her wince, but she forced down the pain, though it brought tears to her eyes.

She stumbled out of the last bush onto asphalt and dashed across the street into another patch of woods. She couldn't hear breaking branches behind her and took that for a good sign.

Florida's vegetation was slowing down her pursuers. Viper, however, was nowhere in sight. *That* wasn't a good sign.

She made it to the street in front of her house. Fire was burning half of the woods on the other side but had stopped at the dirt path the bulldozer had cleared. In the middle of the road, she peered over her shoulder. She couldn't see the men yet, and she didn't want to bring this danger straight to Donovan. Her searching eyes landed on the mountain of dirt, grass, bushes, and tree roots in the middle of the road. She hoped Florida's vegetation would be on her side again as she climbed halfway up the pile. She sank onto her knees, heart pounding, and started to pull clumps of grass and palmetto branches over her body. Her gaze kept ticking toward the woods, afraid the men would emerge before she had a chance to completely conceal herself. Then she'd have nowhere to hide.

A moment after she draped the fronds of palmetto branch over her head, one of the men trampled through the vines onto the street. Seconds later, he was followed by his partner. They stomped to the middle of the road.

"Where'd da bitch go?"

They circled around, scanning the area for her. One of them faced the mountain where she hid. He raised his gun and popped off three bullets along the length of it. The final one came close to Beth. She could hear it rip through branches.

She held her body still, not wanting to give away her position. Her heart was thumping so violently she thought the nature covering her must be vibrating with every beat.

"Hey!"

The sound of Viper's voice made Beth hold her breath. He sauntered out of the woods. While his friends appeared disheveled and pissed after chasing her, Viper looked cool and calm.

"Da bitch got away," one of the men said.

"That's fine," Viper said. "She probably ran to her bitch ass husband. We'll get 'er. We need to go back to the car, but we'll come back."

From beneath the vegetation, Beth watched the three of them walk down the street and into the smoke. Wanting to run back to Donovan right then, she restrained the urge to make sure they were really gone.

Her arms stung from the scratches and itched from the feel of grass and branches rubbing against her skin. She tried not to think about bugs or ants, but the need to escape was unbearable. She clenched all her muscles to stop herself from itching and counted to thirty. When she finished her countdown and couldn't see or hear anyone in the vicinity, she burst out of the branches and leapt off the pile.

Dirt fell off her in clumps. Pieces of grass were in her hair, and her clothing was stained, but she didn't care. Now that she found her safety, she wanted Donovan.

Chapter Nineteen

Donovan ran to the end of the street. His heart pounded viciously against his chest, as if it wanted to break free and fly after the car that took Beth. He skid to a stop and looked left and right. With the thick smoke, he hadn't seen which way the car had gone, and he couldn't see taillights now. It was gone. His wife was gone.

How can this be happening? He put his hands to his head, grasped his hair, and tugged. Feeling lost, he rotated in a circle. He couldn't piece together a plan of action. *My wife was kidnapped right in front of me. RIGHT IN FRONT OF ME!* His mind screamed that over and over again. He had been powerless to stop it. Where would they take her? What would they do to her? His stomach rolled. *They'll hurt her. They'll kill her.* He spun around and rushed toward a cop. "Sir."

The officer barely glanced at him. "Not now. I have my hands full." He hustled away.

Donovan stared after him. "But my wife was just kidnapped," he shouted. The officer didn't turn back. The roar of the fire and the peal of approaching sirens had swallowed his shout. His hands tightened into numb-knuckled fists. He put his fists against his temple and yelled to the heavens. "Damn it!" Helplessness latched onto his ankles and wrists, cementing him in place. He didn't know what to do.

He peered left and right. What *could* he do? His frantic gaze settled on his truck. In a few strides, he was at the door. He slammed the door shut, ready to search the streets for the damn car that harbored his wife. A snapshot of the car speeding off with Beth replayed in his mind.

Before the smoke had swooped around it, enveloping it, he had seen the license plate. He repeated the figures as he wrenched the key in the ignition. The truck rumbled to life. His hand gripped the stick shift. He yanked it into drive and looked up. A car sped past him. In the rearview mirror, Donovan saw it come to a screeching halt in front of his house. The door opened, and Thorn leapt out.

Donovan quickly shoved his truck back into park, ripped out the keys, and jumped out. "Thorn!"

Thorn whipped around. "Donovan. Beth called me and said Viper was here." He peered around. "Where is she?"

"He took her. The son-of-a-bitch took her."

Thorn's hand fell to his firearm. "Where?"

"Just down the road. The car went this way, but I don't know which way it turned."

"Did you get a good look at it?"

"My wife is in that car. You bet I did." He gave Thorn the license plate number with the make and model of the car; Thorn put out an APV on Viper and that car, so every officer on patrol would keep an eye out for it. After that, he called for backup. Thorn would have every local drug dealer's house searched, and the two of them would search the streets themselves. Donovan trusted Thorn to do what was necessary to bring Beth home safely. Neither of them would let her come to harm. If she did, they'd make Viper pay.

Two police cars rolled up, and Thorn issued orders to both teams. They drove off with their lights flashing. "Come on, Goldwyn. We're going to hunt them down."

Donovan climbed into the passenger's seat of Thorn's unmarked car. He gripped the handle on the door. The thought of Beth in the hands of the snake who left a bloody knife on their porch sickened and enraged him. If he found her and found Viper with her, he couldn't be sure he'd be able to stop himself from committing murder, which was why it was a good thing Thorn was with him.

Thorn started the car and pulled out of the smoky road. Donovan gazed at the side mirror. All he could see behind them was swirling smoke and the red of firetrucks. Then someone burst out of the path the tractors had cleared, onto the road. The figure was slender and tall. Dark hair flew in the smoky breeze.

"Stop. Stop!"

Thorn punched the brake, and Donovan jumped out of the car. "Beth!"

The figure turned. A gust of wind parted the smoke, revealing Beth. *How?* The one-worded question rang in Donovan's head. *How?*

She ran to him and threw her arms around his neck. He lifted her off her feet. His mouth ran kisses all over her face. The fear and anger he had dissipated like mist. Relief was sweet. His love for her made his eyes wet. He had come so close to losing her; Viper wouldn't have made the mistakes his predecessors had made. He had a lot to learn from, a lot of time to craft his plan and make sure he carried it out to the end. But Donovan had Beth in his arms now. He framed her face with his hands. Thin sticks and dried leaves stuck out of her hair. Dirt darkened her forehead, cheeks, and arms.

He picked the nature from her hair. "What happened?"

"I got away," she panted.

Thorn joined them. "My God, Beth." He hugged her. "Tell us everything."

Beth told them about throwing herself out of the car, running through the woods to dodge them, and barely missing bullets. "It was Viper and two other men."

"Damn, Beth, you were lucky to get away alive," Thorn said.

Beth looked at him. "I realize that." Her voice was dry, bitter. She looked between them. "We need to find them."

Donovan usually took the stance that seeking out these men, and making themselves pawns, was a bad idea, but after all this, he was done. He'd take a stand with Beth and Thorn. "Three of them, three of us."

"You're thinking what I'm thinking?" Thorn asked.

"He's thinking what we're all thinking," Beth corrected.

"I don't think they would've gone far," Thorn said and looked at Beth. "I bet they're searching for you. Let's take a ride around your neighborhood and see if we can find them."

Beth turned toward their house. Donovan rubbed her arm. "The firefighters have it under control," he said.

She nodded. "I know. I love our home, but it means nothing if we're not alive to live in it."

He kissed her on the forehead, not minding the

taste of smoke and dirt. "Then let's find these bastards." He opened the front passenger door for her.

She put her hand on the door and started to duck inside but stopped. She faced him. "We're forgetting something."

He frowned. "What?"

"Our guns."

They hurried into their house and to their bedroom. Donovan squatted in front of the safe in their closet. He punched in the code and opened the heavy door. He took out Beth's gun and handed it to her. She checked that the magazine was full before slapping it into place. She clipped the holster to her belt, snatched a flannel shirt from a hanger, and knotted it around her waist to conceal it. Donovan checked the ammo in his own gun. He had a full magazine and one bullet in the chamber. He clipped it to his belt but didn't bother to hide it. As they rushed out, Donovan twisted the lock on the door handle and tugged the door shut behind him. Beth slid into the front seat, and he ducked into the back. In the middle, he positioned one foot on either side of the hump in the floor. Sitting forward, he looked through the windshield as Thorn started the car.

"The two of you armed?"

"Yes," Beth and Donovan answered together.

Thorn chuckled. "The two of you are armed *without* guns." He drove the car through the firetrucks and made a right turn. As they passed streets, they craned their necks to look for the black car. "They last saw you in this area, so they probably figure you're still around here hiding. They know you wouldn't run past your house but would try to go back to it."

Donovan shook his head. "Viper has balls doing

this with a slew of firefighters and cops so close."

Thorn nodded as they crawled past another street. "He knows they're busy and a lot is happening. The fire is a good distraction."

Beth turned in her seat to look at the two of them. "He set this fire."

Thorn glanced at her. "What?"

"You said it yourself. It's a good distraction. Maybe he's not the arsonist trying to burn Florida off the map, but he could be a copycat using this fire as a cover."

Thorn shook his head. "Copying isn't Viper's style."

"Maybe his boys were the ones going around lighting those other fires to make it look like random hits, not a planned attack," Donovan offered.

They were silent as they let that sink in. Thorn turned the car onto the main road. When he reached another street that lead to their neighborhood, he turned onto it.

"Shit," Beth whispered after a moment. "Are we to blame for the fires?" She looked at them. "Are we to blame for the houses that have been burned down? Lori's house?"

"No," Thorn said. "This is Viper. If it's true, he committed arson, not you."

They stared out the window, and none of them spoke. Donovan knew that if it was true and Viper was responsible for the fires, Beth would forever feel guilty for all the houses lost, all the acres burned.

They were rolling up to their street when a black car sped through the stop sign and swerved in front of them. Thorn jabbed the brake. "Son-of-a-bitch!" In the next instant, he flipped a switch and the red and white lights flashed on the dash. The car picked up speed. "What are the fucking odds of that?" The car's engine roared as Thorn took chase.

There was no mistaking it; the car in front of them was the car Donovan had chased after. The idiots had cut off a cop car searching for them. Little did they know Beth and Donovan were in that car.

"Buckle up," Thorn spat as he edged closer to the Camaro. "This isn't going to end gently."

As Beth clicked her seatbelt into place, Donovan pulled the lap belt across him, tightened it, and gripped the handles on the back of the seats.

Thorn urged the car forward. When the tires ate up the distance, he maneuvered the car to the other lane. "Hold on," he said through clenched teeth and made contact with the side of the Camaro. Performing a Precision Immobilization Technique, Thorn made a sharp right turn, forcing the Camaro to turn to the left. The Camaro lost control and spun into the grass, facing the opposite direction. As soon as the Camaro cleared Thorn's car, Thorn shot their car around in a wide U-turn. The Camaro continued to bump along in the grass. The right-side tires were in a ditch. Low-hanging tree branches smacked the Camaro. It hopped onto the road and swerved a moment before straightening out.

"Damn it. That's why there's usually a second car," Thorn said. "I had called for backup when you two went to get your guns, but they're ten minutes away. If I can stay on their tail, we'll be able to corner them." He picked up his radio and spoke into it, giving a location and direction to the units listening to the channel.

The Camaro floored it around a turn. Tires squealed.

Thorn stayed close behind it.

In the backseat, Donovan couldn't stop his right foot from digging into the floor, as if he was the one controlling the car's speed. His arm muscles flinched whenever Thorn turned the wheel. He wanted to catch the car. He wanted to get his hands on Viper.

The Camaro stayed ahead of them, driving wildly. Both cars raced down the middle of the road. Thorn didn't let up, though. He kept his foot on the gas pedal and road on the Camaro's ass. When the Camaro swerved onto another street, Thorn followed it.

They were now back in the area where the fire was burning. To their right were burned trees and a few patches of fire still feasting on nature. At the end of the road, the Camaro didn't turn but shot across the road and leapt into a flaming patch of woods.

"I'd let you guys out but—" The car accelerated. "—I can't stop now."

They were going in after the Camaro.

Beth braced her right hand on the dash and gripped the bar above her door. Donovan clenched his jaw and planted his feet. In seconds, the car zoomed across the road and dove into the woods. Flames flashed on either side of the car. Ahead of them, the Camaro's tires were throwing ash into the air. Thorn drove the car over burning earth. The chase became more dangerous as the two cars snaked in and out of trees.

Donovan looked at the woods with a fresh dose of fear. The treetops were bursting with fire. Fiery pieces dropped from the trees to the ground.

Thorn stayed close behind the Camaro. Flames

licked the side of the car as they tore through the woods. Then something slammed onto the hood. Beth let out a yelp as sparks showered over the windshield. A burning branch blocked Donovan's view.

"I can't see a fucking thing," Thorn shouted. "If I stop, we'll lose them."

"I can get it," Beth said.

Donovan lurched and caught her arm when she sat forward. "Don't even think about it."

"Donovan, I can reach it. Look." She pointed. "The end of the branch is sticking out, and it's not on fire. I just have to open my window and reach for it. It's right there." She tugged her hair into fast bun.

"You could get burned."

"I won't if Thorn stays away from the flames."

"Thanks for the pressure," Thorn muttered. "I can see through that side. There's no fire."

He glanced at Beth and gave her a nod. "Do it."

She removed her seat belt and pushed the button for the window. Heat and smoke swooped in through the opening. Donovan swallowed as she pressed her body into the door. She stuck out her head. With one hand on the door to keep herself steady, she reached for the branch. Donovan strained to see through the tiny section of the windshield that wasn't blocked with flames. He couldn't see any fire on that side. Yet. But he knew it was only a matter of time before they reached an area where the fire burned on the right, and then she'd be in trouble.

"Beth, hurry up," he shouted.

She inched farther out the window. Her fingers curled around the end of the branch. The car bumped up and down, causing Beth to lose her footing and her hold on the branch. She reached again. The branch had slid farther down the windshield, so she had to squeeze farther out of the window. Her hand wrapped around the branch, and she tugged on it, but it didn't budge.

"It's stuck on a wiper," she called into the car.

"Beth, watch out!" Thorn twisted the windshield wiper switch. The wipers squeaked loudly as they moved across the dry glass. Pieces of the branch broke off and flew through the air. Beth flinched away from the sparks. Then she grasped the branch and flung it off the hood. Donovan watched it soar past the car.

"Get back in now!"

Thorn's shout had Donovan rotating back to look out the windshield. Two trees stood on either side of the path they charged down. Flames consumed a tangled mass of veins. If Beth wasn't back inside the car in a few seconds, she'd get burned. Badly.

She tucked her arms close to her body and ducked back through the window. The second she was inside, the car rubbed against the fiery vines. Fire filled the opening. Beth fell to the side, shrinking away from the flames. Heat dominated the inside of the car. When they cleared the burning trees, Beth sat up and compressed the button until the window was back in place.

Donovan shoved his shoulder between the seats. He reached for Beth, turning her face to him with his hand. "Are you okay? Are you burned?"

"No. Not a lick. I'm okay."

Despite her words, he turned her head from side to side, checking her cheeks and neck. He pulled her arms to him, making sure she didn't have a single burn mark on her. His heart calmed a fraction. She was smudged with soot but not burned.

"Looks like Viper's having trouble."

Donovan looked to see the Camaro stuck. The wheels spun, kicking up dirt, but the car wasn't going anywhere. And Thorn didn't slow.

"I can't fit them all in my car, yet I can't leave the two of you here," he said as they got closer. "And I don't want the bastards to burn to death."

Donovan bit his lip on that last one. If they were the ones responsible for the fires, he thought it was what they deserved. The car's speed escalated, and Donovan knew just what Thorn meant to do. Heaven help them.

They slammed into the Camaro's bumper, launching it free. The Camaro sped off, and Thorn followed it. The path snaked one way for a minute and then curved back. What Donovan saw before them made his breath catch. A wall of fire. There was no escaping it. He looked left and right, searching for a gap in the flames, but there wasn't one.

The Camaro didn't slow. It plunged right in. The flames closed around it, swallowing it whole.

"Guys," Thorn said. "We're going in."

"Oh shit." Beth's voice was a whisper.

Donovan braced. For all they knew, there was a tree directly in front of them. They could collide into it and die. Or die from the flames. His heart pounded. When the car dove into the flames, he captured his breath in his lungs. The fire was blinding. It was all around them. Time seemed to stand still. Then they erupted from the red, orange, and yellow storm, and a road appeared. Thorn whipped the wheel. The car swerved in the path of an oncoming vehicle. Donovan grasped Beth's arm as Thorn jerked the wheel again to avoid the car. They careened into a ditch and took down a mailbox before coming to a jolting stop.

Thorn jumped out of the car with his gun in his hand. He aimed at the Camaro as it escaped. Two gunshots sounded. A back tire blew. The Camaro swayed from side to side but veered around the turn and disappeared. Thorn shouted into the radio, telling his backup where the Camaro was headed.

As Donovan got out and rushed to Beth's side, Thorn hurried to the other car that had stopped after the near-collision. Donovan caught Beth's hands and pulled her to her feet. Wrapping his arms around her, he tucked her close to his body.

"That was close, too close." He wasn't just talking about the fire or the accident, but that he had almost lost her. Cradling her face in his hands, he drew her into a kiss. She leaned into him, as if her knees had dissolved. Her body was pliant against his solid chest. One of his hands slid down her side and molded around her ribs. His thumb rubbed the fleshy curve of her breast. His other hand cupped the back of her head. He tilted his head, deepening the kiss. Desire clouded his mind. He wanted to carry Beth into the shower, wash away the soot on her body, and make love to her against the slick, tiled wall. He eased back before his urges could grow to proportions that would be impossible to hide. He held her to him a moment longer, though, not wanting to let her go. Finally, he released her.

He ran a finger down her cheek. "We need a vacation."

Beth laughed. "Our vacations tend to be deadly."

Despite the morbid truth of that, he smiled. "One

day, we'll have a normal vacation."

She nodded and pressed her lips to his. "One day."

After Thorn made sure the driver of the other vehicle was unharmed and helped the home owner to put his mailbox back in the ground, he drove Beth and Donovan home. Except, they wouldn't be staying there. They unpacked their vehicles, put a few items back into the house, and moved the duffel bags and backpack of important documents into the trunk of Thorn's car. Once they were sure the fire wasn't a threat to their home anymore, they left.

Thorn took them to a motel. While he paid for a room with cash, they sat in the car. With Viper on the loose, they couldn't stay at home. No matter how exceptional their alarm system was, it wasn't safe for them there.

Thorn came back with a room key. He drove the car to 4F. He checked to make sure the coast was clear before ushering them inside. The walls were white. The comforter on the bed was a hideous blue and pink. A small, box TV sat on the dresser. Behind a small wall was a tiny kitchen, a plastic table, and four metal chairs. It was a crappy motel room, but as Thorn would remind them, the police department was paying for it, and it was clean.

They dumped their belongings on the floor. The three of them stood in the cramped room, unsure of what to do next.

"There's going to be a police car keeping an eye on your room every second you're here." Thorn hauled one of the metal chairs over to the window. He placed it in the corner. "But, for tonight, you'll have me for company." He set his gun on the AC, shut the blinds, and sat down so he could see through the crack between the blinds and the window frame.

Having Thorn in the motel room all night wasn't what Donovan had in mind. Donovan wanted to make love to Beth as if they had never been together before, but he couldn't do that with Thorn there. However, given the threat Viper posed, Donovan wouldn't feel comfortable unless there was a high level of protection for Beth. If that meant Thorn would stay with them, then he'd just have to rein in his libido.

Beth dropped onto the edge of the bed. "A slumber party. How fun."

From the window, Thorn snorted. "Just pretend I'm not here." He paused. "Wait. Never mind. I take that back. Please, remember I'm here."

Donovan shot him a look. "Believe me, I wouldn't be able to forget. You've already ruined my plans for the night." He tweaked Beth's chin. Her cheeks turned pink.

She got up. "I'm going to take a shower. I smell like smoke." She rooted through her duffle bag, pulled out clean clothes, and hid her bra and panties under her T-shirt on the pile. "I wish I had been smart enough to grab the shampoo and conditioner. Now I'm going to have to use the hotel's tiny bottles of crap." She stepped toward the bathroom door. "I won't be long."

She closed herself into the bathroom. A moment later, the shower turned on. Donovan turned to Thorn who hadn't moved in his chair. "No visualizing what's happening in that bathroom," he said.

Although Thorn didn't look at him, he could see Thorn's cheeks lift with a grin. "Or what, Goldwyn?"

Ten minutes later, Beth came out of the bathroom.

She had on jeans, a black T-shirt, and socks. Beneath her shirt, Donovan could tell she had on a bra. At home, if it was the two of them, she'd forgo the restriction, and he'd be able to see the shape of her naked breasts and the points of her nipples. Thank God, she had the forethought to include her bra when she selected her clothes. No way would he let her walk around bra-less with Thorn in the room.

"I feel a lot better."

Donovan went to her. He secured his arms around her waist and smelled the soap on her skin. "You look it," he whispered in her ear. On impulse, he caught her earlobe between his teeth. Her hands gripped his hips. They needed a release, but they couldn't have it.

She pushed him away. "You should shower. It'll help." She brought her lips to his ear. "But maybe for you, it should be a cold one."

Grinning, he picked out clean clothes and went into the bathroom. Taking Beth's advice, he iced his lust with a cold shower. He came out after a fast rub down with the bar of soup and found Beth stretched out on the bed watching TV. She had stripped the bed of the questionable sheets and comforter and replaced them with their own. Donovan sat down next to her and put his arm around her. She nestled into his side. Together, they watched the news. There was no mention of her near-kidnapping or the car chase, because the three of them were good at keeping secrets. The only ones outside of the motel room who knew the details were the Orlando Police Department and Viper.

A knock on the door made Donovan flinch. His hand fell on the gun he had set next to him on the bed. He started to slip it out of its holder, but Beth put her hand on his. "It's okay. I called for pizza while you were taking your shower."

"Oh." He rose to answer the door.

"Wait," Thorn hissed. He held up a hand. "One of the officers is checking him."

Donovan froze. He hadn't thought about Viper intercepting the pizza delivery person, killing him, and putting someone else in his place to kill them. The thought twisted his gut.

"Okay. It's clear," Thorn said. "But I'll open it. If Viper is watching, I don't want him to see you. Get out of sight."

Donovan took Beth's hand and tugged her into the kitchenette. They listened to Thorn open the door, pay for the pizzas, shut the door again, and lock it. Donovan didn't budge until the chain clattered into place, and Thorn told them it was okay to come out. The three of them ate pizza—Thorn ate with his eyes trained out the window—until they were stuffed.

Sitting on the bed, Beth leaned against the wall and yawned. Her face was pale with exhaustion. Her eyes were ringed with dark circles. He laid a hand on her cheek. "You should get some rest."

She looked at him. "So should you."

He shook his head. "I want to keep an eye on things."

"That's what Thorn is here for," she said in a low voice.

He touched his forehead to hers so he could talk to her without Thorn listening in on their conversation. "I need to make sure you're safe."

"I am safe." She put her hands around his neck. "We both are. We've had a long day. Neither of us will be able to do much if Viper comes, unless we get some sleep."

"I'll sleep later." He traced a fingertip over the dark smudge under her eye. "I want to watch you sleep for a while."

She pressed her lips to his. "Okay." She crawled beneath the covers and glanced at Thorn before turning her back to him. "This is so awkward," she muttered.

Next to her, above the covers, Donovan leaned his back against the wall. Her hand rested on his thigh. While staring down at her, he watched her eyelids drift close. She let out a slow breath. He thought she was drifting off to sleep when she called out, "Night, Thorn."

Thorn chuckled. "Nighty-night."

Chapter Twenty

Beth stirred a few hours later. She rolled over, and her eyes drifted open. A low light lit the room. Donovan sat upright next to her. She looked up at him, expecting to see his chin down on his chest as he dozed, but his eyes were open, alert. She sat up and put her head on his shoulder. His hand reached over and caressed her cheek.

"You didn't sleep a wink, did you?" she asked.

He shook his head.

She sighed. "Donovan, you have to get some sleep."

"I'll sleep when I'm—"

"Don't," she cut him off. "Don't say that. Everything's going to be fine while you sleep. A cop car is outside, and Thorn is ever vigilant." She stole a glance at Thorn. He was in the same position. Silent. Watchful. He didn't even peek at them. "Just lie down with me." She patted the mattress. "Let yourself go."

He exhaled. "Okay, but only for a little bit."

She nodded, though she had no intention of waking him if he did fall asleep. She scooted back down, and he lay flat on his back. Her fingers combed through his hair, gently massaging. His brown hair was feather-soft against her fingers. She moved her fingertips in swirls along his scalp. Each time she swept her fingers through his hair, he fought to keep his eyes open.

"Close your eyes," she whispered to him and pressed her lips one at a time to his eyelids.

When she eased back, his eyelids didn't so much as flutter. Smiling, she continued to soothe him.

Her fingertips brushed back and forth along his forehead, from temple to temple. Her heart ached for him. He was so dedicated to protecting her that he exhausted himself. And he didn't care that he did.

As he slept, his features were lax. Seeing his face calm, without a drop of worry or anger, made her want to kiss him all over his face, but she didn't want to wake him. He looked so peaceful it tugged her heart strings into knots. Her love for him swelled in her chest.

Her fingers brushed his hair to the side. She didn't always get to comfort him like this and being able to do it now made her happy. The last time she had indulged in caring for him was when he had broken ribs in San Francisco. He had admitted to her then that he despised having to own up to his pain and weaknesses. After being with him for two and a half years, she knew when he was pushing the limits. Although, he hated being cared for as if he were a child, she enjoyed providing it. Seeing his vulnerabilities brought out her motherly instincts.

She stroked his forehead with her fingers. How she longed to touch him with her lips, but she restrained herself. Her own eyelids started to lower. The hand holding up her head lost its strength, and her head fell onto her arm. Her other arm became heavy. Her fingers traced lines down his cheek and neck before her palm settled on his chest. Sleep pulled her quickly into the sweet, serene darkness of unconsciousness.

****

Sometime later, a loud breath made her eyelids peel apart. Donovan's chest fell as he exhaled. She looked at his face. He was in a deep sleep. Her gaze shifted to the window. Thorn still sat there. His back leaned against the chair, and his eyes were pinned on the tiny gap between the blinds and the windowpane. He had been sitting there for hours. His butt had to be numb by now, his neck aching, his eyes tired. She carefully lifted her hand off Donovan's chest and slowly slipped away from his warm body. She rose off the bed and took cautious steps, not wanting to wake Donovan. At Thorn's side, she put a hand on his shoulder. "You should be allowed to catch a couple of winks."

He shook his head marginally. "This is my job."

She stepped behind him to see through the crack. Light posts lit the parking lot. She could see a few cars parked out front and knew one of them across the way was a cop car. Nothing moved. The wind wasn't blowing so much as a candy wrapper. No one was out there.

"It looks quiet," she said.

"It always looks that way…until something happens."

She nodded. He was right. When something was about to go down, it was always uncharacteristically quiet. "Would you like some coffee to keep you awake? I saw a few packets of coffee in the kitchen."

He reached up and lay his hand over hers. "That would be nice."

She tiptoed past the bed. In the kitchen, she filled the coffee maker and emptied the ground contents of a package into a filter. Hoping the gurgling of the machine wouldn't wake Donovan, she flipped the switch. While waiting for the coffee to brew, she leaned against the counter. Arms and ankles crossed, the noise of the machine lured her into a partial sleep, although her eyes were open. When the grumbles stopped, she roused from her state and poured coffee into a Styrofoam cup. She snapped a plastic lid on top and took it to Thorn. Passing the bed, she was relieved to see Donovan was still knocked out.

"Here." She handed Thorn the cup.

Thorn took it. "Thanks, Beth."

"No problem." It was the least she could do. Wanting to keep Thorn a little company, she went back into the kitchen for a chair, which she set next to Thorn's. She sat down. "Have you seen anything interesting?"

"Well, I saw a hooker leave a room a few doors down. She was counting some bills as she left. Then a drug deal went down by the stop sign."

Beth blinked. "And the cops posted out there just let both slide?"

"They have their orders." He took a gulp of coffee.

Beth bit her lip. "Of course." She caught a glint of silver as Thorn lowered the cup. It was the band he habitually wore on his right ring finger. "Since Donovan's asleep, I'm going to use this opportunity to get to know you more."

"Say that any louder, and Donovan will wake up to beat my ass." He smirked as he took another sip of the hot brew.

Beth nudged his arm. "I mean talk to you. There's something I've been wanting to ask you for a long time." She paused. "When I was in the hospital in

Oahu, I saw your ring." The moment she said those words, she noticed his thumb start to rotate the band. "For as long as I've known you, you've worn it, but I know you're not married. And, as far as I know, you never were. So, what does the ring symbolize?"

Thorn took the top off the cup and drained the rest of the coffee. He lowered it and looked out the window. After a tense moment of silence, he finally spoke. "It was my dad's. He died when I was fifteen. My mom gave it to me, but I thought it was weird to wear my father's wedding band, especially since she still wore hers, so I kept it in a drawer. When I joined the force, I put it on. He had been a detective, too, and was shot on the job. I wanted to feel close to him, as if he was there with me through training and on my side on the job, keeping me safe, keeping me smart. I've kept it on ever since."

Beth swallowed. She had no idea he had lost his father. What sort of friend was she? "That's a great way to honor him."

"My father was a good man. He was a fierce protector of the people he loved. He always told me that if I protected my loved ones like a guard dog, I'd never feel guilty." For the first time, he met her gaze. "That's what I try to do, because I don't want to feel guilty if something happened to you. Or to Donovan."

He looked away, and Beth smiled. "You're a great friend, Thorn. The best brother from another mother a girl could have."

Thorn laughed softly. "Thanks."

"I mean it. I probably wouldn't be here if it weren't for you." When Jackson Storm's men had taken her hostage, she had called Thorn, and he had travelled from Florida to Oahu to save her. He had managed to get a SWAT team to help him charge the building where she had been held, and they found her, half-dead, in a janitor's closet. Without him, Donovan would never have known she was alive after the tsunami. Without him, she would've perished while waiting for a miracle.

Thorn squeezed her knee, but he didn't say anything.

She decided to change the subject. "Does the ring prevent women from hitting on you while you're on the job?"

On the side of his mouth, Thorn's dimple winked at her. "Not always. Some of the drunk ones wouldn't be able to see it if I held it up to their faces. You'd be surprised how often I'm hit on while making an arrest."

Beth gave a breathy laugh. "I can imagine." She tilted her head as curiosity filled her. "Since I've known you, you've never had a girlfriend. A girl hasn't caught your eye?"

His fingers turned the cup around and around. "Well, you know I flirt with you to tease you and have fun, but I'm not the kind of guy to go after another man's woman. I've only ever looked at you as a friend, but there is someone who recently caught my eye."

Beth couldn't hide her smile. "Amanda?"

Thorn's thumb poked a hole through the Styrofoam cup. "Yeah." His voice was hoarse.

"So, why haven't you asked her out?"

Thorn's head whipped around. He gaped at her a moment before his head snapped back to the window. "I thought you'd neuter me if I did."

Beth covered her mouth with her hand. "No, I

wouldn't neuter you." She giggled. "But if you screw up, I might."

His fingers dug into the cup, shredding it. Pieces of Styrofoam fluttered to his feet. "I haven't asked her out, because she makes me nervous." He risked another glance at Beth. "She scares me."

Beth frowned. "Why?"

Thorn's Adam's apple bobbed. "Because she's special."

His statement couldn't be truer. "She is," Beth agreed and lay a hand on his arm. "But so are you."

He shook his head. "I can see the hurt in her eyes. Someone put it there." His thumbs broke the thick bottom of the cup in half. "I'm afraid if I try to get close to her, she'll run away."

Beth looked down at the Styrofoam snowflakes on the floor. His fear was a very real possibility. She knew all about Amanda's past and what brought her to seek self-defense lessons. It wasn't up to her to tell Thorn the details, but she could give him something so he could understand.

"Amanda's ex hospitalized her." Her words made Thorn's arms flex. She almost got up to retrieve another cup for him to tear apart. "He gave her scars. The physical ones, she covers. The mental scars are what you can see in her eyes." She paused before saying the next part. "Men scare her."

Thorn turned his head away from the window, but he only did it for ten seconds as he took a couple of calming breaths. His hands were fists.

"It took her a year before she could talk to Donovan and make eye contact with him, but she's getting better. She shook your hand."

He tilted his head to her. His gaze flicked to her. "What does that mean?"

"For the longest time, she didn't like people to touch her. That's how badly her ex hurt her. But she gave me a hug when I hired her as my assistant. That was the first time she had done that since I've known her." She leaned closer. "Your reaction wasn't the only one I noticed when I introduced the two of you. You were a stranger to her, but she shook your hand. For her to do that, that means she felt something, too." She lowered her voice. "The next time I saw her she asked about you. As a matter of fact, she blushed."

Thorn's chest rose and fell slowly.

"She wanted to know what your first name was, but I told her she'd have to ask you yourself to find out." Beth grinned when Thorn looked at her. "The two of you would make a good match." She peered over her shoulder at Donovan. "Like Donovan and me."

Thorn stared out the window for several heartbeats before saying, "Thanks for that."

She squeezed his arm. "You just have to be patient with her."

"I can do that." He nodded. "For her, I'll take it slow. I'll talk to her until she trusts me."

"For how long?"

"As long as it takes."

Beth nodded. "You're a good man, Thorn." She got up to get him a fresh cup of coffee. He accepted it with a nod. The two of them sat silently. She didn't have to guess what Thorn was thinking about. She thought about Amanda, too. Amanda was a diamond in the rough, and Beth hoped she would step out of her comfort zone enough to let Thorn in. He could be the one to heal her and protect her. Beth hadn't told him how Amanda was still afraid of her ex, because the bastard continued to haunt her—not just in her nightmares and memories but in real life. He wouldn't leave her alone, and Amanda lived in fear of the day he'd come for her again.

Beth stared out the window with Thorn. She wished he'd take a break, but she knew he'd refuse. This was his job, which he took seriously. He was trained to be on long stakeouts, but she couldn't help but feel concern for her friend. Fatigue and exhaustion weren't good things for a cop to have while on the job.

A dark shape passed beneath the streetlight across the parking lot. Beth sat forward. "Did you see that?" She pointed a finger. "Someone is by the streetlight."

Thorn lifted his radio. "Unknown person your nine o'clock."

Beth's heart tripped in her chest like a rock tumbling down a cliff. Her mouth went dry. The figure meandered across the parking lot with a haltering gait. When it came on the sidewalk, Thorn picked up his firearm and held it in his hands.

Beth didn't blink as the figure turned and ambled in their direction. The person was a couple of rooms away and still coming closer.

Thorn slowly rose from his chair. He pressed his back to the wall and angled his head to watch as the person approached. His hands were in front of him, cradling his firearm.

Beth followed his motion and got out of her chair. If that person burst through their door, she couldn't be sitting on a chair like a moron. She had to be on her feet, ready. She looked toward Donovan, who was sound asleep. Should she wake him?

The figure came to their door and stopped.

Beth held her breath.

A hand reached out and fiddled with the door handle.

Her gaze landed on the door handle on her side of the door. It shook. Beth's hands clenched. It was then she realized she didn't have her weapon. Her gun was on the nightstand, and Donovan's gun was on the bed next to him. She could get it in a couple of strides, but she didn't want to budge from where she stood.

The man stumbled back and stood facing the door for several seconds. The same hand that had rattled the door handle lifted to scratch the man's head. He lumbered around and continued walking. Beth eyed him as he swayed from side to side and passed the window where the two of them stood on guard.

Neither of them moved. Not even after the man's shadow shrank up the sidewalk.

"Looks like a drunk. We've got eyes on him," a soft voice said from Thorn's radio. A moment later, "All clear. The drunk found his room two doors down."

Thorn dropped into his chair. He set his firearm back in its place and clicked the radio. "Ten-four." He stood the radio next to his firearm. Then he lowered his head and raked his hands through his hair.

Beth lowered into her chair. Thorn's anxiety bounced off him in waves. "You need a shot of something strong and probably a good massage." His shoulders looked as tense as concrete, as if the morrow in his bones had been replaced with cement.

Thorn gave a dry laugh. "I probably do."

"When this is done, drinks are on me."

"And what about the massage?"

She smirked. "You're on your own with that one. You could always ask that hooker next time she comes around."

He sat back. "I'll pass."

Beth felt bad. Thorn was on edge, worried for them, and the one woman he would want to be alone with was too frightened to even speak to the male species. She sighed. "Can I get you anything?"

"No." His voice was gruff.

"Come on. There has to be something. More coffee? A slice of pizza?"

"I have to take a leak."

Beth paused. "Okay, so go."

"I can't."

"Sure, you can. I'll keep lookout for you."

"No."

"Thorn, if your bladder bursts, you won't be good to anyone. I can sit here and keep my eyes trained out this window for as long as it takes you to use the bathroom." She got up and nudged him with her knee. "Come on."

"Fine," he growled and got up. With his hands around her shoulders, he shifted her and gently pushed her into his chair. "Stay here."

While he was gone, she kept her gaze glued out the window. He wasn't even gone a minute before he returned. She swapped places and sat with him until she couldn't stop yawning. She brought him a slice of pizza and refilled his coffee before she crawled back into bed with Donovan. When she set her head on his shoulder, his arms came around her. She watched Thorn as he studied the night. Her eyelids lowered as she sent out a wish for him and Amanda. The two of them deserved happiness and love, and Beth had a feeling they'd find it in each other's arms.

****

The room was bright with sunlight when she woke. Donovan wasn't in bed next to her. She sat up and stretched her arms over her head. Poor Thorn was still in the chair. The torn Styrofoam still littered the floor at his feet, but the second cup she brought him was whole and no doubt empty.

"Morning," she said.

Thorn bobbed his head. She couldn't even begin to guess how tired he was. He had stayed awake all night to keep them safe. He rose stiffly from the chair. "Now that you're up, I'm officially off duty."

Guilt gripped her. She glanced at the clock on the nightstand. It was seven-thirty in the morning. "If you were waiting for me to wake up, you should've woken me up. You didn't have to let me sleep."

"I can't wake a sleeping woman."

She smiled. "You're cute."

Donovan stepped out of the kitchen. "Excuse me?"

She rolled her eyes. "Good morning, dear."

Donovan chuckled. "Good morning." He bent down to kiss her on the top of the head.

A knock at the door had their backs going straight.

Thorn lifted a hand. "Relax. I asked the next shift to bring the two of you breakfast." He opened the door. A man in plainclothes stood on the other side with a white paper bag in his hand. "I hope they like egg and sausage sandwiches."

Thorn accepted the bag and slapped the guy's shoulder. "Thanks, man. I appreciate it."

"The other car is rolling out in five, and then I'll be on duty."

"See you later." Thorn shut the door. "Here." He set the white bag on the bed. "Eat up."

Five minutes later, a voice came from Thorn's radio. "In position."

"Ten-four." Thorn let out a sigh as he clipped his radio on his belt and put his gun back in the holster. "I'm outta here, kids. I'll check in after work."

Beth frowned. "After work. You have to go in? Shit, Thorn. You were up all night."

"Criminals don't rest," he said matter-of-factly.

Beth got off the bed and hugged him. His arms came around her slowly, as if stiff. He looked down at her with shadowed eyes and gave her a weak smile. This was not the jubilant Thorn she knew. He looked between her and Donovan. "Stay safe." He gave them a half-hearted salute before slipping out the door.

Donovan locked the door. "It's about time."

"Hey, he—" Her words were cut off when Donovan scooped her up with one arm, crushing her to his body, and claimed her mouth with his. She was going to tell him how devoted Thorn was to their safety, but all words vanished from her mind. She saw stars. Donovan kissed her so thoroughly her toes tingled. Every part of her body hummed to life.

"I've been wanting to do this since you came back to me," he said against her lips. He lifted her off her feet and settled her on the bed. The weight of his body made her mouth water. His hands sought her flesh as if he had never touched her skin before, as if he didn't know her texture, her heat. He stripped off her clothes, tossing them left and right. She couldn't stop a laugh from bubbling up her throat.

His eagerness made her lust explode like grenades throughout her body. His hands fondled every part of her. She let out a moan of pleasure. His mouth stole tastes as she reared up at his touch. He was driving her so mad she bit her bottom lip. The pressure of her teeth intensified the more he explored her. She tasted blood; her teeth had cut into the tender flesh of her bottom lip. She sucked it away as her hands groped his naked body. When he sank into her, she let out her first cry. They worked together. Their movements were in sync, pushing each other to the brink. Beth announced her final release, and soon after Donovan followed.

Shuddering, Donovan collapsed next to her. Beth panted beside him. Her body quivered. He looped an arm around her slick body and held her as she shivered. It took them several minutes to recover.

Donovan pushed off the bed and went to give her a kiss but stopped. He brought his hand to her face and swiped her bottom lip with his thumb. "Did I do this?"

Beth looked to see a streak of blood on his thumb. She touched her bleeding lip. "No," she said, feeling her cheeks blaze. "I did. I was biting my lip." She touched the tiny gash with her tongue and tasted the metallic flavor of her blood. "Then again, you're partly to blame." She smiled. "I was biting my lip because of what you were doing."

His dark eyes sparkled. "Next time, I'll have to make sure you're not biting your lip. I can't let you hurt yourself." He touched his lips to hers. "I like to kiss these lips too much."

Chapter Twenty-One

After eating their now-cold breakfasts, Donovan pulled out his laptop from the backpack, opened it on the plastic table in the kitchenette, and connected it to the motel's Wi-Fi. Beth pulled a chair next to him. "What are you doing?"

"I figured it was time we got to know the person who's coming after us." He opened a search engine and typed in Viper's real name—Keon Roberts. The screen filled with links offering arrest reports and news articles. He clicked website after website, gathering the information. Beth leaned forward to read the facts with him. Viper had been arrested seven times since he was seventeen, and these were just the ones that were public record. The first time was for possession of marijuana. A year later, he was charged with theft. An article detailed the incident. Around Christmas, he had broken into a church and stolen all the donations. A surveillance camera had caught him. Days later, the police made the arrest. In his bedroom, they had found electronics and wrapped presents, linking him to a string of thefts that had occurred in a couple of nearby neighborhoods. He had stolen Christmas gifts that parents had worked hard to provide for their children.

"What an asshole," Donovan spat.

Beth nodded in agreement. "It seems every year we hear about someone breaking into houses and stealing the presents right out from under Christmas trees. Makes me sick."

Donovan scrolled down. Viper's next arrest was for statutory rape. He had been eighteen at the time, and the girl had been fifteen. Donovan dug deeper, uncovering details about the case. According to news sources, he attacked a girl at a high school football game. At the time, he had been a senior, and she had been a freshman. He had followed her into the girl's bathroom, grabbed her sexually, and made lewd advances. When she threatened to scream, he slammed her head into the paper towel dispenser. He shoved her into a stall, beat her until she compiled, and raped her against the stall door.

Donovan's blood became acid as he read the details. He clicked on an image that had circulated through the media. She had a gash above her brow, stitches holding her top lip together, a black eye, and bruises along the left side of her face from Viper's blows. Beside him, Beth covered her mouth. A before picture had been placed next to the image showing a beautiful, dark-skinned girl with shapely lips, arched brows, and high cheekbones. She had the face of a model.

A later article said the victim had dropped the charges against Viper, claiming she had consensual sex with him in the girl's bathroom during the game, but after he left, two men came in and beat her. She said her confusion was due to a concussion. No other suspects had ever been found.

Donovan clenched his jaw. "She changed her story because he threatened her."

Beth sighed. "Yup. No doubt it aggravated the

police and her attorney, but they can't do anything if a victim decides to change their story or drop the charges." She pointed at the battered image of the young girl. "He could've been locked up for quite a while for this."

Viper's next offense was for DUI at nineteen. He lost his license, paid a fine, and spent a short time in jail. As Viper got older, his crimes became bolder—battery, sexual assault, and arson. Donovan froze when he read that last one. Viper and four others were arrested for setting fire to an occupied house. The men living in the house were part of known gang. They escaped the house and identified Viper as one of the men seen fleeing the premise. Two of the four other men charged with Viper plead guilty and vouched for Viper's and the other two mens' innocence. The fact the three of them had been there, though, had made them accomplices. Viper spent two years in jail and a year on house arrest with an additional year after that on probation.

Beth pointed at the screen. "Two men got off with Viper." She held up her fingers. "Two. How much you wanna bet those are the same two Viper's been hanging around with since he escaped work release? They're bringing back past times." Her voice lowered. "Past crimes." She looked at him. "They're setting these fires. Or at least the one that started right behind our house. They lured me right where they wanted me."

Donovan put his hand on her thigh. "You're smarter than them. You got away." And he'd make sure they never got a chance to lure her into their trap again.

He scanned the rest of Viper's arrest records. His most recent charges were for drug distribution, drug manufacturing, possession of illegal weapons, and resisting an officer with violence. Those were the ones Beth had a hand in when she went undercover.

Donovan lowered the laptop's screen. "Viper has been racking up the charges and working his way up to bigger, worse crimes."

"Like murder?"

Beth's soft voice was like a knife to his heart. He cupped her face with his hands. "Hey, that's not going to happen." Her gaze avoided his. "Look at me, baby." She let out a slow breath before shifting her gaze to his. "They're not going to get close to you again. You're tough and smart. I'm not going to let you out of my sight, there's a cop car out front, and Thorn won't let anything happen to you either." He glanced at his closed laptop. "Although, after reading all of that, I have to question why Thorn asked you to go undercover in the first place. If he hadn't, this wouldn't be happening."

Beth shook her head between his hands. "That's not fair. I volunteered to go undercover to find out where Buck was hiding. None of this is Thorn's fault. Or mine." Her fingers curled around his wrists. "Or yours."

His hands fell from her face to his lap.

"I talked to Thorn last night while you were sleeping. He has a powerful need to protect the people he cares about, and we are on that list." She paused. "I think we're at the top. I'm sure he regrets putting me undercover in Viper's house now that Viper is out to get me. None of us can take that back, and I wouldn't want to. If I hadn't helped him, we wouldn't have gotten Buck."

"But if we hadn't gone to San Francisco, Jackson Storm wouldn't have come into our lives." Jackson Storm and his minions would forever be at the front of Donovan's mind for what they did to Beth.

She lay her hand on the side of his face. "But maybe we wouldn't have fallen in love."

He frowned at that.

"Think about it," she urged.

Without their trip to San Francisco, they wouldn't have bonded as much as they did, fought side by side to catch a killer, or fought through an earthquake ravaged city to find each other. Their love intensified during those post-disaster moments. If none of that had taken place, who knows where they'd be. Donovan refused to think that they wouldn't be together now, but if they hadn't gone through those events, would they love each other as intensely as they did now? Maybe not...

He pulled Beth's hand from his cheek and kissed it. "You're right." He wished he could take back the things that hurt the two of them, but if he did, he would be erasing their entire relationship. That sobering thought made him realize he needed to let the past go. Whether he was the one who brought those things on them or not, he had to forget it. They were together. They were alive. That was all that mattered.

****

Thorn stopped by after six o'clock with a box of chicken, mashed potatoes, macaroni and cheese, and biscuits. He also had a few files tucked under his arm. He dropped them onto the table. "Your requested files, Your Highness."

Donovan lifted a brow as he picked through the files.

Beth held out a drumstick to Thorn. "You get cranky when you're tired."

Thorn grumbled. He took the drumstick and tore off a chunk with his teeth. "Let's just say there's no leads to Viper's whereabouts."

"That's why we asked for these." Donovan opened two of the files and lay them flat. "Take a look, Beth."

The two files were for the men who got off the hook for the arson. Mugshots for both of the men were clipped to the front with fingerprints and pages of case details. Beth bent over to study the images. One of them had dreadlocks, and the other had a short afro. She gave a small nod. "That's them." Her gaze rose to Thorn as he put his hands on the table across from her. "These are the two men who were with Viper."

Thorn lowered into one of the chairs. "That's a lucky break." He pulled the files to him. "Anthony Morris and Omar Morris are cousins." He looked up. "They're best known for arson. And they're a bitch trying to nail down. We think they're homeless. Always on the move."

Fire roared through Donovan's veins.

"My guess is Viper let these two have fun, so when he came for the two of you, the fire would look like a random attack with the rest of them. No one would think twice."

"We did," Beth said.

Thorn nodded. He took another bite of the drumstick. "If Viper is with these two, it may be impossible to pin his location. These two are skilled when it comes to staying hidden, undetected. They quickly ditch cars and never use the same one twice."

"Except for the black Camaro," Beth added. "I saw

that car once before."

Donovan's head snapped up. He had been reading Viper's file. "What?"

She tore off a flaky piece of biscuit and popped it into her mouth. "The day I went to Lori's house, a black car was parked at the end of the street. When I noticed, it sped off. It rattled me, but I thought maybe it was someone just interested in seeing what happened there and felt embarrassed or ashamed they had been caught. The car I saw then was the same one they used to pick me up."

Donovan clenched his hands on the table. "You should've said something."

She lowered her fork with a few macaroni needles speared on it. "I didn't think anything of it the first time I saw it. And yesterday, there was a lot on my mind, so I forgot. Besides, it doesn't help us any. You gave them the license plate number, and it's still nowhere to be found."

That statement made Donovan's glare shift to Thorn. "How is it possible the entire Orlando Police Force is aware of this car, but it hasn't been spotted yet?"

"Anthony and Omar are experts at this. They've pushed cars into canals and ditched them at scrap yards. They don't just swap out license plates. If they did, we'd be able to pull over every black Camaro Z/28 on the street. And, believe me, we have been." Thorn swallowed another bite of chicken. "Investigators compared the wheel prints they found outside your garage with the wheels on the footage from my car's dash cam. It matches." Thorn shrugged. "I know we already figured out Viper was the one responsible for hijacking your truck, but this confirms it. We can place that car on your property. It adds another bar to his jail cell."

After a moment of silent eating, Beth said, "If they're so smart at ditching their cars, why did they use the Camaro multiple times?"

"Before his arrest, he drove a Dodge Viper." The corner of Thorn's mouth tilted up. "He's cocky when it comes to his reputation. But considering the cousins are smart about cars, my guess is Viper liked the Camaro. He's vain enough not to ditch a car he likes. We ran the plate, though, and it turns out it's a fake. A damn good one, too. No one would be able to look at it and realize it isn't real, which would be the cousins' doing." Thorn dusted off his hands. "The night we raided Viper's house and arrested him, a black Camaro Z/28 was parked in the driveway. We wrote them all down to track later, if need be. I just found that connection a few hours ago. The Camaro from that night belonged to one of his buddies, Jarome Cook. Since Viper went to one of his old buddies from the day he was arrested, there's a chance he went to more. We're currently tracking them all down and searching their homes. So far, nothing."

"At least it's a start," Beth said.

Donovan had to agree with that. It was better than nothing.

The three of them ate their chicken dinner. When Thorn finished, he got up. "Well, kids, I'm out."

"You're not staying?" Beth asked.

Donovan gently pinched her arm. "Don't encourage him."

Thorn sneered. "As much as I'd love to stop

Donovan from getting any sex, I have more work to do. A new cop just took the night shift a moment ago, and the two of you are armed and dangerous. I also think I'll be more help out there."

"Speaking of armed and dangerous," Donovan said. "Do you have duct tape?"

Thorn retrieved a roll of duct tape from the trunk of his car and gave it to him. Donovan held it in one hand and his holstered gun in the other. "We need to hide our guns someplace."

"Why?" Beth asked.

"While it's nice to have a gun right next to us, if someone comes in and tries to disarm us, it's prudent to have them hidden from sight where only we know they are."

Pursing her lips, Beth nodded and scanned the room. While she searched for a hiding place, Donovan went into the kitchen. He crouched by the table and pulled a strip of tape off the roll. Ducking his head, he affixed the gun in its holster to the underbelly of the table. It wasn't in the middle, as that would be hard to reach, but within reach of the chair that had its back to the wall dividing the kitchenette and the room.

"Under the table?"

Donovan turned to see Beth and Thorn watching him. "What's wrong with under the table?" he asked.

"Along with the toilet tank and freezer, it's one of the most common places to hide a weapon," Beth stated. "It's where everyone looks."

He crossed his arms. "Okay, Jane Bond. Where would you hide yours?"

"Give me the tape." She held out her hand for it.

He slapped it into her palm. In the bedroom, she

tugged the bed a few inches away from the wall and crawled on top of it.

"I'm liking her idea already," Thorn said.

Donovan glared at him and was given a toothy grin.

On her knees, she ripped off a strip of tape. Slipping her hands behind the wooden headboard, she affixed her gun to the back of the headboard. She got off the bed and nodded with satisfaction. "That way we're close to it when we're in bed, but it's not in the nightstand or attached to the frame underneath, which is where people check for weapons in bedrooms."

Donovan squinted his eyes at her. "You watch too many cop shows."

****

The next day, Thorn checked on them to—in his own words—make sure they were still alive. He looked as though he might've actually slept the night before, which Beth was glad about. But their request to see their house immediately put him back on edge.

"The two of you are supposed to be keeping your mugs from being seen by Viper and his henchmen."

Beth forced a smile. "I also want to check in on my studio."

Thorn grabbed the hair on the sides of his head. "I've said it before, and I'll say it again...the two of you are a pain in my ass." He dropped his hands. "Fine, but I need to disguise you guys and get another cop car to follow us. Before you even get close to your house or studio, we're going to make sure the area is clear."

Cursing under his breath, Thorn left. He was gone for thirty minutes and returned with a blonde wig for Beth and a baseball cap for Donovan. "This is the best I

258

could do."

Beth tucked her hair beneath the wig and stared at herself in the mirror. Bright lip stick, large sunglasses, and denim shorts completed her look. She hoped it was enough of a change to hide her identity. Donovan wore the cap and dark sunglasses. The stubble growing thickly along his jaw helped to hide the rest of his face.

Thorn checked the parking lot before telling them to go to his car. Keeping her head down, Beth walked to Thorn's car. She did her best not to run or look around. Once inside Thorn's car with Donovan and Thorn, her body relaxed.

They parked a few streets away from their house while the cop car escorting them went ahead to make sure it was safe to get closer. Beth examined her surroundings. Through charcoal trees, she could see the roof of their house. Relief settled over her heart; it was still standing. Even though the firefighters had the fire under control when they left, it could've flared up again and overpowered their efforts. The fact there wasn't a single brush truck in the area was a good sign. The fire department was confident the fire was out.

Out of the corner of her eye, she saw a bright flicker. She turned her head. A foot-tall flame waved at her from the woods. After growing up in Florida, she knew that hot spots were a danger with wildfires. One hot spot could start a new blaze.

"Guys, there's a hot spot over there." She pointed.

In the front passenger's seat, Donovan went to open his door.

"No," Thorn said. "The two of you are staying in this car." He unbuckled his seat belt. "I'll take care of it. When I get out, lock the doors."

Thorn stepped out, and Donovan hit the locking mechanism the second Thorn's door closed. Thorn tromped over the smoking ground to the flame. As he came closer, the flame stretched taller, as if challenging Thorn. But it was a wisp of a thing. Thorn kicked dirt and ash over it and stomped his boot over the smoldering spot until the embers were squashed. He came back to the car, and Donovan unlocked the doors for him.

Thorn's radio sounded. "The premise is clear, but the house still needs to be checked."

"Ten-four," Thorn said into the radio. "We're on the way." He put the car in drive and drove up to their house. "Stay here while we make sure the house is clear."

Beth fiddled with her fingers as Thorn and two other cops went through the front door with their weapons raised. Could Viper really be in there, waiting for them to get comfortable before blowing out their brains? A dozen images flashed through her mind—Donovan and her sitting side by side on the couch, two bangs sounding one right after the other, and blood spraying from their heads. Another image was the two of them asleep in bed, bang, bang, and blood pouring across their pillows. Would she ever feel safe in their house again?

Her heart raced faster as the minutes ticked by. She hadn't heard a gunshot yet, but that didn't stop her from fearing for Thorn's life. Viper would put him down without a thought. And they had left their guns back at the motel room. If something went down, they wouldn't be able to assist. They wouldn't be able to do a damn thing.

Her palms sweated. She tried to imagine Thorn and the two cops searching their house, checking every corner, every closet, every nook and cranny. Finally, Thorn came out, leading the two cops. All three of them had their guns back in their holsters. Thorn lifted a hand and waved them to come.

Beth stepped out of the car. The smell of burnt nature assaulted her senses. On the driveway, she rotated in a full circle, taking in the charred trees and telephone poles, the blackened ground, and the sparseness. She could see the houses several streets down. All their privacy had been burned away. Seeing all the black where the fire had scorched was shocking. Her whole life, she had stood on this driveway and seen green. Even with the addition of new houses, there had always been trees and brush. Now the nature that had thrived there for so long was gone.

Hand in hand, Beth and Donovan trudged to their backyard. On the right side, a few yards of green grass stood between their house and the burnt line of where the fire ended. In the backyard, the pool was a puddle of blue plastic on the ground. Burnt splotches marred the green lawn from the pinecones that had dropped like bombs from the treetops.

"Look." Donovan indicated a patch of woods in their backyard.

Beth's heart lifted. Could it be? Their shoes crunched over ashes and crisp sticks as they trudged to the small section of surviving nature. They rounded a group of palmetto trees and came to a halt in front of Beth's childhood fort. It was still standing. A smile dawned on her face. The igloo-shaped fort was made entirely of pine needles. It could've easily gone up in flames with a single ember, but it made it. That little miracle gave Beth hope. Smiling, she peered at the rest of the devastation and felt it would be okay. One of her memories endured, and she knew, given a couple of years, what was black now would be bursting with life again.

They walked along the other side of the house, and Beth saw, for the first time, just how close the fire had come to stealing her home. A foot was all that remained between the wall of their house and the fire's reach. *A foot.* Even at a wider distance, the roof could've caught on fire. She stepped to the side, over the burnt ground, to take a look at the roof. Not a single smudge of black showed. The fire hadn't been able to so much as lick a shingle. She recalled how Donovan had fought the flames with a hose and squeezed his hand. His efforts might've tipped the odds in their favor.

Back on the driveway, Beth gazed at her house. Happiness filled her. Once this nightmare ended, she could go back home.

A high-pitched sound made Beth's ears perk up. She tilted her head. Was it a hawk? The call came again, but it hadn't come from above her. It was behind her. With her arms crossed, she turned around. Her brows lowered. What was it?

Meeeeooooow.

Her head whipped to the side, and she saw Misty, Mrs. Caraway's cat, sitting in the middle of the road. "Misty." She hurried to the cat, picked her up, and held her to her chest. Misty's fur was matted with dirt and smelled like smoke, but she was okay. Even her paws were clean of burns. Beth pressed her cheek to the top of the feline's head. Tears burned the back of her eyes.

This silly creature had been on her mind off and on since Misty had run off toward the fire. Beth had prayed the cat would survive, and here she was hugging the furry critter. She looked up when she heard scuffling feet approach her.

"Your cat?" Thorn scratched Misty's head.

"No, my neighbor's. I need to return her. I'll be right back."

"You can't go by yourself. I'll come with you." He fell into step with her. His hand resting on his firearm didn't escape her notice, but she ignored it as she cuddled Misty.

At Mrs. Caraway's house, she knocked on the door. Misty purred loudly as they waited on the doormat for an answer. Beth rang the doorbell. She glanced toward the empty driveway when there wasn't a response. "She must not have come back home yet." She bent down and picked up the ceramic lady bug for Mrs. Caraway's spare key. She unlocked the door, but before she could push it open, Thorn stopped her.

"Let me check first," he said.

"This is an old lady's house," she reminded him.

He removed his firearm. "Just let me do my job, okay? What's her name?"

"Mrs. Caraway."

Thorn pushed the door open with his foot. "Mrs. Caraway, this is the Orlando P.D. I'm coming in." He stepped inside.

Beth waited on the doormat with Misty cuddled in her arms. A few minutes later, Thorn returned. "No one here."

Beth shut the door behind her and set Misty on the floor. She immediately ran to her food dish and began gobbling down the kibble. In the pantry, Beth found a plastic container of cat food with a scoop. She filled the bowl to the rim and put fresh water in the other dish. "There you go, little girl." Squatting next to Misty, she petted the feline from head to tail. Her long coat was a mess. Beth picked out stickers and twigs from her fur.

"Here."

Beth looked up. Thorn held out a cat comb. Smiling, she took it and set to work making Misty presentable for her owner's return. Once her coat was smooth and shining again, Beth wrote a note on a flowered piece of stationary. She didn't know whether Mrs. Caraway had a cell phone or not. If she did, Beth didn't have the number. A note was the best thing she could do under the circumstances. After rooting through a few drawers, she found tape and stuck the note to the front door, so Mrs. Caraway would be greeted with good news when she came home.

Misty's safe return elevated Beth's mood even more. She smiled all the way to her studio. Corissa and Amanda were the only ones there, since it was lunch time. Beth used her key to get in. Both women stared at her as if she was an intruder.

"Excuse me, ma'am, I don't know how you got a key, but you—" Amanda fell silent when Donovan and Thorn came in after her. A flash of fear lit Amanda's green eyes. Beth had forgotten all about the wig she wore.

"It's okay," she said. "It's Beth."

The women blinked at her. Beth watched Amanda's eyes skip over to the men behind her. Donovan had on a hat and dark glasses, but Thorn was the only one who still looked like himself. Recognition crossed Amanda's face.

Corissa stepped forward. "Oh my gosh, Beth. You dyed your hair?"

"Not exactly. It's a disguise."

"What's going on?" Amanda asked.

The girl knew the signs. Not coming into work and using a disguise weren't normal actions. Amanda had employed the same tactics in the past to hide from her ex.

"We're okay," Beth said, wanting to reassure her, but the frown didn't leave Amanda's face. "How has everything been here?" She paused, knowing her next question would only deepen that frown. "Had anyone come here looking for me?"

Amanda and Corissa exchanged glances. "No," they said together.

"I'm going to make sure the studio is secure," Thorn said. He stepped away from them and slipped his firearm from the holster at his hip.

Amanda stared after him as he maneuvered with stealth to the back of the studio. When he was out of sight, she spun back around. "Is this about me? Has *he* contacted you?"

Beth took Amanda's hands. "No. This is about me. You're safe here. Corissa knows what to do if Damon comes around." Corissa nodded confirmation, and Amanda's shoulders lowered a fraction.

Thorn came back out into the main room. "Safe and sound," he announced.

Beth nodded, liking his choice of words. Amanda's fear probably hadn't escaped him either. Not with his cop eyes and instincts. "Thanks, Thorn." She couldn't help but notice the shy smile Amanda gave him and the way Thorn seemed to freeze where he stood when they made eye contact. Damn, if there wasn't attraction there. Beth could feel it humming in the air. She wished she could give them a shove right into each other's arms, but it wouldn't work that way. Baby steps. Or, more precisely, insect steps.

The five of them talked briefly. Beth asked how the classes were going and if anyone else had any fire scares. She was grateful to hear none of her other students had been threatened by the fiery beast set loose by Viper and his goons.

"I almost forgot," Corissa said. "The other day, someone dropped off a little package for you, Beth. I put it on your desk."

Beth's gaze jumped to Donovan and Thorn. A package? Her heart raced. What if Viper had left her the heart of the pig he had slaughtered? Her stomach flip-flopped.

Thorn gave Amanda and Corissa a charming smile. "I actually think that's for me. Beth and I will go and get it real fast." He glanced at Donovan. Beth felt a silent order pass between them. Thorn didn't want to upset Amanda and Corissa, so he wanted Donovan to stay there to show them the package wasn't dangerous.

Beth walked to the back of the studio with Thorn matching her steps. Her gaze flicked to his holster. His hand wasn't on his firearm, which she knew must've taken a lot of restraint. They turned into Beth's office. Right there in the middle of her desk was a padded envelope. Not what she had been expecting. Her mind went wild trying to figure out what could be lurking inside it. Another dead snake? Anthrax? Or maybe it wasn't evil, after all. It could easily be business related, like the fliers she had ordered or a bill.

She reached out for it, but Thorn snatched her hand away before she could touch it. He pulled a pair of latex gloves from his back pocket and gingerly opened the envelope. He peeked in, and his jaw tightened. His protected fingers pulled out a bloody switch blade.

Beth's throat constricted. Was it more pig's blood? Or would it be human blood this time? She didn't want to know.

Thorn slipped out a note. He flipped it open. His gaze hardened.

"What does it say?"

He turned it around. Scribbled on the piece of torn paper was "UR NXT!"

Beth swallowed. "You're next." She nodded. "Message received."

****

Beth and Thorn came back into the main room. Thorn held a bubble envelope, but his fingers were pinching the corner, as if he didn't want to disturb any prints. Amanda and Corissa might not notice that, but Donovan did. His interest piqued.

Thorn held up the envelope with a smile. "Turns out it is for me. Thanks for letting us know." He leaned casually against the counter. "If another package comes, can you let me know? Corissa, you should have my number." He tilted his head at Amanda. "Do you still have my card?"

Amanda nodded. A blush crept across her cheeks. "I keep it on me at all times." Her hands lifted, and her fingers pulled back the corner of her workout top. She pulled out his card. Her curves had bent it. She smiled. "Actually, I could probably use another. That way I can keep one here, and the other can be in the pocket of my normal clothes."

Speechlessly, Thorn took a card from his pocket and handed it to her. He had to clear his throat to speak. "Well, I have to get back to work."

"And he's our ride," Beth said. "So, we have to go, too. The two of you are doing a great job here while I'm gone. I wouldn't trust The Fighting Chance to anyone else." She hugged them.

Donovan held the door open for Beth. "Take care, ladies," he said then closed the door.

Once they were on the sidewalk, heading to Thorn's car, Donovan heard Thorn say, "Damn. My business cards are lucky."

****

Beth and Donovan spent two more days locked up in the motel. On the third day, Thorn told them they were getting the boot. Despite the threat, Chief Cormac was pulling the guard after that night, and they would be free to go home in the morning.

"Do you think it's safe?" Beth asked Thorn.

He sighed. "I can't say for sure. Viper hasn't shown up anywhere. Maybe I scared him enough he dropped his whole plan. Since we determined the note was delivered the day of the fire, we can't prove he's still after you, especially since nothing has happened since the fire."

"That's bullshit," Donovan said as anger clashed inside him, raging to break free. "You know he's not going to forget or let Beth go so easily. He's still out there."

Thorn wrenched his head left and right. Bones popped in his neck. "I know. Damn it, Goldwyn, I know, but my hands are tied. There's nothing more I can do. You can pay for this room and stay here longer, and I'll continue to check in every day, but that's the only option we have right now."

Beth groaned. "I don't want to stay in this room any longer than we have to." She peered up at Donovan. "I want to go home."

He cupped her chin with his hand and stared into her eyes. She was tired of living this way, and so was he. "Okay," he said. "Tomorrow morning, we'll check out."

Thorn got up. "I'll be back then to take you home. Sleep tight."

Donovan locked the door after Thorn's exit. He went back to Beth, who sat at the end of the bed. He held her face in his hands and leaned over to kiss her. Her lips were plush and warm. They responded under his, parting to caress his lips. He tasted something sweet, sugary. Was it lip balm? Did she just suck on a piece of candy? He didn't know, but it heightened his hunger for her. His tongue flicked the inside of her lips. The tip of her tongue came out to tease his. Then her mouth opened, accepting him. He sought the sweetness. It seemed as though her tongue was made of honey. He groaned as he tasted, took.

Beth pulled away, much to his protest. She pushed her body backward across the bed until her back touched the headboard. "We may be stuck here for the night, but we can make it enjoyable," she tempted.

His breathing was heavy. Every part of his mind seemed hyperaware, aroused. All he wanted was to plunder her mouth. "Why the hell do you taste so sweet?" His voice sounded deep even to his own ears, as if he were a bear roaring at a honey tree, starving for the goods inside. Beth responded to his voice in ways she couldn't control. Her pupils dilated. Her lips parted. Her legs flinched as her thigh muscles tightened.

"It's peppermint." Her voice was breathless.

He didn't know if peppermint was an aphrodisiac. He knew it stimulated the brain, and damn, he felt stimulated. He crawled over the bed. The closer he got, Beth scooted down, so when his body was poised over hers, they were eye to eye. He lowered himself, but not all the way. The front of his T-shirt fell with gravity and settled over her chest. Propped above her, as if he was holding a push-up, he brought his mouth to hers. He savored the candied taste of her lips, her tongue, her breath. Soft sounds of pleasure purred from Beth as he relished in her flavor.

Beth finally turned her head away, breaking the contact, ending his feast. She panted. Smirking, he nuzzled the side of her neck. His nose moved along her throat. He didn't touch her skin with his mouth. Instead, he let his nose give her Eskimo kisses.

"Damn," Beth gasped. "You've never kissed me like that before."

She turned her head, but still didn't let him have access to her lips. He smelled her skin and moved his nose along her jaw and down the length of her neck. It turned out Eskimo kisses over the body were just as invigorating as the real thing. Her hands slipped beneath his T-shirt and molded to his ribcage. Her nails softly bit him.

"Stay with me, kid, and I'll kiss you in a million different ways."

She turned her head back to his. Her eyes were so

black they glistened. "I'm in."

Her word choice only made his arousal stronger. Stripped of their clothes, he hovered over her. He wanted to make love to her in a way they never had before. No, they wouldn't be trying an outrageous position. What he had in mind would give them a deeper connection. At the moment, he wanted to be as bonded to Beth as was humanly possible.

"Keep eye contact with me...the whole time." He slipped into her. Her eyes fluttered. "Keep eye contact with me," he repeated.

Her gaze met his. He could feel her uncertainty at first. Holding someone's eye contact could be an uncomfortable feeling for most people, but as he stroked inside her, her eyes widened as her pleasure built. He could see her fully let go. She was giving him all of herself. Gazing into her eyes, seeing her changes, only increased his own desire. He breathed with her, inhaling and exhaling to the speed of their love making. He kept his pace slow so he could take it all in—the feel of her and the sight of her. Her mouth opened to release the cries bottled up inside her. Seeing and hearing it made him groan. It was a beautiful thing to witness. Only at the moment of release did they break eye contact.

****

In the morning, Donovan woke excited to leave the cramped motel room and take Beth home. He kissed her shoulder. Her sleeping mouth quirked up at the corners. "Are you ready to go home?"

Her head nodded on the pillow. "Mm-hmm."

He smiled and kissed the delicious curve of her bare shoulder again. "I'm going to take a shower."

"Okay." Beth spoke without opening her eyes. "I'll make us breakfast."

The other day, Thorn had dropped off a few groceries for them so they could make breakfast and sandwiches for lunch. Donovan couldn't wait to have more food to eat than the few items in the fridge. For dinner, he was thinking about steak and potatoes. "Thanks, babe."

On his way to the bathroom, Beth said, "If I make breakfast, can you do something for me?" She was sitting up in bed, holding the comforter to her chest.

He leaned his shoulder against the doorjamb. "Sure."

She offered him a dazzling smile. "Can you shave?"

Chuckling, he ran his hand over his cheeks. "You don't like my whiskers?"

"I think you're handsome either way, but I like to see…and kiss…all of your face."

He rubbed his jawline. His mouth tilted up. If your wife wanted to kiss your face, then you shaved so she could. He nodded. "I'll get my razor."

****

Eggs scented the air when he stepped out of the bathroom. Beth stood in the kitchen with the bedsheet wrapped around her body like a dress. He sucked in a breath between his teeth. "This is a great way to seduce me."

She turned around. In her hand, she held the spatula.

"Even better," he said.

She peered at the spatula and threw her head back in laughter. "Very funny." She sauntered up to him.

272

With her other hand, she caressed his smooth cheek. Then she pressed her cheek to his. "Mm. I like this a lot."

"And I like this a lot." His hands molded to her hips. "I'd like it even more if it was off." His fingers reached for the knot of fabric between her breasts.

Beth swatted his hand and slunk from his reach. "Thorn will be here soon, and I need to take a shower." She slid eggs onto a plate. "You can eat. I had a piece of toast."

"Not hungry?"

"Not really. The smell of the eggs is actually making me a little queasy." She waved her hand in the air. "It's nothing. I get nauseas sometimes before my period."

Donovan frowned and put his arms around her. "Maybe that stomach bug you had isn't fully gone."

She shrugged. "Maybe."

But he didn't remove his arms as he continued to study her face. She didn't look sick. Her face wasn't pale. Her eyes sparkled, and there was a touch of pink to her cheeks.

She placed a quick kiss on his lips. "Seriously, I'm okay. I'm going to shower."

He reluctantly released her. While she showered, he ate his eggs and toast and then gathered items from around the motel room. He set the duffle bags and backpack on the bed and started to pack for their return home. What would they do to stay safe while at home? Sure, they had an advanced security system, but that wouldn't stop Viper from breaking into their house.

He wished they had a panic room, but he didn't have the kind of money it would cost to build one.

Donovan lowered onto the edge of the bed as he thought about what they could do if Viper came for them at home. Without police posted outside, they'd be on their own. Only one defensive tactic came to mind— fight. Followed by another—kill. Viper would try to do that, so they'd have to do the same.

Beth came out of the bathroom wearing a black T-shirt and jeans. Her hair was in a high ponytail that swayed as she moved. She picked up her sneakers and sat down on the bed next to him to slip her feet into them. "I'm going to go checkout and return the room key. Thorn should be here in a minute." She tucked the baseball hat Donovan had worn onto her head and took a step toward the door.

"Wait." Donovan pounced to his feet. He went to the corner where Thorn had sat during the first night they were there. He scanned the parking lot. A cop car was still sitting across the way, in full view of their room. The rest of the parking lot was empty. He shifted to get a good view of the sidewalk that led to the right. A few rooms down sat the reception room. He would be able to keep an eye on her the whole way there.

He nodded. "Okay. I'm going to watch you."

"You mean, make sure I'm not kidnapped again?"

His gaze flicked to her. "That's not funny."

"You have to admit, though, I have an impressive streak."

"Still not funny."

"I know. It was a pathetic attempt at lightening the situation." She kissed his cheek. "I'll be back in a few minutes." She unlocked the door, stepped out, and shut the door behind her.

She walked along the sidewalk at a steady pace.

Her head stared straight ahead. He was proud of her for not looking around and tipping off anyone who could be scrutinizing her. She got to the reception room and entered it, moving out of Donovan's line of sight. He glanced at the cop car, satisfied they'd monitor her return.

He unceremoniously stuffed their dirty clothes into the duffle bags and zipped them closed. The final item he had to pack was his laptop, which he slipped into the backpack. He piled their luggage beside the door.

Our guns. He had almost forgotten about them. He took a step toward the headboard, but a knock on the door made him stop. *That was fast.* At the door, he peered through the peep hole. Beth wasn't on the other side, though. It was Thorn. Donovan took off the chain, spun the deadbolt between his fingers, and opened the door.

Thorn's hands were lifted on either side of his head. The stance amused Donovan. "What are you surrendering for?" he snorted.

Thorn's dark gaze penetrated Donovan. The despair there struck Donovan in the chest. Thorn's head marginally shook from side to side. His eyes shifted to the right.

Donovan's spine straightened. Ice laced his vertebrae. His hand went cold around the door handle. The barrel of a gun came into view from behind the wall and touched the right side of Thorn's head. Another barrel appeared from the left.

Donovan swallowed. His heart pummeled his chest like a sledge hammer trying to break through a concrete wall. A shape shifted into his line of sight. His gaze latched onto Viper as he stepped from behind Thorn, placing yet another gun to Thorn's head.

"He's surrendering to me," Viper sneered.

Donovan prayed Beth had caught sight of what was happening and had sought refuge in the reception room. He wanted her to stay away. Far away. He looked past Viper to the cop car. Behind the windshield, the two cops were motionless.

"Don't worry about them," Viper said. "They're dead." He moved the gun from the back of Thorn's head to over his shoulder, pointing it at Donovan. "Invite us in, so we can get this over with." He jabbed the barrel into Thorn's head again, knocking Thorn's head forward. "Or I'll blow out his brains. If I'm lucky, the bullet will take you out, too."

Donovan took a step back. He had no other choice.

Two men forced Thorn in. One had dreadlocks to his shoulders—Omar. The other had a short afro—Anthony. They were the cousins Beth had identified. Omar redirected his aim toward Donovan. He refused to put his hands in the air, but he let the man muscle him into the kitchen. When he was pushed toward the table, he tried to go to the middle chair where the gun was hidden, but the man shoved him into the adjacent chair. Anthony pushed Thorn into the opposite chair. Neither of them would be able to reach the gun without them noticing.

"I'm sorry, Goldwyn, they snuck up on me," Thorn said.

"Shut up!" Anthony rammed the butt of his gun into the back of Thorn's head. Thorn cursed and winced from the pain, but he kept his shoulders back, his spine straight, and his head up. "No one said you could talk, pig."

Viper leaned against the kitchen counter. He crossed his legs and held his wrist over his belt, so his gun was always visible.

Viper smirked at Donovan, revealing a gold canine tooth. Donovan thought about punching him until that tooth fell out of his mouth. Oh, how badly he wanted to do that. "We'll just wait here for Beth to return," he said. "And I know she'll be back."

"How'd you kill those two cops?" Donovan asked.

"Easy. Their windows were rolled down. We snuck up and popped a bullet into their skulls." He lifted his gun to mimic the action. "Bang, bang." He laughed. "A better question you should ask yourself is how we knew you were here."

Donovan didn't give him the satisfaction of asking.

Viper turned his leer toward Thorn. His gold tooth flashed in the fluorescent lighting.

"The detective here led us straight to you."

Donovan's gaze shifted to Thorn. Thorn's jaw was tight. His hands were balled into fists on the tabletop. Donovan knew Thorn was mentally beating himself up for failing.

"I couldn't find you until we decided to tail your friend." Viper's smirk widened. "I saw your government license plate, so I hunted for your car in the P.D.'s parking lot. When you came and went, I was behind you every single time, but not the same vehicle each time. These boys know how to pick up discreet vehicles."

Omar and Anthony laughed.

"You had no idea you were being followed," Viper told Thorn. "Cops never think criminals can or will get so close, and that was your downfall."

Viper faced Donovan. "He came here every day before and after work. Either he was getting laid, or he was stashing his friends. Then I saw Beth through the opening as this dumbass left last night. It's too bad you hadn't left a moment ago. I could've offed her, and you'd still be alive." He studied his silver gun. "I guess it's better this way." He grinned. "No loose ends."

Donovan tried to move his hand from his lap toward the gun, but when his arm started to stretch more than he wanted it to, he had to stop. He couldn't afford to make a stupid move or let Viper know they had a weapon beneath the very table at which they sat.

His heart fell into his gut when he heard the door open.

Beth!

Chapter Twenty-Two

Thorn's car was parked a few spots from their motel room when Beth stepped out of the reception room. She was glad to see it, as she couldn't wait to get out of there. Hotel rooms for a vacation were one thing. Crappy motel rooms to hide out from people who wanted you dead was another thing entirely. She nearly skipped back to their room, but she restrained herself from acting silly in front of the cops watching her. Her gaze slid over to the cop car. She could see the cop in the driver's seat through the opened window. His head was back, leaning against the headrest, probably napping after the long night while his partner kept watch.

She turned to the door. She twisted the handle by instinct. Her eyebrows lowered when the door opened; Thorn had been a stickler for locking the door even when he was there. She pushed it open. Sunlight filtered into the room from behind her. Their duffel bags were stacked up by the door, ready to be stuffed into the trunk of Thorn's car. Her gaze swept across the room. She had expected to see Donovan and Thorn standing there, waiting for her to come back, but the room was empty. She pushed the door closed and locked it.

"Hey guys, where are you?" She stepped toward the kitchenette. "If Thorn brought food, I want some.

My stomach feels better now, and that toast did nothing to fill me."

A figure stepped into the open. He wore black jeans with a diamond-encrusted dollar sign belt buckle. A black tank showcased a snake head tattooed on a dark bicep.

She stopped mid-step. Her body flinched as if she had run into a brick wall.

No. Her heartrate tripled. Her underarms dampened. *No!*

Her thoughts jumped to her gun taped to the back of the headboard. Could she get to it before getting shot herself? She didn't know, but she had to take the chance. She leapt in the direction of the bed and made two frantic dashes when the lamp in the corner shattered. The sound of it made her yelp. She ducked her head, hunched her shoulders, and lifted her hands. Frozen in place, her heart raced. She held her breath as she braced for a bullet to strike her. A year ago, she had felt the bite of a bullet. She didn't care to ever feel it again.

"Beth!" Donovan's yell came from the kitchen.

Her shoulders lowered a fraction. *He's alive. Thank God! But what about Thorn?*

She slowly rotated to face Viper. He had a silver gun pointed at her. It looked like the same one she had seen resting in his lap while he lounged in a leather chair, like a king on a throne while his serfs got high all around him. The only difference was this one had a silencer. Her mouth was dry as she waited for him to unload his clip in her chest. Would it be a quick death? Or agonizingly slow?

"Hi, Beth." Viper smirked. "Or should I say…hi,

Felicia?"

Beth tried to swallow the lump that had formed in her throat.

"Come on. We're having a party in here." He flicked his gun at her, motioning for her to move toward the kitchen.

She took a halting footstep. Her body screamed for her to run. But her heart told her to stay. If she got shot in the back while attempting to flee, she wouldn't be able to help Donovan or Thorn. She'd be condemning them to death. She couldn't do that. Forcing her feet to lift, one after the other, was tough, though. Each step brought her closer to Viper. Her stomach whirled. *Please don't let me puke now.* Not only would that be demeaning to do in front of Viper, but it wouldn't help things. She wouldn't be able to defend herself while shaking from illness.

When she was close enough, Viper grabbed her arm and tugged her into the kitchenette. The two men she had seen in mugshots were standing on either side of the table with their guns pressed to the backs of Donovan's and Thorn's heads.

Her gaze landed on Donovan then sprang to Thorn. They looked okay. *But they're not okay. They have guns pointed at them. And so do I.*

Viper poked the barrel of his gun into her temple. "Sit, bitch."

She lowered into the chair between Donovan and Thorn. Her body was rigid. A million questions circled in her mind. What was Viper going to do to her? How would he kill her? Would he kill Donovan and Thorn, too? How the hell could they flip the scales in their favor and overpower Viper and his peasants?

Viper stood across from her. She stared at him, not knowing what to expect. He could pop a bullet into her forehead at any moment. Her breathing was fast. She tried to slow it, but her heart rate wouldn't ease by a single heartbeat.

"If you want me," she said, "you have me. Why not let them go? You could kill me and get out of here before they have time to call for backup."

Donovan glared at her. She could practically hear his thoughts screaming at her to shut up, but she couldn't. If she could find a way to spare them, she'd take it. Her odds of surviving this was slim, anyway.

"I already explained that to them," Viper said. "I don't like loose ends." He pointed his gun at Donovan. Beth's heart came to a shuddering stop. "Loose end number one." He waved his arm through the air, so the gun was now in Thorn's face. "Loose end number two." The gun came back in her direction. He cocked his head to the side. "Which loose end should I snip first? I'll let you choose."

She clenched her teeth. Her temples throbbed.

"No? That sucks. Now I'll have to do it at fucking random." His smile became manic. "But random can be fun." He swayed the gun back and forth, aiming it at Donovan, then Thorn, then back to Donovan. "Snip, snip, snip—"

Back and forth. Back and Forth.

Beth's heart punched her chest. She felt like she was going to be sick, spewing her fear and anxiety all over the table. *What can I do? What can I do?*

"Snip, snip, snip." The gun stopped in front of Thorn. "Snip."

Horror stabbed Beth in her heart. Not Thorn. Not

her best friend. Not the man who deserved something so much more than this bloody ending.

"No!" Beth's panicked shout echoed in the kitchenette.

Viper's gaze flashed to her. A sick gleam sparked in his eyes. "Ah. Do you have a soft spot for the detective?" He tilted his head at Donovan. "That's interesting."

Beth's hands tightened in her lap. He was thinking she had something with Thorn and was trying to taunt Donovan with it. *That's not going to work.*

"Maybe I'll do you a favor, man, and get rid of this piece of shit first." He modified his aim. A muffled bang sounded.

Beth screamed.

Thorn bent forward with a shout of pain.

Beth tried to go to him, but Viper's arm swung toward her. "Nuh-uh. You stay right there."

Tears blurred her vision and choked her. She looked to Thorn. He sat up, clutching his arm. His eyes met hers. They were drowning with pain. "It's okay," he said and felt his wound. "It was just a graze."

"Just a graze for now," Viper corrected.

Beth gripped her knees. Her perspiring palms soaked her jeans with sweat. The cotton of her T-shirt was also wet with sweat under her arms. *Please stop this, God. Please stop this.*

Viper let out a hideous laugh. "This is fun. Hell, I don't need to rush. I think I'm going to enjoy this a little longer." He gazed at Beth. "After all, I've been imagining this for a while." He pulled out the chair across from her and sat down in it. His body slunk down low, and he spread his legs. He hooked his left arm over the back of the chair and set his right hand, with the gun, in his lap. Everything about his posture exuded confidence.

Beth wanted to spit at him from across the table.

She looked to Thorn. Blood slithered down his arm. The smell of gunpowder tinged the air and crept into her nostrils. Her stomach whirled faster.

"You okay over there?" Viper turned his head to Thorn.

"Fuck you, asshole."

Viper laughed. "I can see why she likes you." He winked at Beth before turning to Thorn. "You're not so bad, pig. You've got guts. I like that."

Beth was flabbergasted. *This guy is psycho.*

She looked at Donovan. He held her eye contact for a moment, and then his gaze lowered to the table in front of her. She lowered her gaze. Nothing was there. Her gaze ticked back to him. He gave her a slight nod. She peered back down at the table. *What is he trying to tell me? There's nothing there.* She glared at the table as if she had X-ray vision. The image of Donovan's gun taped to the bottom of the table flashed in her mind.

Her chest expanded. She tamped the urge to release a gasp. She stole a glance at Thorn.

He was looking at her, too, as if he knew what Donovan had hinted. In his eyes, she saw hope. *She* was their only hope of getting out of this alive. The weight of that bore down on her.

"Why are you going after Beth?" Thorn asked, drawing Viper's attention. "Sure, she went undercover in your domain, but she wasn't there for you. She was there to get information about Buck. *I* sent her there. No one else. Me. And I was the one who got SWAT to go to your house to arrest you and everyone there. Not Beth. If you should kill anyone, it should be me. And me alone."

While Thorn spoke, Beth lifted her hands off her knees and turned them slowly so her palms faced the bottom of the table. She felt the leather of the holster housing the gun and the texture of the duct tape fastening it in place. Holding her breath, she carefully slid the gun from the holster. In her hands, it felt cold and heavy. She had killed a corrupt cop years ago, and now, she'd be killing again. Although it was in self-defense, she was well aware her count was going from one to two. It was a dark thought that would stain her for a long time.

"You're more involved with this than I thought," Viper said to Thorn. "I had just thought you were their bitch."

Beth propped her hands between her knees. Looking at the table, she traced the line between her legs across the table to Viper. Based on her aim and Viper's horrible sitting posture, she'd get him right in the chest.

"I've made up my mind," Viper said. "I'll shoot you, Detective. Then I'll shoot the husband. Finally…" He met Beth's glare. "I'll end you."

She felt for the lever on the side of the gun and toggled it up, taking it off safety. "You've underestimated us," she said. Without thinking about it another second, she squeezed the trigger. The bang rang out loud and clear. Viper flinched back. She squeezed the trigger two more times. Viper fell backward, knocking over his chair.

During the moment of shock, Thorn propelled

back, out of the line of fire, and grabbed Anthony's hand. He wrenched the man's arm across his chest. A bullet escaped the gun and hit the wall. Thorn thrust up his uninjured arm, cracking his elbow into Anthony's face again and again. When his hand loosened, Thorn ripped the gun away and pointed it at Anthony's head. "Don't move."

On the other side of the kitchenette, Donovan had shoved Omar into the wall. His fist crashed into Omar's face several times. When Omar toppled to the ground, Beth stomped on the hand that grasped the gun and lined up her shot. "Try it, and I'll shoot you dead."

Donovan kicked the gun out of the Omar's hand. Out of the corner of her eye, she saw him do the same to the gun clamped in Viper's hand. Then he bent over him. Beth's heart still hammered in her chest.

Donovan came to her side. "He's dead," he whispered. His hands wrapped around hers, and he slipped the gun from her fingers. He took her place, training the gun on the man at their feet.

"Beth, call 9-1-1. Tell them two officers and a wanted criminal are down." Thorn paused. "Make sure to tell them two other wanted criminals are waiting to be arrested for attempted murder."

Beth hurried into the bedroom. She dropped onto the bed and picked up the phone. Her hand shook as she jabbed the three buttons. *I had to do it. Just like before. I had to do it.*

"9-1-1, what's your emergency?"

Chapter Twenty-Three

A crime scene unit van, an ambulance, a coroner's van, and three cop cars clogged the motel's parking lot. Cops handcuffed Anthony and Omar, and paramedics quickly ushered Thorn and Beth to their bus. They cleaned and bandaged Thorn's arm. For Beth, they wrapped her in a blanket and gave her oxygen because she was hyperventilating. The two of them, joined by Donovan who was not letting his wife out of his sight, sat in the ambulance, shaken by the events that had just unfolded. Donovan rubbed Beth's arms as she shook and wheezed for breath. He whispered to her, hoping to calm her. Several minutes passed before she had a handle on her adrenaline crash.

After Donovan explained his side of what happened to the cops, he walked over to where Beth sat on the curb. The blanket had slipped off her shoulders. He sat down next to her. Slinging his arm around her, he pulled her close.

"It's strange," Beth said, ending their silence. "I had thought I'd care... At first, I thought I did care...that I had killed another person. Shooting Chewy hadn't really fazed me because I didn't know him. He was a murderer, and he had a gun on us. So, I thought adding Viper to that list, making it two people, would've impacted me more. But Viper was just a person I confronted once while in a disguise. I had forgotten all about him. Then when he started all this, he became a nightmare I wanted to end. I killed a nightmare." She turned to him. "I wasn't hyperventilating because I had killed Viper, but because the two people I love the most were almost murdered by him. That is what I cared about…you and Thorn. Nothing else mattered. When it was over, the realization of how close it came hit me hard."

Donovan framed her face with his hands and pressed his lips to her forehead. He understood and didn't have to say so. Kissing her, holding her was more powerful than saying, "I understand."

She laid her head on his shoulder and looked toward the ambulance. Thorn still sat on the tailgate while the medics looked him over. "Thorn's helped us and come to our rescue time and time again," she said. "I never thought we'd pull him into our mess like this. We should hold a barbeque in his honor. The first person on the invite list will be Amanda."

Donovan smiled. "He'd like that."

****

The next day, Donovan picked up his monster truck at his mechanic's garage. Beth came with him. The first thing he did was pop the hood and check for any sign of a snake's head painted on the metal. Nothing. He examined the body of the truck for things that shouldn't be there. He paused next to the cobra posing to strike on the side of the truck. Viper had used snakes as his symbol, and he had used them to taunt Beth.

"Maybe I should change my truck's design."

"You can't do that." Beth's hand slid over the cobra's body. "You have fans. *Venom* will always be your truck, and the cobra will always be your symbol. You can't change it. You shouldn't." She faced him. "And I don't want you to." A sly smile took her lips. "I have fond memories of this truck, and I plan on making more of them with you."

Donovan grinned. Yes, they had fond memories with his truck. Like the first time he had taken her for a ride around his track. It had ended with a steamy encounter.

He transported his monster truck back to his private garage. Seeing the truck back in its rightful place felt good. "It's good to have it back." He reached up to pull the door down.

"Wait." Beth stopped him with a hand on his arm. "Let's take it for a spin."

"You're sure?"

"Definitely."

In the driver's seat, he slipped the keys in the ignition. He twisted the key, starting the massive engine. Beth sat in the seat next to him. He grinned at her. "Ready?"

She turned to him. Her eyes sparkled. "Always."

Epilogue

One week later…

Beth paced the cold tile in their master bathroom. Back and forth. Back and forth. She wrung her hands. Her heart pounded. When she reached the door, she spun on her heel and passed three different pregnancy tests sitting on the counter. She anxiously counted down the seconds until the results would come through.

She had to be sure.

In the past, every time she took a test, the results had crushed her. She had taken several without Donovan's knowledge and kept the negative results from him, not wanting him to have the same disappointment that ripped at her heart. But that morning, she woke up in bed alone and had to rush to the bathroom. After releasing the contents of her stomach, she sat on the floor and wondered, *what if this isn't a bug? What if this is morning sickness?*

It made sense. She usually never had an illness this long, and she'd been experiencing nausea every day after lunch and dinner. She had sent out a prayer as she peed on the test strips.

She paused in front of the counter and studied herself in the mirror. Her skin seemed to have a luminescence to it. Her eyes glittered. Even her hair seemed shiny with vitality. She cupped her breasts. Did they feel heavier? They were a little tender, but they usually were before her menstrual cycle, except her period was late by two weeks.

She turned sideways and examined her belly. Of course, there was no difference, but she tried to imagine herself with a large belly heavy with a baby. What would she look like pregnant? She balled up a towel and stuffed it under her tank top. With her athletic body, the bump extending from her belly looked out of place but cute. Her eyes lowered to where the towel poked out from under her tight top. The teal color where her skin should've been ruined the moment. Rolling her eyes, she ripped the towel away.

She checked the timer. Another minute remained. She forced her gaze to stay off the little strips, though their power was magnetizing. She knew they there, working their magic. But would that magic be good or bad?

Her gaze roamed around the bathroom. *Maybe I should clean the toilet. That'll take some time.* But considering she had just thrown up in it, she really didn't want to do that. She looked around for something to distract her. *Why the hell don't we keep magazines in here?* Although she doubted she'd be able to concentrate on a magazine, she could flip the pages and stare at the pictures. That would be a lot better than going out of her mind.

She started to pace again.

Back and forth. Back and forth.

Positive or negative?

Back and forth. Back and forth.

She thought about Donovan holding a pink bundle, as a wail pierced the air. Her chest tightened. *Damn, he would look so sexy as a new father.* Her cheeks warmed at the thought.

But if the results were negative—three, bold, screaming negatives—she wouldn't tell him. She'd shelter him from the devastation, and she'd take out her grief on a punching bag.

Back and forth. Back and forth.

Positive or negative?

Back and forth. Back and forth.

The rattle of the egg timer going off made Beth freeze. She took a slow, deep breath, bracing herself for the news, and turned to the counter. Eyeing her reflection, she took a step toward the counter. *We can do it, Beth. We've got this.*

Her gaze lowered.

The first test strip had a blue plus sign in the window—Pregnant.

The second test strip had two pink lines in the window—Pregnant.

The final one said it simply—Pregnant.

She clamped her hand over her mouth. Her knees gave, and she sank to the floor. Happy tears plunged down her cheeks. Her shoulders shook as she cried. *Finally.* After months and months of trying to get pregnant, after the bitter disappointment and the guilt, finally, she was pregnant.

She clutched the counter, as if it was an anchor that would keep her from floating with pure delight. She dropped her hand from her mouth and a laugh escaped. A laugh through the tears.

Finally.

She stayed on the floor another moment while she let her emotions ebb. Then she rose to her feet.

Automatically, she double-checked the results, afraid her eyes had tricked her, but the results were the same.

She splashed water onto her face and schooled her breathing to keep more tears from coming. Now she had to tell Donovan, and she didn't want her face to give it away. She gathered the three test strips. Her hand clutched them as if they would vanish, taking away the positive results and all her dreams with them.

Donovan was sitting at the kitchen table with a cup of coffee. "Hey, baby."

She smiled. The term of endearment made her stomach jitter and her excitement soar.

She bent over, giving him a kiss on the temple. With her free hand on his shoulder, she stepped behind his chair. "I have something to show you." From behind his back, she selected the strip with the two pink lines and set it in front of him.

He looked at the pregnancy test and lowered his cup of coffee to the table.

After a moment, she placed the second one next to the first.

He didn't move.

She set the last one down.

He launched to his feet and faced her. His eyes were wide and glistening. "You're pregnant?"

Heart bursting with love, she nodded. "I'm pregnant."

Donovan swept her up in his arms.

She wrapped her legs around him as his mouth sought hers. She tasted the saltiness of their tears as they kissed.

She now had everything she had ever wanted—a man who was her soulmate, a home they could build memories in, and a baby who would have the best parts of both of them.

www.ingramcontent.com/pod-product-compliance
Lightning Source LLC
Chambersburg PA
CBHW051522260626

47170CB00003B/744